DANAE PENN

FALSE RUMOURS

Cover design: JD Smith

Published by Nichol Press

ISBN: 979-10-97586-01-0

Printed by Lightning Source

DANAE PENN
FALSE RUMOURS

A BELINA LANSAC
MURDER MYSTERY

NICHOL PRESS

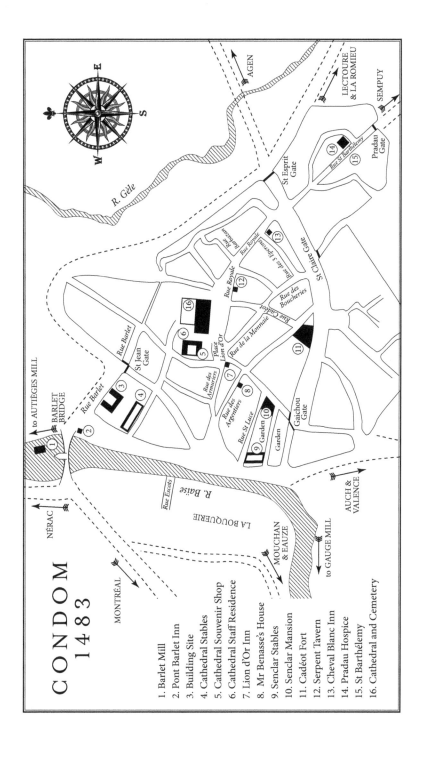

CONDOM 1483

1. Barlet Mill
2. Pont Barlet Inn
3. Building Site
4. Cathedral Stables
5. Cathedral Souvenir Shop
6. Cathedral Staff Residence
7. Lion d'Or Inn
8. Mr Benasse's House
9. Senclar Stables
10. Senclar Mansion
11. Cadéot Fort
12. Serpent Tavern
13. Cheval Blanc Inn
14. Pradau Hospice
15. St Barthélemy
16. Cathedral and Cemetery

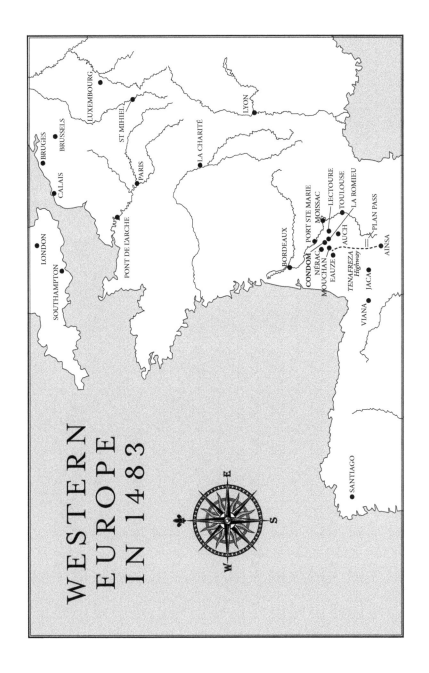

WESTERN EUROPE IN 1483

LONDON
SOUTHAMPTON
CALAIS
BRUGES
BRUSSELS
LUXEMBOURG
ST MIHIEL
PARIS
PONT DE L'ARCHE
LA CHARITÉ
LYON
BORDEAUX
PORT STE MARIE
CONDOM
NÉRAC
MOUCHAN
EAUZE
MOISSAC
LECTOURE
TOULOUSE
LA ROMIEU
AUCH
PLAN PASS
AÏNSA
TENAFREZA Highway
JACA
VIANA
SANTIAGO

W S E N

CHAPTER ONE

30th August 1483

The storm broke in mid-afternoon as Belina was waiting her turn in the apothecary's store. To curb her impatience she gazed at the porcelain jars on the shelves, trying to decipher the Latin scripts on them. Everyone jumped at the sudden clap of thunder and the apothecary spilt the arsenic he was transferring on to a tiny cloth square lying on his poisons scales. He cursed and began again.

A small man in a physician's red gown pushed his way to the front of the line, elbowing Belina aside. "Dame Senclar is waiting for her medicines. Hurry. Serve me first."

The apothecary took no notice of the man and continued to weigh out two ounces of crushed arsenic for his customer's rat poison.

The physician banged his fist on the counter so hard that everything upon it bounced. The blacksmith in the doorway growled. So did his dog.

The apothecary looked up at the man. "I have already spilled this arsenic once, and I do not intend to do so again," he said. "You will wait your turn." He finished concocting the rat poison and looked towards Belina, "Dame Lansac, what can I get for you?"

"A dozen phials of *aygue ardente* and two dozen pots of foot balm, please."

The physician scowled at Belina. "Young women should never drink *aygue ardente*. Dame Senclar would disapprove of you buying such firewater."

Belina stared at him and refrained from answering, well aware that she dare not deliberately offend the richest landowner in Condom.

Rain began to lash the cobbles outside the store and the crowds of Saturday shoppers ran to take refuge inside the cathedral. Belina paid her bill and followed them in, holding up the skirt of her tunic and taking care not to be pushed against the heap of rubble piled just outside the doorway.

It was dark and very noisy in the nave, with everyone complaining about the storm and how it would ruin the grapes. Pilgrims wandered around, glancing at the side chapels, deciding whether or not to spend the night in one of them. Several pilgrims had spread cloaks on the floor and were drinking wine from their gourds while discussing what to do next.

"This is the worst summer I have known for pilgrimage," declared a wiry, sunburnt pilgrim, "and I have been walking the Way of St James for over fifteen years."

"Have you committed that many crimes?" asked a passing chorister.

"Don't be cheeky. I walk to Compostela every year because I'm paid to by people who have inherited such an obligation. Instead of wasting four or five months going to Galicia and back they pay me to fulfil the vows of their ancestors." He drank from his terracotta flask and hooked it back on to his belt. "And to pray for them," he added. But the chorister had already disappeared into the vestry.

Belina looked at the pilgrim's flask, admiring its engraving. She was about to ask him where he had acquired it when a hand reached out to grab one of the newly bought a*ygue ardente* phials in her basket. She thumped the hand, turned and stamped on the thief's foot.

"I was only looking,"the thief whined, withdrawing his hand.

"Then look with your eyes, and keep your hands to yourself," Belina retorted. "If you want to buy some it will cost you two *sous*."

He tried to bargain with her, but she was adamant. The cathedral treasurer set the price and she was forbidden to lower it. The unsuccessful thief cursed the treasurer and limped away empty-handed.

Belina held her basket close to her damp tunic and watched a group of pilgrims shuffling from one side-chapel to another, praying before each statue. Their progress was hampered by the cloaks spread out on the floor near many of the statues, but no one was dropping alms into the coin boxes placed prominently in front of each chapel. Until March that year the coin boxes had been smaller and less obvious. Rocca, the new treasurer from Paris, had changed that. All the cathedral staff had received orders to keep their accounts up-to-date and to submit their ledgers to Rocca's assistant, Loupmont, every Wednesday afternoon. Quiteira, Belina's colleague in the cathedral shop, could read but not write so Belina had to find time to comply grudgingly with Rocca's orders.

She edged her way through the crowd of pilgrims, avoiding the wine gourds swinging from the tops of their staffs, and joined a group of local shoppers and street tradesmen who were shouting at each other about the demonstration that morning against fines and evictions. Two ribbon sellers maintained that protesting had done more harm than good but several shoppers voiced loud disagreement. In their view, the French habit of taking to the street to demonstrate was something a Parisian like Rocca would understand. Now that Gascony had become part of south-west France, its inhabitants needed to adopt French ways of behaviour, they said.

Belina stopped listening to the argument and thought about how she would spend Sunday with her husband: getting up late, a quick Mass, and then walking with Guillaume down to the wharf and along the towpath of the river Baïse to the fishponds at Cahuzac. Perhaps they would get further, to the Beauregard mill where long ago her aunt had fed her delicious *merveilles* to eat while her cousin Christau took her back by boat, letting the current wash them gently down to her grandmother's mill at Autièges, saving his strength for the more arduous row home. Now she was looking forward to eating those same honey cakes with Guillaume at the end of a special dinner in the Pont Barlet inn, a celebration he had promised for her birthday two weeks ago. His promise had been broken: the Bishop of Condom had ordered him to take an urgent message to Archdeacon Marre in Auch, and Belina's indignant protests had been brushed aside.

Back to the present, she saw that people were leaving the cathedral. The rain had turned to drizzle. It was a good opportunity for her to walk back to the shop in case the storm returned.

Quiteira had removed all the small objects from the display counter and brought them back inside the shop. She scowled at Belina's greeting. "You have been a long time."

"I got caught in the rain and had to shelter in the cathedral. Someone tried to steal one of the *aygue ardente* phials from my basket."

"A pilgrim or a soldier?" Quiteira asked.

"Don't know. Might even have been a local person."

Quiteira shook her head. Gascons did not steal, even though so many of them were hard up now-a-days, what with the king's taxes and the bishop's taxes and the bad harvest.

Belina had had enough of listening to complaints that afternoon. She walked into the inner storeroom and arranged the firewater phials inside the cupboard and the foot balm pots on a high shelf, forgetting the moans of the citizens of Condom and beginning to hum at the thought of spending the morrow in her husband's company. She went over to the copper basin and glanced at her face in the tin mirror, admiring the aquiline nose and large black eyes which had first attracted Guillaume to her, or so he often told her.

She unwrapped her soggy head-cloth and hung it on the rail. Her glossy dark hair tumbled down her back and she smiled at herself in the mirror. She picked up her empty basket and returned to the shop.

Quiteira was putting on her pattens and grumbling about the muddy street outside. "It's all right for you, Belina, you live here. All you need to do is cross the courtyard and go up the stairs." She sighed and flexed her left foot on its patten. "While I have to walk all the way to rue Cadeot. It's not fair."

Belina took no notice. Instead, she went outside and began to pull up the shutter. A passerby helped her and then pulled the awning down for her spattering them both with drips from the storm. Belina's hair clung to her cheeks and she laughed at the sudden chill touch of the water. Her helper gazed at her with great interest, and Belina supposed that he presumed her unmarried because she was not wearing a head-cloth.

"Thank you so much," she said with a small smile and walked briskly back inside the darkened shop, colliding with Quiteira.

"Look where you're going." Quiteira tried to flounce off down the street, but found it difficult to walk in her pattens on the muddy cobbles. Belina lit a tallow candle so that she could lock and bolt the street door of the shop. She went through the darkened shop to the courtyard door, unlocked it and blew out the candle, wrinkling her nose at the smell.

She locked the door behind her and rushed up the stairs, her mind full of happy plans for the next day.

CHAPTER TWO

Belina ran down the corridor towards her front door but to her annoyance and puzzlement she found it locked. Where was Guillaume? Had he got caught in the storm? She fumbled at the key ring hanging from her belt, selected the second largest key and pushed the heavy door open.

Guillaume was there. That was the good news. She gazed at their bed which was covered with clothes and papers in neat piles. Her husband was kneeling beside a chest and taking his best slippers from it.

"Shut the door please."

Not much of a greeting. Belina stood still instead of rushing forward to kiss him. "Whatever are you doing?" she demanded.

"Packing, as you can see." He put the slippers on the bed.

"Why?"

"Because I am off to Bordeaux at dawn tomorrow." He put his bag of spurs beside his riding boots and stood up.

"But tomorrow's Sunday. You promised to take me to dinner. You promised to make up for not being here for my birthday. You......"

"Yes, I know I did, but we shall have to postpone it a second time." Guillaume replied and continued packing his clothes into his travel bundle. "And where is your head-cloth?"

"In the shop, drying out. Perhaps you haven't noticed that

there has been a thunderstorm?" She wriggled out of her damp tunic, walked over to the sink and wrung the drips from the muddy hem.

"Why were you not in the shop? That storm had been threatening all day." He put his toothscraper and Castilla soap in their tiny hemp bag while she extracted an old shirt and a faded cotte from her clothes basket.

"What's so urgent about Bordeaux?" She put on the shirt and the cotte and began lacing its bodice. "Why is it always you who has to go on these unplanned journeys? Or have you known about this for days and days?"

Guillaume dropped his spare shirt on to the floor and unlaced Belina's bodice, caressing her breasts. He told her that he had only that day been ordered by the archdeacon to take a message to Bordeaux and that he had tried very hard to suggest that someone else go instead. Someone not married, someone who did not have the 'most beautiful wife in Gascony'.

She let him kiss her and fondle her for several minutes, trying to forget that her husband always obeyed instructions from the archdeacon.

Then she pulled away from him before things went too far. "Why? What's so urgent about the message? Why can't someone else deliver it?" She kicked one of his riding boots across the room, narrowly missing the cat. "Sorry, Minet." Belina bent to stroke the animal. "Who is this precious message for?"

"The senior legal adviser to the Archbishop of Bordeaux."

"Why him?"

"Rocca is planning to send a lot more money and, even worse, cathedral treasure to Henry Tudor in Brittany." Guillaume continued his packing. "The Earl of Richmond."

"The English count who gets our money? The reason for the demonstration this morning?" Belina picked up Minet and sat on the edge of the bed, determined to find out the real reason for her husband's sudden departure for Bordeaux.

Guillaume took his spurs out of their bag and examined

them. "The Earl of Richmond's mother is plotting against the new English king, Richard III."

"Why?"

"Lady Margaret Beaufort has been personally inconvenienced by his ambitions to ensure justice for poor people. King Richard insists on preventing greedy landlords from exploiting their tenants. That does not suit Lady Margaret at all. She is an enormously rich landowner."

"In that case," said Belina, "she could afford to lose a bit of rent from poor tenants."

"Of course she could afford it. But the trouble with the excessively rich is that they are also excessively greedy. They don't care how much anyone suffers."

"Like Dame Senclar, you mean," said Belina, thinking about Condom's main enemy rather than people in a faraway country.

"Far, far worse than Dame Senclar." Guillaume put the spurs back in their bag. "It's not only that. What is really frightening is her ambition for her son, Henry Tudor."

"Dame Senclar is very ambitious for *her* son, Henri," Belina observed, stroking the cat again.

Guillaume abandoned his packing and sat down beside Belina. "The same thing will happen in France soon," he said, "King Louis will not last much longer. Indeed, he might already be dead. His son Charles is only thirteen which means that his elder sister, Anne de Beaujeu, will rule France for the next few years. The nobles will not like being ordered around by her - or her husband, come to that. They will rebel, copying the plotters in England who are planning to stir up a rebellion against King Richard by pretending he has murdered his nephews in the Tower of London. King Richard could be killed in revenge for such a terrible crime and then the English will be forced into being ruled by this Welsh upstart living in Brittany. Someone who knows nothing of England, and who is only twenty-six years old. A year younger than me."

"How do you know all this?" Belina asked.

"My father heard about the plot in Southampton. It will harm the wine trade between Bordeaux and England, and hurt my father's wine import business."

"And the wine shipping business of your family in Bordeaux too, I suppose," said Belina, trying to keep her voice from sounding as bitter as she always felt about the Bordeaux wine trade.

"Of course," he agreed. "I will take advantage of being sent to Bordeaux on the archdeacon's orders so that I can discuss all this with my half-brothers. Indeed, the archdeacon asked me to report back to him any news I gathered from the Bordeaux wine shippers."

"Why?" Belina asked sharply, fearing the delay in Guillaume's return to Condom.

"Lots of reasons. If Henry Tudor rules England, the English will become too poor to import wine and they will have to drink cider all year instead. Henry Tudor will have to commandeer ships so that he can invade England from Brittany. Transporting wine will become too hazardous and difficult, perhaps even impossible. And the expense of mounting an invasion from Brittany has led Lady Margaret's friend Bishop Morton to order Rocca to send Condom cathedral's treasure to Brittany to be melted down to finance Henry Tudor."

Belina gasped. "So the demonstration here this morning was justified?"

"I suppose so, although the demonstrators did not know the real reasons for sending treasure to the Earl of Richmond." He got off the bed and stood in front of Belina, staring down at her face. "You are not to tell anyone about all this. Promise me."

She promised, and asked about how much the archdeacon knew of the plot.

Guillaume doubted the archdeacon knew about the plan to murder the princes in the Tower, although he had been investigating the reasons behind Rocca's 'thieving' for some time. The archdeacon had flatly refused Rocca's request to have the treasure 'stolen', as he put it, and sent north to Brittany. He had had the locks of the cathedral safe room changed. "He told me that the groom of a newly-arrived Parisian lawyer had been seen tampering with the existing locks."

Belina had stopped listening to Guillaume. She was too upset at the idea that he would be absent for such a long time so she missed Guillaume's sour comment about the Parisian lawyer being lodged in Rocca's chamber in the cathedral staff residence. She sighed, realising that her husband would take advantage of being in Bordeaux – yet again – to see his family there and discuss the wine trade. Did the people of Bordeaux ever talk about anything else? However, discussing the wine trade was much safer than planning for an English invasion of Bordeaux. Guillaume referred to that as 'the Bordeaux *Reconquista*' and was supporting it vigorously. Belina was scared stiff that Pierre de Beaujeu would be told about the plot and that Guillaume would be arrested.

She walked over to the window, picked up the carafe, sniffed it and poured some watery wine into a goblet. The thunderstorm that afternoon had not cleared the air and she was thirsty and sticky.

Guillaume took the goblet and drank from it. "*Mercés.*"

She snatched the goblet back. "I hope you've left me some."

But before she could begin to drink there was loud banging at the door.

"Messire Lansac, it's Jeannot from the hospice. Brother Pierre needs you urgently."

"Go and see what the Recteur wants," Guillaume told her, "but don't say that I'm off to Bordeaux tomorrow."

She opened the door a little. An urchin tugged at his forelock. "Dame Lansac, there's been another pilgrim died and Brother Pierre insists that Messire Lansac comes at once. I'm not to return without him."

"You go and wait downstairs in the courtyard and Messire Lansac will be with you in a moment."

Belina closed the door.

"Well?" Guillaume looked up from sorting out his wax tablets, brushing away strands of his fair hair from them, and checking that the wax had been scraped clean of previous jottings.

"A pilgrim has died and you're needed to investigate why and how, and make one of your reports. So, there will be no early morning start for Bordeaux. Your reports take hours to draw up." She grinned.

"Nonsense, my love." Guillaume counted out wax tablets and set them aside to put in his travel bundle. He added three styli to them. "You can go along to the hospice and investigate what's happened. It will keep you occupied in my absence."

"I could do no such thing," Belina spluttered. "You know I couldn't," she replied.

"Yes, you can. You've often helped me. Just take a very good look at the corpse and its surroundings, question Brother Pierre, note down his comments on your tablets, get him to strip the corpse and wrap it in a shroud and return here with everything worn or carried by the pilgrim. Absolutely everything."

"In this weather the body will go off very quickly." She shuddered, sweat dripping from her face.

"That, fortunately, is Brother Pierre's problem, not yours. No wonder he's told Jeannot that it's urgent. Urgent doesn't mean important." He hugged her and started to kiss her.

But Belina was not to be cajoled. She picked up the rectangle of white lawn which was her spare head-cloth and wound it round her head, looking in the tin mirror to check that most of her hair was covered. Guillaume handed her his investigation bag with its special wax tablets, styli and sample phials, and she took a honey sweet from the jar on the table to give to Jeannot.

Guillaume hugged her so tightly that she fell back on to the bed and lost one of her slippers. He picked it up and said "Don't go out in these slippers in the mud."

"I'm not going to. My pattens are downstairs in the shop."

He held the door open for her and kissed her nose.

"You will be all right. Don't worry. I have the utmost faith in you."

She went down the corridor, trying not to trip over the cat.

CHAPTER THREE

It was difficult to keep up with Jeannot who was rushing through the cemetery behind the cathedral. The thunderstorm had made the grass slippery and Belina's pattens slowed her down. As she struggled through the crowd gossiping in the cemetery she heard snatches of conversation, discussing the demonstration in the cathedral that morning.

"Jacme has been arrested for theft of a sheaf of wheat..."

"...Rocca must be behind that..."

"...My neighbour's parents are in debt to Rocca's nasty assistant and he will have them evicted..."

"...Farmer Fogerat's crop has been ruined by hail and Rocca is seizing his sheep as compensation..."

"...The Mézards have been fined for arrears of rent. They will be paupers before the year's end..."

"...They say that Rocca is stealing from us so that he can send our money to Paris."

"No, not Paris. He sends it to an English count in Brittany."

Belina's ears twitched at the sound of this last exchange. Rumour was afoot already, it appeared, truth mingled with lies and invention. She wished she had listened more carefully to Guillaume just now instead of fulminating about his departure for Bordeaux. She really did want to know more about the English count everyone had been talking about for several weeks. Although she was the only person in Condom who knew it, Guillaume's mother was English, accounting for his fair hair. He had been born in England, near Southampton, and christened William. But Guillaume took great care to pretend that he was completely *bordelais*, born and brought up in Bordeaux. Now that Gascony was administered by France it was prudent to conceal his ancestry. She knew that her husband was very worried about the English count because he was supported by Lancastrians, the enemies of King Edward, and therefore enemies now of King Richard. The Lancastrians thought only of amassing wealth for themselves and cared little for the suffering of the English people or the uncertainties their poor administration caused to business, including the Bordeaux wine trade that Guillaume was so devoted to.......

Jeannot interrupted her thoughts. "Do hurry, Dame Lansac. Brother Pierre will be getting anxious."

She felt anxious too as she followed Jeannot through the market hall and into rue Royale, glad to be walking on cobbles instead of grass and mud. She took care to keep away from the central drain and its filthy puddles. Her progress was slowed by the horse-drawn carts descending rue Royale on their way to the Saint Esprit Gate and Jeannot was way ahead of her, beyond rue Barbazan where a donkey was trying to squeeze past a group of old peasant women sheltering in the vaulted alley. Soldiers were staggering from the Cheval Blanc at the end of rue des Trois Eperons. Their singing and whistling reminded Belina of her brother Geraud. She hoped he was still as joyful and carefree, and that he did not regret going with other young Gascons to join the army and fight the Moors in Spain. She had not heard from him for over a year. Was he still alive? Was he a prisoner in a Moorish fortress? She wiped away sudden tears and struggled on down the crowded street, pushing her way past the people, animals and carts waiting to go through the Saint Esprit Gate. She walked as briskly as possible down rue Saint Barthelemy until she was near the church. Friars were coming out of it, talking to pilgrims cluttering up the end of the street. She threaded her way through the crowd and entered the Pradau hospice by the door opposite the church. Her heart was thumping with apprehension and she clutched the investigation bag tightly enough to hurt her thumb.

The Recteur's assistant was waiting for her."I was expecting Messire Lansac," he said reproachfully.

"He's too busy with something very urgent for the cathedral," explained Belina, "and he has asked me to come here instead."

The assistant raised his eyebrows and stared at her. "You'll have to be quick," he whispered as he led the way to the pilgrims' dormitory, "I can't keep the pilgrims out of here much longer. They're tired from travelling in this rotten weather."

Belina greeted Brother Pierre at the entrance to the dormitory and explained again why she was standing in for Guillaume.

"No problem, Dame Belina. You have often helped your husband with his investigations. I am sure you will know exactly what to do."

He stopped in front of a shroud-covered body and gently pulled the shroud away.

Belina peered at the corpse. She had watched Guillaume many times in this situation, but it still offended her to see an unknown naked body. She was not the sort of young woman to frequent the étuves, although she and Guillaume had gone to the public bath houses twice when they were courting.

She saw a muscular man aged about twenty-five, quite tall, brown wavy hair, naturally balding rather than tonsured. His face was set in a terrible grimace. His eyes were wide open, as if staring at her, trying to tell her something.

"Do you think he was poisoned?" she asked Brother Pierre.

"With a face like that, I would suppose so. But it could have been a heart attack."

"Tell me more," Belina prompted him.

She gathered that the pilgrim had arrived just after the thunderstorm that afternoon. He said he had come from Mouchan and walked through Condom, getting soaked by the heavy rain. He hadn't wanted to walk any further that day and asked to stay the night. He had given the porter a coin and been shown into the main hall which was where the pilgrims waited to have their feet washed and to be given their evening meal.

"What was for supper?" Belina asked.

"A bit of fish stew, mostly bread really."

"And wine?"

"Yes, but it is a bit sour by now. It's not long to the next vintage."

"Who washed his feet?"

"No one. Brother Martin saw him have his boots removed. But then he asked to go to the dormitory saying he had already eaten a cake in Condom and wanted to rest."

"Mouchan is not that far away. He can't have been that weary," said Belina.

"Perhaps he felt poorly," suggested Brother Pierre.

Belina knelt on the dusty floor and peered at the dead man's eyes, trying to estimate how cloudy and flattened they were and from that to deduce how long he had lain dead in the dormitory. She pressed her forefinger on his shoulder. It was still warm, but it turned white under her finger.

"Suppose he has been dead three hours," she said to Brother Pierre, "when did you find him?"

"Perhaps an hour ago." But he didn't sound very sure.

Belina tried another tack. "How many people witnessed his death?"

"Nobody. Everyone was in the main hall having their feet washed or eating their supper."

She touched the pilgrim's face, working his eyelids and lower jaw for signs of stiffening.

"What about the hospice staff?"

"Washing lots of very dirty feet and bringing food into the dining hall. What with the mud and the sweat of the stinking pilgrims and the food beginning to go off in the hot weather, they had plenty to do and not enough time to do it."

His reply was logical, but would Guillaume have believed it?

"Who found the body, and when?"

"A group of pilgrims, accompanied by Brother Martin. They came into the dormitory together and were jostling for the best places to put their belongings."

Belina looked at the long dark dormitory, and listened to the insects buzzing in the stuffy gloom.

"Are we in the best place, as you call it?" she asked.

"Yes. This corner by the north wall is cooler and less stuffy. Less noisy too." He pointed to the corpse. "He must have been an experienced traveller to have chosen this spot."

"But not a particularly sociable one," said Belina, peering into the gloom at the changing colour of the corpse's skin. His chest was becoming pale and his heels were turning purple. She lifted his right arm and saw that his nails were white and his fingers were turning blue. His arm felt much cooler than his shoulder. She felt various parts of the corpse, pretending to herself that she was Guillaume and not Belina, seller of medallions, carvings and *babioles*, former accounter at a flour mill. The arms and legs were definitely cooler than the rest of the body.

"Are you quite sure that no one was in here with him?"

"No, Dame Belina, I'm not completely sure. But it is unlikely."

"Are you certain he arrived alone?"

"Yes. I remember watching him arrive myself. As I told you, he came into the hospice earlier than they usually do and alone. I am sure about his arrival. Definitely sure."

"Are lone travellers so unusual?"

"Very unusual. They find safety in numbers. And if they are

going to get lost they can do it in a group. So even pilgrims who did set off from home alone, escaping their families and creditors and enemies – or whatever – soon join a group. By the time they reach Condom they are always in a group. Always."

"Perhaps he is not a pilgrim," she suggested. "Or rather, *was* not."

She looked at him again and saw that his thighs had a few old scars and his right shoulder was more heavily muscled than the left one. From bearing weapons, perhaps.

"A soldier?" she asked Brother Pierre.

"Possibly. Many pilgrims are. Soldiers have many crimes to atone for. That is why they walk to St James in Galicia. That way they receive indulgences for their wickedness and violence."

"Brother Pierre, what is your opinion about the cause of his death?"

"I do not have one. That is Messire Guillaume's task, I think."

"Yes," said Belina quickly, "but I'm sure he would like to know your opinion."

"As I said, I do not have one."

"You must have had sufficient doubts, or you would not have sent Jeannot to fetch my husband."

"Too many unknowns," replied Brother Pierre.

Belina took a wax tablet from Guillaume's investigation bag and looked at the dormitory again, screwing up her eyes in the fading light. She counted her paces to the doorway and noted where the pilgrims had left their meagre possessions. Staffs had been dropped in several places near the corpse. A mouse was trying to get inside a satchel. A pilgrim's wide-brimmed hat lay beneath one of the windows, and there was another near the wall opposite the corpse.

She sat down under a window and sketched the room on her tablet, showing the body and the various objects, the door and the three windows and the places where the dust had been disturbed. She paused and stared again at the darkening room, estimating its length and width. She frowned at her arithmetic. She had forgotten the precise length of her paces, when compared with Guillaume's measuring system.

Reluctantly, she examined the corpse's face again. It was hideous with pain. Maybe he had suffered a fit? Or a heart attack? Better than poison. And yet there was all that vomit and filth around him.

She put her sleeve over her nose and bent down to get a closer look at the vomit. Brother Pierre pulled her back.

"Don't do that, Dame Belina. If that's poison you risk breathing it. Don't touch it. Forget about it."

"I cannot do that," she whispered, trying to stop herself choking.

"Sit over by the window," said the friar, "while I put a sample of this disgusting stuff in Messire Guillaume's sample phial."

Without waiting for her reply he fished out three little phials and tore Guillaume's straw in half. He put a gobbet of vomit in the first phial, a smear of excrement in the largest phial, and two urine-soaked fragments of rush matting in the third one. He inserted their stoppers and placed the phials back in the investigation bag.

"Thank you so much," said Belina. "Please would you be able to turn the body over?"

"Of course." The friar heaved the inert corpse on to its front. The back and buttocks were pale apart from a thick horizontal stripe of purplish skin down the back of the body.

Brother Pierre pointed to the purple stripe. "That means he died here, on his back." Belina nodded.

She got to her feet and walked back to the corpse. She looked at the heap of clothes beside the body. Surely Guillaume had assumed the corpse would still be clothed?

"Who removed his clothes?" she asked.

"I did, whilst waiting for your husband. In this heat, I need to get the body into the coldest cellar as soon as possible."

"Yes of course. But don't bury him until my husband has said that you can." She picked up a fresh tablet from the investigation bag, and sat down on the clothes. The rush matting all around her looked, and smelled, filthy. She put the tablet on her knee and looked up at Brother Pierre.

"What is his name?"

"Robert. The doorman only writes down Christian names."

"A pity," sighed Belina.

"Many people only have Christian names," explained Brother Pierre, "especially Flemish pilgrims."

"Is he Flemish?"

"No idea."

Belina scratched a summary of what she had observed and learned so far. It was not much. She got up and looked through the clothes, the pilgrim's hat with a scallop shell sewn on to it, the long wooden staff, the boots, the gourd and the satchel. She put everything inside the light summer cloak except for one of the *chausses* which she used to fasten the bundle to the pilgrim's staff.

"I will get a hospice porter to escort you back to your residence," said Brother Pierre. "You will have to hurry because of the curfew." He walked to the dormitory entrance and looked at the crowd of pilgrims peering through the doorway.

"Please stand back and wait here for at least twenty *paternosters*," he told them, then beckoned to his anxious assistant hovering beyond the crowd. "Brother Martin, help me carry the body down to the cellar please, and Jeannot, you watch over this bundle of clothes and the staff. You're not to touch them. Keep everyone away."

Belina unhooked the lantern and led the two friars down the steep steps and into the cool damp cellar. "I hope rats don't get at the body," she said.

"No chance of that. We will put him in this spare sarcophagus and cover it with the old *chrestia* door over there." He pointed to a door leaning against the wall.

The two friars lowered the pilgrim's body into the stone coffin while Belina watched them. The sight of a dead body being lowered into a grave always brought back the grief of her mother's funeral long ago. Belina gulped and brushed away her tears as the friars picked up the small wooden door and placed it over the sarcophagus.

Belina led them with the lantern back up the cellar stairs and Brother Pierre picked up the pilgrim's bundle and accompanied Belina to the hospice entrance hall. He told a hospice porter to carry the pilgrim's staff and bundle and the porter shouldered it slowly, complaining that it weighed a lot. Belina wondered why it was so heavy.

The curfew bell started to ring its first series of long chimes and they had to walk very quickly up rue Saint Barthelemy and into rue Royale as the bell began chiming for the second time. They walked up rue Royale with difficulty because it was getting dark. The best street in Condom had the highest houses, each built of stone and topped with a tall tower, and the buildings cut off what little daylight was left. Servants were pushing back the shutters for the night to let what breeze there was waft into the stately rooms facing the street.

The curfew bell began its third chiming, and Belina hoped that the Watch was in a different part of the town because theoretically she should not be walking outside after curfew. She must be home before the final five sharp rings of the curfew bell had finished. They stopped discussing the demonstration that morning against Rocca's harsh behaviour, walked quickly past the crumbling cathedral and reached the shop. She took the largest key from her belt and unlocked the door, and then found a taper so that she could light a candle from the porter's lantern. "Be careful with that candle," the porter said. "If the Watch see it you'll be in trouble. They don't want any more fires especially in this hot weather."

"It's all right," she whispered, "I'm just getting my staircase lantern organised. And I will leave all this heavy stuff for my husband to carry upstairs." She lit the taper. "How will you get back to the hospice now that the final bell has gone for curfew?"

"I won't try. Much too risky. I'll walk along to the Lion d'Or and ask them to take me in."

"Will they?"

"Yes. My cousin works there. They know me well."

She thanked him again and locked the door behind her, propped her pattens beside it, put on her slippers and stepped around the bundle of the pilgrim's clothes still attached to his walking staff. Carrying the lantern, she negotiated her way through the chests and urns on the floor of the shop and unlocked the door to the courtyard. By now it was almost dark and she climbed up the steep wooden staircase with great care.

The door to their chamber was locked, much to her annoyance. She banged on it, hurting her fist.

"You've been a long time," said Guillaume. It wasn't much of a welcome but after three years of marriage she was used to his terse preparations when he was about to go on a journey. She saw that he had shaved in preparation for his early start and that he was cleaning his riding boots. His travel bundle stood on the floor and the untidy room she had left was now in good order. She smiled in spite of her tiredness.

He handed her a goblet. Expecting it to be full of watery wine she gulped half of it down and spluttered at the unexpected *aygue ardente*. She made a face. "You might have warned me that it is firewater."

"After what you've been through you need some of the best local medicine."

She sniffed at the brandy and sipped a little more of it.

"Where are the pilgrim's possessions?" Guillaume demanded.

"In the shop. They were much too heavy for me to carry upstairs."

"Heavy? How can a pilgrim walk any distance with heavy clothes? You must be very tired."

She sat down on the bed. Yes, she was tired, but not so worn out that she had forgotten her surprise at the weight of the pilgrim's clothes. His *besace*, on the other hand, had seemed light for a pilgrim's satchel.

Guillaume returned with the pilgrim's bundle swinging from the staff. He went into the inner room, untied the makeshift tape and placed the staff in the far corner. Then he opened the bundle very gently.

"Did you make a list of all these things?" he asked her.

"No. I didn't even try. Brother Pierre was in a hurry to remove the body from the dormitory so that the pilgrims could get into the room. But I noted down as much as I could see of the body. He seemed to have been poisoned. His face was horrid, really horrid."

Guillaume put his arm round her shoulders. But only for a moment. Then he was back on his knees examining the pilgrim's few possessions, handling them with great care.

"No use in this candlelight," he said after a few moments. "You'll have to look at them carefully tomorrow and make a detailed list." He hung the gourd on its hook near the top of the staff.

"And you?" she asked.

"Me? I'm leaving for Bordeaux, like I told you."

"How can you? It's more than enough to look at a dead body in the hospice. Now, the rest of the investigation is up to you, Messire Rapporteur."

"I don't have the time. You can do it all. You're perfectly capable, and it will occupy you in my absence."

"I have plenty of my own work to do, thank you, without having to do yours too," she retorted. "You can keep your work problems for yourself."

"Consider it a challenge." He grinned, and went back to giving his riding boots a final polish.

She let down her hair and undressed while he went on

rubbing his boots, humming softly. "Stop that humming, and polishing, and come to bed," she called to him. But he took no notice.

CHAPTER FOUR

Belina woke before daybreak. Guillaume had already washed and dressed and was leaning against the wall, chewing a chunk of cheese pressed on to a crust of yesterday's bread. Three apples and a peach awaited his attention.

"*Adiu*, my love," he called out, examining the peach.

She got out of bed and scowled at him. "Surely you should stay here and investigate that pilgrim's death?"

"No. You can do that. Better than selling *babioles* to pilgrims - or to false pilgrims."

"Some of them are genuine," Belina retorted.

"Yesterday's corpse might not be. His clothes were too heavy."

"I know," she admitted. "I am going to slit open the lining of the cloak to see if there's money inside it. But even if there is, it might just mean he is a prudent pilgrim."

"Of course, especially if he has set out from somewhere very close to Lectoure or Agen and still has a hoard of coins for his journey."

"I don't think so. He was coming back from Messire Saint Jacques in Galicia. He's got a scallop shell. And he told the Recteur that he had walked here from Mouchan."

"Then he may well be a false pilgrim," replied Guillaume."Or a thief." He finished the peach and started on an apple. "If he is a penitential pilgrim on his way back from St

James he would have a letter of certification confirming that he's completed the pilgrimage. So you could search for that."

"I will look through the satchel as soon as I am back from Mass," said Belina.

"Don't talk about it yet in the cathedral. Just keep your eyes and ears open. See if there are any strangers."

"Of course there will be strangers. What with pilgrims and soldiers and pedlars and tax-collectors and merchants, Condom is becoming invaded," she replied.

"In that case you will have plenty to look at and listen to," was Guillaume's laconic reply.

She felt like hitting him, or even pulling his fair hair. Instead, she stroked it. "You're a stranger too," she said.

He kissed her nose."That's why I'm telling you to watch them – instead of concentrating on your usual suspects, the Senclar family."

"I am sure that Dame Senclar is a poisoner, and a witch."

"That's what everyone says."

"Maybe she poisoned this pilgrim," Belina suggested.

"Unlikely. She wouldn't bother. She only poisons her enemies."

"Definitely not. They say that when she was a child in Lectoure she poisoned lots of paupers, just to try out her potions," Belina insisted.

"By now, at the age of forty and living in Condom, she will know which potion does what," he replied, shifting slightly against the wall. "Less guesswork for Dame Senclar nowadays."

"She scares me,"said Belina. "Is she really only forty?"

Guillaume nodded. "Yes. She is a rich heiress who was married aged twelve and had a baby at thirteen. She was lucky to survive that. She must have had a horrible, cruel mother to wed her to such a scoundrel." He ate the last apple. "Lady Margaret Beaufort was the same."

"The mother of the English count who lives in Brittany?"

"Yes, alas." Guillaume leant out of the window, reached

downwards and picked a peach from the tree beside it. "More Welsh than English, actually, because he was born and brought up in Wales."

"Is that the count who gets money from Rocca?" Guillaume nodded. "Our money, our treasure. Why should he be getting it?" Belina banged her fist on the table. "The archdeacon must stop any more going to him."

"He is trying to stop it, as I told you yesterday, but Rocca is very powerful." Guillaume began to eat the peach. "He is protected by Archbishop Cato in Paris, who is the confidant of King Louis."

"Does King Louis approve of our money going to Brittany?"

"Of course he does. If Henry Tudor becomes king of England he won't try to invade France, which we hear that King Richard is planning to do."

"How can you be so sure about Henry Tudor not invading France, Guillaume?"

"He will prefer to sit in his counting-house knee deep in the English money he extorted from the peasants and shop-keepers to pay for Bishop Morton's business interests."

Belina asked if these interests included the Bordeaux wine trade, but Guillaume maintained that they centred on property transactions. Moreover, as soon as Morton became Archbishop of Canterbury he would exploit the Sussex iron ore and make an enormous profit from ironworking. He would drain the Fens. He would....

Belina stopped listening. She had no idea where Sussex or the Fens were. Even Bordeaux was a far-away city from her point of view. Guillaume's birthplace, Southampton, seemed like the end of the Earth. She knew her husband wanted to take her there some day, but she dreaded the voyage even more than meeting his English family.

Guillaume interrupted her thoughts with a quick embrace. "Don't forget to play chess with Sir John in my absence. It will take his mind off the dangers to his beloved England now that

King Edward has died. I know he approves of the Duke of Gloucester – he fought beside him in Scotland."

"King Richard, you mean," said Belina.

"Oh yes, King Richard. God help him." Guillaume pulled on his boots, picked up his travel bundle and bag of spurs, and clattered off downstairs.

She watched him cross the courtyard and open the door outside. He turned and blew her a kiss, pushed his hat over his fair hair and disappeared from sight.

She washed her face and hands and put on her Sunday gown. She brushed her long black hair and coiled it on top of her head. She ate the remaining dry crust and said her prayers, asking Our Lady for forgiveness for her unloving speech with Guillaume and asking for him to be protected in his journey to Bordeaux. "And, especially please, let him be back here soon," she added.

She draped the pilgrim's cloak over Guillaume's work table. She knew well that her husband would have stretched it out on the bed, risking fleas and other insects hopping inside the bedclothes. She had passed many a scratchy night after he had done that.

No sooner had she smoothed the cloak out on the table than the cat jumped on to it and began to wash itself.

"Minet, get off," she scolded, carrying her through to the bed in the main room. But the cat returned at once to the table and curled up on the middle of the old worn cloak. She began to purr.

Trying not to disturb Minet, Belina examined the cloak. It was more dusty than dirty, and had been carefully darned in several places. She felt the hem, still wondering why the homespun cloth was so heavy. Turning part of it over, she saw that a large area of it had been re-hemmed with bigger stitches. Belina fetched her scissors and cut away some of the stitching.

She gasped at the sight of so many gold and silver coins.

They represented many weeks' takings in the shop. Even more puzzling, the coins were from different countries. She took a couple of the largest to the window, but even in the better light she was unable to identify them.

She rummaged through Guillaume's chest and picked up an old *chausse*. Then she listed the coins as best she could describe them on a tablet and dropped each one into the *chausse*. She took out her winter cotte from her clothes chest, wrapped it round the *chausse*, and placed that at the bottom of her chest.

Next she examined the rest of the pilgrim's possessions. A typical wide-brimmed hat with a scallop shell, a battered satchel, good quality boots, stinking *chausses* which she stuffed inside the left boot, a grubby tunic, and the pilgrim's staff with the drinking gourd which Guillaume had tied to the hook on the staff. Belina sniffed the empty gourd. It smelled sharp and sour. She wrinkled her nose and put the staff and the gourd back in the corner. She turned her attention to the large leather purse that held a few coins. There was no sign of a letter of certification certifying that he was a penitential pilgrim.

Belina frowned. She could not understand why a pilgrim coming *back* from his pilgrimage to Galicia would have so much money. Was he a thief? Surely, he could not be a real pilgrim? Perhaps he was just very mean and had stayed in hospices to save money? Perhaps he was a gambler and had won all these coins? She could not make sense of it at all.

Minet sniffed the open satchel, removed a piece of cheese and gulped it down.

Belina emptied out the rest of the satchel's contents. They included two wood carvings wrapped in cloth. One was of St Roch, a patron saint of pilgrims. The other was of a boy peeing. When she looked closer, she saw that the heads of both carvings had been stained, probably by wine.

She listed all the contents on her tablet, and replaced them in the same order, as Guillaume used to do.

"Why aren't you here when you are needed?" she asked

the empty room. She strode across it. "No answer came the stern reply," she said. She sat down at the table and listed her observations of the pilgrim's dead body. What poison had he taken? Why had such a rich pilgrim taken poison? If he was the victim of a poisoner, why hadn't his murderer stolen the hoard of gold and silver?

The cathedral bell interrupted her thoughts. She put on her Sunday head-cloth, folded back its front brim (but perhaps not as neatly as she should have done), picked up a coin from the wooden box on top of the corner cupboard, and looked out of the window to check the weather. It was not dry enough to wear her normal outdoor slippers and so she had to spend time hunting for her shoes. By the time she was organised to go to Mass, the bell had stopped ringing. She would be late.

She entered the cathedral by the south door as usual. The maintenance expert had reported last spring that the tower at the west end of the nave was unstable and might collapse at any time. Either it had to be buttressed carefully, and expensively, or the whole building would have to be pulled down and replaced by a sound, new one. Meanwhile, everyone had been asked to contribute to the tower-strengthening fund. It was this fund which people said had been spirited away to Henry Tudor, the English count in Brittany.

She stood among the other cathedral staff and their families, listening to the music resonating from the crumbling painted walls of the damaged cathedral. A very pretty girl with an elegant pale green wired head-cloth tried to stand next to the cathedral staff, but they pushed her away. "No strumpets here," said the head groom. "Go back to La Bouquerie where you belong."

On the far side of the chancel sat the consuls and their families. The first pew was occupied by the Senclars, Henri in the middle, between his bosomy wife Jeanne and his tiny, skinny mother, Edith the Poisoner. Beyond Jeanne were his twin daughters by his first marriage. Next to Edith sat René

Chezelle, her physician, rumoured to be the provider of special poisons that he found for Dame Senclar in the vicinity of a town called Châtellerault. Belina had no idea where that town was, and she hoped it was far away from Gascony. Henri Senclar was whispering into Jeanne's ear while fondling her left breast, which was almost exposed. His mother was frowning at him, but he took no notice. He might be a consul of Condom, but he was still a spoilt greedy little boy.

Belina turned her attention to the mystery of the dead pilgrim. She went over what she had observed in her mind, what Brother Pierre had said (which was not much), and what she had picked up during the last six years selling *babioles* to pilgrims. How many pilgrims were genuine? How many of their relics were genuine? Guillaume called that question 'opening Pandora's box'. Apparently, Pandora was a Greek, which was yet another thing Belina found difficult to understand. When she had asked Guillaume if Pandora's box contained a relic and if so of what saint, he had laughed and hugged her. She knew quite a lot about Greek medical ideas, the four cardinal humours, for example. But the nuns who had taught her to read, write and count had never spoken about Pandora and her box.

A hand on her shoulder brought Belina back to the present. She spun round and stared at her elder brother Jordi.

"We have to talk urgently," he whispered.

Belina flicked away the bits of flour his hand had left on her shoulder. "Let's leave now," she whispered back.

They tiptoed outside and walked to the shop. Belina pretended to check the shutters, waiting until the street was empty.

"What's the matter? You look as if you haven't slept for eight days."

"Not yet eight days." He sighed.

Belina waited for his explanations. It was unlike Jordi to be so taciturn. Like all Gascons, he was normally very talkative.

"That accursed assistant of Treasurer Rocca deserves to go down with the plague."

Belina stared at him in amazement. "Don't talk like that, it's unlucky."

"It's unlucky that we have such scoundrels here in Condom. Rocca and Loupmont should go back to their birthplace, Saint Mihiel, and stay there for ever."

"I thought they came from Paris," said Belina.

"Before they turned up here, yes. But originally they are from the Barrois."

"Where's that?"

"Hundreds of leagues to the east. The Duchy of Bar."

This meant nothing to Belina. She waited to hear the reason for her brother's anger and anxiety, taking care that no more flour fell on to her Sunday gown.

"Loupmont has made an official accusation against me."

She gasped. "What for?"

"Cheating on the weight of the bishop's wheat."

"Did you?" she whispered, staring into his eyes, just like Guillaume did when questioning a suspect.

"Of course I didn't. I'm not daft. Millers have a reputation for cheating on grain and flour weights, but that doesn't mean I would cheat the bishop."

They stared at each other. Bishop Montbrun was not much liked, nor personally respected, but he was their bishop and the owner of the Moulié family mill at Gauge. He could turn them out if he wanted to – or even if the archdeacon felt like it, and they knew very well that the archdeacon was too harassed and overworked to check the truth of spiteful false charges. The accusation was very serious.

"I'd like Guillaume's advice, Belina." He started to open the door of the cathedral staff residence next to the shuttered shop.

Belina hesitated. How could she tell her brother that Guillaume was away from home?

"It's the wrong time to disturb him," she lied. "He's busy on one of his long reports for the bishop."

"Damn his long reports."

"I agree," said Belina, "so let's walk down to the river and try to find a solution. But wait in the courtyard first while I go upstairs to change out of my Sunday gown."

Belina returned wearing her everyday tunic and carrying her satchel of tablets.

"What do you need all those tablets for?" he demanded."

"For later. I need to check the poisonous plants in the Senclar garden."

"Why?"

"Guillaume has asked me to draw them on these tablets," she replied.

They reached the Barlet Bridge and Belina looked up at its high tower and gate through which people from La Bouquerie and other visitors from beyond the town were walking or riding horses, mules, and donkeys. She gazed at the river Baïse as it flowed fast and deep below the solidly built bridge. A week of August thunderstorms in the Pyrenees had turned the water brown and it carried tree branches, dead ducks, and planks from smashed jetties upstream.

They worked out a possible solution to the problem of Loupmont's accusation as they looked at the skilful way their cousin Christau was handling his boat in the tricky, dangerous currents. They went to meet him at the waterside, where Jordi helped Christau tie the boat up, unload some sacks of flour and store them in their shed near the wharf. Then the three of them watched the panicky manœuvres being made by Bernard Troubat and his crew in the imposing boat that belonged to Henri Senclar.

"Why does the consul employ such an incompetent fool?" muttered Jordi.

"Because the consul never travels anywhere by boat," replied Christau. "But mostly because Troubat's main job is more important to Consul Senclar."

"What job?"

"Didn't you know? He is responsible for the transport of the consul's strumpet, the head-cloth maker who lives in La Bouquerie. She has to be ferried across the river whenever the consul wants to sample her favours, which is often."

Belina felt embarrassed. She gritted her teeth and gazed downstream, watching a mass of vegetation being swept northwards over the weir. She listened to branches crashing against the mill wheel and the splashes made by objects hurtling over the weir.

"If she is so vital to the consul's needs, why doesn't he ensure that she is transported more safely? Or why doesn't he send a groom on a horse over the bridge to fetch her?" Jordi asked.

"They say he doesn't fancy her smelling of horses."

"But she still has to walk up the path to the rue des Argentiers and along to the Senclar mansion," said Jordi, adding that she would get her clothes muddy and her head-cloth blown away.

"The consul keeps a so-called boathouse opposite La Bouquerie. Whore-house, more like."

Belina's embarrassment grew. She pulled at her head-cloth, crossed her arms and looked down at the muddy stone wharf.

"Once she's inside the whore-house her head-cloth comes off, and so does everything else. Very quickly," Christau continued, chuckling.

"How can you know that Christau?"

"Us boatmen peer in through the holes in the boathouse back door." He grinned. "The consul is very energetic, but his strumpet can keep him going for hours. She's got lots of interesting ideas and methods." He whispered in Jordi's ear for several minutes and they both laughed.

Belina had had enough. "It's time you got back to the mill," she told her brother sharply. "Catalina will be wondering where you are." Christau hurried away back to his boat. "Will you tell her about what we plan to do?" Belina asked, more gently.

"Not really. She's too gossipy. And her mother's even worse."

"Is her mother still giving you trouble?" Belina asked, even more gently.

"Oh yes indeed. She is always dropping in and criticising us. And always wasting our time too, as well as spoiling the children."

"All grandmothers do that."

"Our stepmother doesn't," he retorted. "She never bothers to see the children."

"She's much too young to be a grandmother," Belina replied. She kissed him farewell and strode away without waiting to watch Jordi and Christau moor the boat securely and walk upstream along the riverside path to the mill at Gauge.

CHAPTER FIVE

As she made her way through the heat of the day along the wharf to Consul Senclar's stables, Belina heard scraps of conversation as she swatted at the swarms of flies that were gathering by the river. Crops had been damaged in the storm – that meant less grain for her brother's mill. The grapes had swelled too soon in the heat and had then been crushed by the rain. Table grapes ripening in town gardens had been worst hit. Shopkeepers were repairing shutters. The ground was still damp and strewn with rubbish, attracting more flies. Belina put her hand over her nose as she stepped round a really noxious mound of filth, averting her eyes.

It was a relief to reach the Senclar stables. She peered inside, looking for Tomas Forgues, the brother of Guillaume's groom Antoni. It was difficult to identify him among all the other grooms, busy rubbing down fine horses. Surely the consul did not need twenty riding horses? Belina was puzzled by all the activity.

"*Adishatz*, Dame Belina."

She turned round and smiled a greeting at Tomas. "You seem really busy," she said,"I hope I am not disturbing you too much."

"Doesn't matter if you are."

"Has the consul been buying lots of horses?" she asked.

"No. Most of these belong to yesterday's arrivals from

Eauze. Rich pilgrims on their way back from Compostela. All displaying their scallop shells to show they have been to see Messire Saint Jacques in Galicia.

"They will be tired after such a long journey," said Belina.

"Depends on whether they really got as far as they say. Quite a lot of pilgrims turn round at Bierzo and don't reach Galicia at all. And then there are others who are merchants in disguise trying to find trading possibilities with the new war in the south of Spain."

"Where are this group returning to?" She pointed to the horses.

"This lot live in Luxembourg."

"Where's that?"

"In the east, between Flanders and Lorraine."

"Is that where Saint Mihiel is?"

"Never heard of it. What's interesting about Saint Mihiel?"

"I don't know if anything is. My brother mentioned it." She stopped talking, reluctant to say anything more in case she gave away Jordi's secret.

"Luxembourg is a duchy belonging to the Counts of Saint Pol. The young Dame Senclar especially likes Luxembourgers to stay here." Tomas began rubbing down another horse. "Probably because Dame Edith doesn't like Luxembourgers. She doesn't like anyone except French nobility."

"But she's not noble," Belina objected.

"No, but she's educated and proud that she can read and write Latin. She despises the young dame for her lack of book-learning. She is always mocking her in front of visitors."

"Perhaps she's just jealous of the young dame's youth," Belina suggested.

"Is Messire Guillaume's mother like that?" Tomas asked.

"She's dead."

"Oh, sorry about that. Easier for you then."

"Yes," said Belina. She needed to turn the conversation away from an interrogation concerning Guillaume's family.

She knew very well that his mother was not dead (or, at least, she was very much alive last time they heard from her) but Guillaume had made Belina promise not to tell anyone that his mother was English.

"I was wondering if you could possibly show me round Dame Senclar's *potager*", she said.

"Of course I can, but why do you want to see a lot of soggy vegetables?"

"My husband has asked me to look at them, and the herbs, to get an idea of what is growing at the moment."

"Do you want to eat some of them?" he grinned.

"No, no," she replied hastily. "I have to make a list of the ones that are poisonous. Guillaume is investigating the poisoning of a pilgrim in the Pradau hospice."

"And you really think that he was poisoned by Dame Senclar?"

"No, of course not," Belina said.

"Actually, you never know," said Tomas. "The mistress has a very bad reputation. Personally, I would never eat or drink anything she gave me."

Belina longed to prod him for more information but she realized that there were too many people nearby who might be listening and could report back to Dame Senclar. She changed the subject, and explained to Tomas that because the pilgrim had died in a religious building it was her husband's responsibility to investigate the death and report his findings to Bishop Montbrun. She wished the Senechal's staff would do the investigations instead.

Belina followed Tomas through the stables and he showed her into the kitchen garden. She took out a wax tablet and began to draw a plant, her stylus scratching on the much re-used tablet. She pinched a leaf and sniffed her fingers.

"Don't do that, Dame."

She looked up. A young kitchen maid carrying a basket of peaches was frowning at her.

"That there plant can give you a nasty bellyache. The master cook is very particular about us never touching it. Especially never touching it and then rubbing our eyes."

"What's it called?"

"*Arnic*, or something like that."

"What other plants are dangerous?" asked Belina.

"I'll show you." The maid put down her basket of peaches and led Belina round the squares of herbs and vegetables, pointing out the dangerous ones and waiting while Belina drew them on her tablets. She told Belina her version of the name of each plant.

"However do you remember all these names?" Belina asked her.

"The master cook insists that we know them all so that we can fetch whatever he orders," the maid explained.

"But why would he order poisonous plants?"

"To kill rats and moles and suchlike of course."

"You could get a cat to catch rats and mice," said Belina.

"The family don't like cats. They like dogs, especially grey-hounds. That way they feel grand, like King Louis."

"They are grand anyway," said Belina,"even without all the dogs and horses."

"Oh yes. And they have lots of jewellery, even the consul."

Belina knew that. Henri Senclar was a good customer of the shop. She had learnt the hard way to avoid him and his wandering hands. He had a way of standing very close to women looking at their cleavage, waiting for ribbons on his codpiece to shake. On one occasion, soon after she had begun working in the shop, he had asked Quiteira to find something special for him from the inner room, and then he had pinned Belina against the counter and put one hand up inside her skirt while with the other one forced her face against his. Luckily, Quiteira had seen what he was doing and pulled him away. Belina wondered if he treated all girls like that, and whether this helpful young kitchen maid suffered from his attentions.

"The consul gave me a lovely bracelet for my saint's day,"- said the maid, "but he made me promise not to wear it when I am working."

"Of course not. You wouldn't want to damage it," said Belina.

"It's not that," the girl replied. "The old and young dames wouldn't like to know that the consul had given me it. They are jealous crabs. Mean shrews."

"So when do you wear your bracelet?" asked Belina.

The girl looked down at the ground. "When the consul tells me to meet him in the étuves." She kept looking at the ground.

"I hope he pays you well for your company,"said Belina.

"Not bad. At least I can put by a bit of money for getting married."

"Are you betrothed?"

"Sort of. My friend Ramon works in the Cheval Blanc and he is putting money by too. We hope to have an inn of our own sometime."

"Does the Cheval Blanc have lots of pilgrims just now?" asked Belina.

"Not enough to pay the staff properly." She shrugged her shoulders. "They had an odd pilgrim the other day who came in dressed as an ex-soldier. Then he went to the cathedral, or so he said, and came back dressed as a pilgrim with a staff and satchel and a hat with a scallop shell. Ramon hardly recognized him."

"Perhaps it was a different person,"Belina suggested.

"No, he had the same funny way of walking. As if he were a horseman who had been wounded in the past."

"Or perhaps he was just worn out with coming back from Compostela?"

"That's the funny thing," said the maid. "When he arrived dressed like an ex-soldier he told Ramon he had come from Abrin, and Moissac before that." She pointed to a plant and told Belina that it was a *fenugrec* which she took with her to her meetings with the consul in the étuves.

"For myself I chew on a bit of yarrow," she announced.

"Why?"

"They say it's a love potion."

"Do you want to fall in love with the consul? I thought you said you were betrothed," Belina asked, trying to keep the surprise out of her voice.

"Of course not. But chewing it makes me not mind being with the consul in the étuves. The *fenugrec* makes him terribly energetic and amorous."

Belina preferred to change the subject. "How do you know when he wants you to meet him?"

"In the morning the Steward whispers in my ear that I have to go there early afternoon because that is the best time for the consul."

"Best time to get away from work or to get away from his wife?"

"Neither. It's his favourite time for sex," the maid explained unemotionally. "Though sometimes he prefers what he calls 'dinner-with-siesta' and for that we meet in his boathouse and we have a small meal, a lot of strong wine and heaps of sex."

"How do you get into the boathouse? Or isn't it locked?" Belina asked.

"I walk down to the wharf and wait for the head boatman who keeps the key on his belt," the maid explained. "Trouble with that arrangement is that the boatman wants his turn too, before the consul arrives. Troubat isn't really sexy, but he helps himself to some of the consul's *poudre de cantharides* and I try to get him aroused. It takes time. Twice the consul has banged on the door trying to get in, but Troubat puts his hand over my mouth and tries to keep still until the consul swears and goes away."

"That means you lose your dinner and the money from the

consul," said Belina. She sketched another plant, hoping the kitchen maid would not notice her shaky drawing.

"No. I wait until Troubat has put his clothes back on and left by a hidden door which I don't think the consul realises is there."

"Perhaps he doesn't really leave," suggested Belina. "Maybe he watches you and the consul." She forced herself to continue sketching.

"I don't care if he does. After all, lots of people can see me with the consul in the étuves. When Troubat's gone I just lie on the lovely silk cushions, chew on my yarrow stalk and wait for the consul to arrive."

"Is he cross when he arrives?" asked Belina. She picked up another wax tablet.

"Yes of course. But that makes him all the more excited. He's quite fun when he is like that."

Belina decided that this conversation was not only improper but was also delaying her plant studies and she sketched the next one – an orris – with an unsteady hand.

The maid took the hint and went back into the house while Belina disregarded the story about the odd pilgrim because he had been in the Cheval Blanc inn and not in the hospice. Instead, she concentrated on plants and poisons.

It became too hot to sit drawing in the garden, so she returned to the stables. By now all was quiet, with horses eating and grooms cleaning the saddles. Tomas was talking to the head groom so she waited for a few minutes before interrupting their discussion about the worrying state of the damp straw. Then she curtseyed very briefly to the head groom and explained that she needed to ask him and all his staff whether they had seen 'her' dead pilgrim.

"No, Dame Lansac," came the quick reply. "All pilgrims look the same. The only difference is in the amount they limp. I keep a careful watch for those likely to be tempted to steal a horse or a mule." He sighed. "These are bad times. I have to suspect everyone."

Belina nodded. "Please could I speak to all your staff," she repeated.

"Yes, but don't waste their time."

He led Belina around the stables, making it very clear to his grooms and stable lads that they should not 'waste the dame's time'. By which he meant *their* time, Belina realised, but she persevered. Several grooms had seen pilgrims coming out of the cathedral after the thunderstorm on Saturday and buy food in the streets, but no one had been near the Pradau hospice on the other side of the town.

Belina turned to Tomas to bid him farewell, carefully not admitting that he had shown her into the Senclar *potager*, but he was concentrating on the head groom's instructions.

"You are to ride to Flaran Abbey straight away and take this package from Dame Senclar," the head groom was saying.

"The elder dame?" Tomas asked.

"Yes, of course I mean Dame Edith. The young dame does not give alms to Flaran. Nor to anywhere else for that matter."

No one likes Dame Jeanne, thought Belina, herself included. "Pushy, sharp-tongued upstart," she said to herself as she walked upstream to the Gachiou Gate, and then through that and on to the common. It was very hot and she found it difficult to walk on the slippery grass so she was glad when she could escape the fierce sunshine and walk between the crumbling ramparts opposite the Sainte Claire Gate and into the shady rue des Trois Eperons to the Cheval Blanc. The street was crowded with noisy groups of soldiers looking at the workshops of saddlers and spurmakers. A blacksmith's apprentice was beating farm implements into shape whilst his colleague sharpened knives. The bridle maker's wife was scolding a goat which was trying to eat a rein hanging from an open shutter.

Belina crossed to the other side of the street. Her tablet bag was feeling very heavy by now, but she dared not put it down. She was concentrating so hard on avoiding the mess left by animals that she collided with a pedlar's bulging bag and was squashed against the nailmaker's stall, grazing her hand on a group of nails hanging from his counter.

It seemed a relief to reach the main door of the Cheval Blanc. Belina hoped it would be cooler inside, but she hesitated before opening the door of the large inn and entering the crowded, noisy room. Soldiers, merchants, and prosperous-looking travellers were quenching their thirst and discussing the bad state of the roads. It made a change from listening to depressing tales of deaths and evictions.

The landlord pushed his way towards her through the crowds of customers. "This inn is no place for a woman on her own," he told her. Taking her arm, he led her outside into the street. "We are not the sort of establishment that encourages women...," he paused, "to entertain our customers."

Belina looked at him in embarrassment, irritated by his insinuations.

"I am not looking for your customers," she snapped, "I am looking for one of your staff, named Ramon."

"You are out of luck. He is already betrothed," he smirked.

"I know that very well. Indeed, it was his betrothed who suggested I should talk to him."

"Well, you can't do that. He's much too busy. We all are. Now, you be off away from here."

She stared at him, still feeling a mixture of embarrassment and annoyance. She pressed her lips tightly together and her head began to shake a little.

"If you still want to find customers to entertain, try the Chat Gris tavern in La Bouquerie. They keep a stock of girls ready to serve their customers."

He strode back through the doorway, leaving her standing in the busy street, with men pushing past her to get into the inn.

She waited for five *paternosters* and walked back inside. To her right she saw a couple of merchants with their wives (at least, she presumed they were their wives), and sat down near them. She tried to concentrate on their conversation, even though their northern French accent was difficult to follow. Their talk was about the dying King Louis and what his death might mean for trade and taxes. The older merchant maintained that it would mean lower taxes, on the grounds that they could not go even higher. The younger merchant foresaw civil war, and therefore higher taxes in addition to destruction and the dangers to trading and travel. Then talk turned to the money to be made from the capture of the kingdom of Granada in southern Spain.

Two soldiers joined in the conversation, explaining that they themselves were on their way to fight the Moors. "We want their women as slaves."

Belina gulped. She wondered if her soldier brother had acquired slaves by now.

"Are you Jews, by any chance?" a third soldier asked the merchants.

"What if we are?"

"Keep out of Spain, messires. They say that Queen Isabel has set herself against the Jews."

"Why is that?"

"So that she can keep both the Church and the rabble in Seville contented. Confiscating Jewish treasure helps to fund the royal attack against the Moors. Better than taxes. It's a very popular move."

"But presumably that is only southern Spain?"

"Don't be so sure of that, messire. They say the Inquisition is coming north and that it has already reached Ciudad Real."

Everyone began talking at once about the Inquisition in Spain, and Belina lost interest. It seemed unlikely that the dead pilgrim would be connected with that horror in any way.

She left the inn, turned right into the rue Royale, walked past the Saint Esprit Gate with its queues of pack animals and then along rue Saint Barthelemy to the hospice.

CHAPTER SIX

Guillaume and his groom, Antoni, had reached Vianne, their first stop-off on their long journey to Bordeaux. They dismounted, paid their toll and went through the ancient gateway to the nearest inn where they left their horses in the stables. They knew the Chapon inn well from their many journeys to and from Bordeaux and the landlord greeted them with deference. "*Bonjour messires*, what can I get you? Some Buzet wine perhaps, with a chicken pie?"

They settled down in a quiet corner and discussed the journey so far. It had been easy enough going along the straight, flat highway to Nérac, but getting through that town had proved tricky because the river Baïse had flooded the tanneries near the bridge. They had threaded their way through unknown alleys, pursued by the appalling stink. The town was very noisy and disorderly and they lost some precious time finding their way out of the chaos.

"We will not reach Port Sainte Marie in time for dinner," Guillaume had remarked. "Best to go as fast as possible through Barbaste and Lavardac and stop at the Chapon in Vianne."

"Suppose there is a flood at Barbaste too?" said Antoni.

"That bridge beside the Tours mill is high enough and strong enough. We will be all right there even if the miller overcharges us to cross it and keeps more than he should for himself instead of handing it over to the *seigneur* of Barbaste."

"But it will be too far for the horses before they eat their dinner," Antoni persisted. "And before we eat our dinner too."

But Guillaume took no notice. His thoughts were on Belina. How was she coping with the task he had set her, investigating the death of that pilgrim in the Pradau hospice? Should he have made her do that? After all, he could have used the pilgrim's death as an excuse to persuade the archdeacon to tell Josep to go to Bordeaux instead. Guillaume was not often arrogant and he rarely thought himself indispensable. And yet, being in Bordeaux would further his chance of playing an important part in the *Reconquista* of Gascony.

As they rode along the muddy highway to Barbaste, avoiding the fallen branches and the swollen streams pouring over the surface of the road, Guillaume concentrated on whether he had taught his wife well enough how to do his inquirer's work.

He had developed his original plan because he knew that he had to make himself available at short notice to help in the *Reconquista* plot, serving his real country rather than France. His secret instructions had referred, albeit obliquely, to helping agents develop a way to get their normal work responsibilities to be done by someone so trustworthy that their own absence from their Bordeaux workplace would go unnoticed. That would not have been too difficult if Guillaume had still been living in the Bordeaux area like all the other secret agents did. But he was many days' journey away, stuck in Condom. Moreover, the only person who he could even begin to trust with his secret was his wife, his beloved Belina. And so he had trained her carefully and slowly, giving her no idea that one day she would have to undertake an investigation all by herself.

Antoni interrupted Guillaume's thoughts. "Messire Guillaume, if you insist on reaching Vianne before we have dinner you will have to ride faster."

Guillaume came back to the present, spurred his horse and

caught Antoni up at the entrance to Lavardac. Past the town, the highway had improved and they rode faster which meant that Guillaume had to concentrate on keeping himself on his horse and his thoughts on the journey instead of on his wife.

It was not until they had reached the Chapon inn and were eating their chicken pie that Guillaume's thoughts turned again to Belina and the difficult work she was doing on his behalf. Was she managing it? He hoped so, of course, but it was the first time she had been alone with a dead body. Would she ask for help? If so, who would she ask? He reviewed the people she might ask and decided that none of them could do such a task.

Antoni broke into his thoughts by setting his goblet down next to the wine jug. Guillaume took the hint and poured some more wine. "This stuff is rather good, even if it is not Bordeaux. Let's have some more." He signalled to the landlord.

When another pewter jug was brought to their table Guillaume asked if this Buzet wine was exported to England – but he did not indicate his own family's interest in the subject.

"We try to, messire, but those terrible merchants in Bordeaux don't let us send any of our wine down to Bordeaux until after Christmas, by which time it is not so good for travelling all the way across the Gulf of Gascony. In any case, the winter weather makes shipping dangerous. I don't like Bordeaux people."

Guillaume smiled, but said nothing. Antoni, however, was less reticent. "I agree. I find them selfish and greedy. I prefer Toulouse." He drank from his goblet. "Better place for horses too."

"Why?"

"They say that there is Spanish blood in them. Spanish horses are best because they are foaled in a high and hard country. Spanish jennets are swift and agile. The Portuguese and the Moors use them too." Antoni drank some more of his wine. "The Moors are very good horsemen, so they say."

Guillaume suggested that perhaps that was because Moors did not drink wine owing to their religion, but Antoni did not take the bait. Instead, once the landlord had moved away to serve other customers Antoni took revenge and said, "my colleagues are all talking about the new arrival in the cathedral staff residence."

"What new arrival? A horse or a person?"

"Both, but it is the person we all talk about. He is a Flemish lawyer who says he is from Paris, but Miqueu has managed to find out that he has been living in England."

Guillaume finished his chicken pie, and said, "and his groom picks locks, or so I have been told."

"I've heard that too," replied Antoni. "But it is the Flemish lawyer who is interesting. He is very good looking, and very successful with women." He paused and looked at Guillaume. "Miqueu has been observing the way he has seduced several pretty young women. He takes them into inns, or finds them there already, and provides them with wine and smiles and hugs." He paused again and stared into Guillaume's hazel eyes. "And much more than hugs," he added.

"Why does Miqueu think that is so fascinating, Antoni?"

"To learn from him, I think. Miqueu is only seventeen." Antoni finished the wine in his goblet, but the jug was too far away for him to help himself to more, so he carried on needling Guilllaume. "Miqueu was saying to us all that this new arrival would be dangerous for Dame Belina."

Guillaume stared at him and frowned. "My wife is not the sort of woman to be taken into inns by Flemish seducers, or by anyone else for that matter."

"Of course not, Messire Guillaume. It's only what Miqueu has been saying." He paused. "But I have seen this man on two occasions already and he is very handsome. Long black curly hair and very fine clothes."

"He can't be Flemish if he has black hair," said Guillaume. "They have fair hair, like myself." He pulled his hat down a bit more as if to hide his hair. "And what is he doing in the cathedral staff residence?"

"No one really knows, but he seems to be a close friend of Rocca and is sharing his chamber."

"So?" said Guillaume. He crossed his arms and stared at his groom. His thoughts went back to his doubts about whether Belina could or would undertake the investigation entirely by herself. Suppose she asked for legal help? Suppose this Flemish lawyer living so close to her agreed to help her? He would, if Antoni's chatter was even half truthful, take advantage of being close to Belina to touch her, smile at her, touch her hair underneath her head-cloth... or maybe remove the head-cloth entirely...

Guillaume shuddered and almost spilt his wine. He frowned, his mind centred on Belina's beautiful black hair.

Antoni interrupted Guillaume's thoughts with a sly hint that perhaps Rocca had arranged for Guillaume to go to Bordeaux so that the seducer could get to know Dame Belina better.

"I repeat, Antoni," said Guillaume, "that my wife is not the sort of woman to be taken into inns by Flemish seducers. In any case, it was not Rocca who ordered me to go to Bordeaux. It was the archdeacon."

"Are you sure?"

"Of course, I'm sure," snapped Guillaume. He called for a third jug of wine.

Antoni tried another hint. "Perhaps the archdeacon was feeling harassed and overworked and could have merely agreed to Rocca's suggestion to send you to Bordeaux?"

"I doubt it." Guillaume grabbed the new jug of wine and poured some into his goblet. He placed the jug out of Antoni's reach.

"Perhaps Dame Belina is friendly and welcoming to every man who comes into the cathedral shop" said Antoni, staring at the wine jug and fingering his empty goblet. "I shall never forget the friendly, welcoming way she greeted you in the shop the first time you met her, after you had delivered some special document from the Archbishop of Bordeaux." Antoni lifted his empty goblet and looked at it disconsolately. "That must have been nearly three years ago, I suppose, when ..."

"Three and a half years," Guillaume interrupted his groom. He smiled, remembering the first time he had met Belina, her lovely eyes, her nose, her blue tunic which hinted at her lithe body within it, her beautiful black hair which he longed to pull down and then kiss her....

"And then you asked to be transferred to the staff of the Bishop of Condom," said Antoni, interrupting Guillaume's thoughts, "even though you were negotiating to work for the Seneschal in Bordeaux with your brother. Falling in love with Dame Belina changed those plans. Of course, the miller's daughter would know how to attract your attention, and trick you into marrying her."

Guillaume stopped smiling. "Stop your impertinence, Antoni. I am well aware that it didn't suit you personally to leave Bordeaux and your easy life there." He finished the wine. "If I remember correctly, you changed your mind about staying in Bordeaux because my successor would have made you work much harder."

"That's not true, Messire Guillaume," Antoni spluttered.

"And neither is it true that my wife would allow herself to be taken into inns by Flemish seducers." He called the landlord and asked for the bill, paid it and stalked out of the inn, his spurs rattling.

They collected their horses from the stable and Guillaume tipped the stable lad a *denier*. They mounted and walked down the street leading to the large square in the centre of Vianne. In comparison with Nérac, it was quiet and orderly, and they walked their horses through it easily and reached the northern gateway, where they paid the toll and set out for the bank of the Garonne to take the ferry to Port Sainte Marie.

During the rough river crossing Guillaume stared straight ahead of him, ignoring his groom completely. He continued to be stern and silent for the rest of the day, trying unsuccessfully to concentrate on his forthcoming meeting with the senior legal adviser in Bordeaux, and trying not to think about the 'Flemish seducer' staying in the same building as Belina. He pictured them together, at first in the Pradau hospice, then walking back to the shop. Would she be inveigled into an inn? He did not think so. Belina was keen on her local reputation. She would not dare to enter an inn with a strange man, she would …

Guillaume interrupted his positive thoughts. At his own insistence, his beloved wife had examined a corpse and had been ordered by him to discover more about that poisoned corpse, to find the murderer. Had he endangered his wife? Perhaps it was not only her reputation that was in danger. Maybe her life was too.

He tried to think logically. Belina's life was not in danger, he was almost sure about that. But her reputation? That was different. And his reputation as a cuckolded husband? He tried not to think about that either. Nevertheless, it filled his thoughts for the rest of the day and all night.

CHAPTER SEVEN

The Pradau hospice porter was busy in the outer courtyard with a group of pilgrims leaving late for La Romieu so that Belina was able to slide through the doorway without him noticing her. She decided to examine the refectory on her left. It was a large room that buzzed with flies and smelled of sweat, urine and sour wine. A cat slunk past her with a squeaking half-dead mouse in its mouth. Another cat was tossing a mouse in the air. A dog nearby was scratching itself. Belina hoped its fleas would not jump on to her skirt. She wondered if the dead pilgrim had chosen not to eat supper in such surroundings - although surely any traveller would be used to conditions like these? Guillaume had described places like this in his anecdotes, and twice he had returned home with his clothes full of fleas. It had taken a good deal of time and patience to get rid of them.

"Dame Belina, good morning," Brother Martin greeted her from the kitchen door. "How is your investigation going? When can we bury that poor pilgrim?"

"It's too soon yet," she replied.

"Maybe that is so, but the cellar will be smelling of him before long." Belina thought the smell of the refectory this morning was bad enough. "Would you like to look at the corpse in the sarcophagus in the cellar?" he asked.

She shook her head and tried to ignore her heaving

stomach. "No thank you. What I need to do first is to question everyone about what they were doing and what they saw on Saturday. I will start with yourself, if I may."

He suggested they sit down on the bench near the window. "It's hard to remember anything special. Most afternoons are similar here. People arrive, have their feet washed, eat their supper, get their shoes and clothes mended, chat to each other about their journey..."

She interrupted him. "When did this particular pilgrim arrive?"

"Oh, rather early in the afternoon, brandishing his *bourdon* as if he wasn't used to walking with a staff."

"That sounds unusual," said Belina.

"Yes, perhaps it is." Brother Martin thought for a moment. "Another unusual thing was that he didn't fill up his gourd. Usually pilgrims' gourds are empty by the time they arrive here and we get them to line up in that corner," he pointed to near the kitchen doorway, "to refill them."

"Are you sure of this?" Belina asked.

"Of course I am sure. As I said, the pilgrims fill up their gourds over there."

"Yes, yes, I understand. But you see, this dead pilgrim's gourd was empty when I examined it yesterday."

He shrugged his shoulders and brushed a fly from his tonsured head.

"Brother Martin," a kitchen boy called out, "you are needed here at once please."

And that was the end of Belina's chance of questioning a key witness. She escaped from the stuffy room and made her way to the outer courtyard. When she thought no one was looking she spat on to the grass verge.

Several old men and women were sitting on benches under a mulberry tree. Four were playing dice. Belina hoped they were not gambling over their game because she knew Brother

Pierre disapproved of that. He had told her several times that whatever Saint Louis was against, friars were against too.

She approached the dice players slowly but noisily and there was a hasty removal of pebbles from the makeshift table. Belina took no notice of that, nor of their discomfiture. She sat down beside one of the old women and, speaking in Gascon, explained why she was there and what she wanted to ask them.

Silence. Feet shuffled among the dust. Someone coughed. The dice players continued, but very quietly and keeping their pebbles out of sight.

"I know," said Belina, "that normally none of you come into contact much with the pilgrims, and that you eat and sleep in a different part of the hospice, but perhaps you could help me in my investigation, just in case you might have noticed something. I would be very grateful for your help."

Still silence. Belina wondered if she should produce a coin to loosen tongues. The oldest man said he had seen a magpie pecking at one of the shutters of the pilgrims' dormitory the previous afternoon. "That's a sure sign of death," he maintained.

Belina agreed, and listened to everyone's tales of deaths foretold by magpies. She tried to steer their conversation towards the pilgrim who had died yesterday. "Brother Martin has told me that the pilgrim didn't seem used to walking with a staff. Did any of you notice a new arrival like that?"

"I did," said one of the dice players. "Chap with a foreign accent. I called out *adishatz* as a friendly greeting, but he didn't understand. A foreigner."

"Do you remember anything else about this pilgrim?" Belina asked. "Did he limp? Did he stoop? Did his feet hurt perhaps?"

The man thought for a while and then told her that the pilgrim did not stoop, and was not that old. He did not limp, but walked more like a horseman does.

"And yet he was staying the night in this hospice instead of at an inn?" said Belina.

"Perhaps he had run out of money," suggested the oldest woman.

It was a good suggestion. But Belina knew how many gold and silver coins had tumbled out of his cloak.

"Perhaps he had quarrelled with an innkeeper?" someone said.

Another good suggestion, especially after Belina's experience that day in the Cheval Blanc.

"Did he arrive here on foot or on a horse?" she asked.

"On foot. Most of them do. Even the ones with a horse or a mule use it for their possessions, not for riding." He paused, and then added, "I noticed him clutching his stomach, and one of the hospice staff carried his *besace* and *bourdon* indoors for him. That's not unusual, though, when pilgrims look tired. And they often do."

Belina asked which member of the staff had done this.

"I'm not sure, but I think it was probably Ferdinan."

"Where would I find him now?" asked Belina.

"In the kitchen, getting hot water ready to wash the pilgrims' feet."

Belina stood up, smiled and thanked them. She went inside the hospice and walked towards the kitchen. Even before she got there she found the noise, heat and smells overpowering.

She stopped one of the perspiring kitchen boys. "Excuse me, could you tell me please where I can find Ferdinan."

"Over there, dame." He pointed to the kitchen fire where cauldrons of water were boiling and vegetables were stewing.

Swallowing her nausea, Belina threaded her way through the busy kitchen and waited for Ferdinan to unhook one of the cauldrons. "Excuse me, are you Ferdinan?" she asked, and introduced herself.

"Yes."

"If you could spare a few moments, I would be very grateful if you could tell me about a pilgrim who arrived yesterday and whose satchel and staff you carried into the pilgrims' dormitory."

"Why do you want to know that?"

"Because that pilgrim died later that afternoon, and I have been asked to enquire into his death."

He hesitated while people bustled around them and cauldrons hissed and bubbled. It was very hot close to the fire. At last he came to a decision, picked up a cauldron and carried it through the refectory and into the main hall. Belina followed, glad to be out of the heat and away from the stench.

Ferdinan set the cauldron down in a corner and fetched two stools, waiting for her to be seated first. "That pilgrim looked rather weary," he began," and I think he was also feeling a bit poorly."

"Yes?" prompted Belina.

"But don't think it meant he was really sickening for something. Many pilgrims arrive weary and feeling ill."

"I'm sure they do."

"What was different about him was his uncertainty," said Ferdinan. "He didn't seem to be a regular hospice user."

"In what way?"

"He wasn't expecting to have his feet washed. Indeed, he didn't think his feet needed to be washed. And I can assure you, Dame Lansac, all pilgrims need to have their feet washed. Absolutely all of them." He held his nose.

"What if they have travelled on horseback?" suggested Belina.

"Rich pilgrims like that don't stay in hospices. They stay in special hospitality houses, like the Senclar mansion. They are made welcome there – at a price of course."

"What kind of price?" asked Belina.

"I don't know exactly," he replied, "but I have heard that Dame Jeanne Senclar charges a great deal. They say that she was hostess in the hospice of Aubrac in the highlands twenty leagues north-east of Rodez, and that her father was Chief Steward there."

"You mean, she learnt hospitality as a kind of servant?" asked Belina, astonished.

"You could put it like that," he replied, "but she herself would never admit it. She's much too grand. Wife of a consul, who is the son of a grand, prosperous Lectoure lady She doesn't think of herself as a servant."

"No indeed," said Belina.

"Look, talk of the Devil, there she is." Ferdinan pointed to the hospice gateway. Jeanne Senclar was striding through it with a fair-haired groom, and Jeannot and other young servants stood back and bowed. The groom stared straight at Belina.

She gulped and wondered what Jeannot might have told Dame Senclar about the dead pilgrim.

The 'Devil' strode past Belina, looking straight through her, as if she were a transparent window pane in the Senclar mansion. Then she turned round and glared.

"Dame Lansac, I trust you are not wasting the time of hospice staff gossiping idly and uselessly." Belina stared at her, unable to reply. "Surely, you should be in my Lord Bishop's shop, contributing to the diocesan finances?"

"My assistant is performing that role," muttered Belina.

"Dereliction of duty on your part, I think," Dame Senclar sneered. "Or perhaps you are trying to create friendships with pilgrims." Belina said nothing. "Your husband is away so often that I suppose you have to find alternative men. How long have you been married?"

"Three years."

"What's wrong with your marriage then?" Dame Jeanne demanded.

"Nothing."

"There must be. A husband who is always away from home is the sign of a failed wife. Or a failed husband." Belina looked away, embarrassed. Dame Jeanne continued relentlessly and even more loudly. "My husband had three daughters by his first wife, and three young sons by me. That is the sign of a successful marriage."

Ferdinan decided to intervene. "How many brothers and sisters do you have, Dame Jeanne?"

"That is none of your business," she snapped.

"They say," Ferdinan continued, "that you are the only child of the Chief Steward of Aubrac hospice. Does that mean that your parents' marriage was unsuccessful?"

Jeanne Senclar swept past him and entered the hospice building. Belina clasped Ferdinan's hand. "Thank you," she whispered.

"Don't mention it. She is a *punaise*, a horrid beetle. It's nice to be important, but it is more important to be nice."

Belina smiled. "Yes indeed." She turned towards Jeannot who had, she regretted, been listening to Dame Jeanne's cruel comments.

"Jeannot, please could you find Brother Pierre for me. I need to discuss the death of that pilgrim with him."

"Please excuse me, Dame Lansac," said Ferdinan, "but I must make a start on washing dirty feet."

"Of course. I wish you well in such a task."

"Thanks. But of course it is a holy task, and the pilgrims are on a holy journey." He paused. "At least, I like to think they are. It makes the job more bearable."

He picked up the cauldron and went back into the refectory. Belina looked at the group of tired and dusty pilgrims coming into the courtyard. They unhooked their gourds and tried to get the last drop of liquid out of them. They dropped their staffs with a clatter on the cobbles and sank down on to the benches in the courtyard. They looked too tired to walk the last few yards to the hospice refectory. Or perhaps, Belina wondered, they knew it would be horribly smelly in there and were postponing refilling their gourds.

"You were looking for me, I think, Dame Belina." Brother Pierre interrupted Belina's thoughts.

"I was indeed," she replied, getting up and curtseying. "I have to show you something I found in the dead pilgrim's satchel."

He led the way to his *bureau* and indicated a chair beside his desk. The room was cool, the herbs strewn on the tiled floor smelled sweet, and only two flies were buzzing about. His pet dog was not scratching, and welcomed its master with a gentle nudge.

"How are the investigations going?" Brother Pierre asked. "Has Messire Guillaume discovered the cause of death yet?"

"No, not yet," replied Belina. "He has asked me to check with some of your staff and residents here to see if they remember the pilgrim."

"Do they?"

"Some do. He didn't seem to them to be a genuine pilgrim."

"Dame Belina, I regret to say that not all visitors staying here on their way to Saint Jacques in Galicia are totally genuine. But I think that all of them are making some sort of pilgrimage in their soul, and in their mind they will feel better for their journey in spite of sore feet and aching limbs."

"Is it true that some walk the *Chemin* for penitence?"

"Occasionally a wayward priest or friar has to do this, but it is very rare. More usual are people who have committed a crime, or several crimes, who walk to Compostela to be granted indulgences for their misdeeds. But here we never ask our guests about their need for pardon of course." He paused. "You wanted to show me something I think."

She took two pieces of cloth from her satchel and unwrapped them carefully on to his desk.

He picked each carving up and frowned. "This one is of Saint Roch, a patron saint of pilgrims, with the wound on his thigh and his dog beside him. But you have already recognised him, I suppose."

"Yes indeed."

He picked up the second carving and frowned at it. It seemed to be of a boy peeing. Like the little statue of Saint Roch the top of its head was stained dark red. Brother Pierre put it down quickly and looked again at Saint Roch's head.

"Dame Belina, pilgrims often show me the *babioles* and carvings they have bought on their way to and from Compostela. I have often seen statues of Saint Roch, and even more often those of Saint James. Sometimes I see statues of Saint Peter," he smiled,"which I expect you sold them."

Belina smiled back at him.

"But this carving is very peculiar, rather unseemly and not at all saintly." He turned the statue of the little boy round so that neither of them could see what the boy was doing.

"Brother Pierre," said Belina less diffidently than she felt,"I would be grateful if you – or a member of your staff – could show these two carvings to pilgrims returning from Compostela and ask them if they have seen the owner on their travels. And then ask them about him. It would help my husband's investigation very much."

He picked up the carving of Saint Roch. "That's a good idea, except that carvings of Saint Roch are rather common, you know."

"Brother Pierre, that is why I am asking you to show this other carving as well."

"I understand that, but I am not going to do this. This hospice is a holy house, and this carving is vulgar." He placed it near her.

"Even if it is of a young boy?" asked Belina.

"Especially because of that." He stood up and went to the door carrying the little statue of Saint Roch. Belina wrapped the offending carving back inside its bit of cloth and placed it in her satchel.

"Thank you for your help, Brother Pierre. I will let you know as soon as I can when the pilgrim may be buried." She curtseyed to him and followed him out into the courtyard.

"*Adishatz.*"

CHAPTER EIGHT

On her way back home Belina passed peasants trudging down rue Barthelemy and queuing to leave Condom through the Pradau Gate. She turned left towards the Sainte Claire Gate so that she could ask the gatekeeper for a drink. Her throat still hurt from the fetid air in the hospice kitchen. All around her people talked angrily about Rocca and Loupmont. Belina heard snatches of conversation about neighbours and relatives who had suffered - and were still suffering - from Rocca's harsh fines and taxes, his persecution of farmers whose harvests had been ruined by thunderstorms, and whose livelihoods had already been endangered by two bad winters when most of their seeds had turned to mush.

"He's from Paris. He doesn't know about the land. He doesn't care who provides food for him. He is a town person. And he hates horses. I think he's frightened of them."

She crossed the grassed-over old town ditch, avoiding the mess left by sheep and goats, and walked wearily up rue des Boucheries. The nearer she got to the cathedral the more muttered threats of harming the Parisian she heard. They hoped he would die, crushed underneath the sheaves of wheat which he was insisting were his, or by the weight of the coins he insisted should be paid to him as fines for rent arrears and other unpaid bills.

Belina could not stop thinking about Henry Tudor, the

mysterious English count in Brittany who was receiving so much money from Gascons and whose mother was apparently planning to have the Princes in the Tower murdered. Why should Rocca be sending the English count so much Gascon money? She was aware that some local Condom landlords and merchants were a bit dishonest and greedy. Indeed, Dame Senclar was notorious for her avarice and her harsh attitude to people in arrears with their rent. But in comparison with Rocca even she appeared sweet-natured and generous. And Belina was not certain that Jordi had been totally honest in his calculations of weight of grain and of flour. Perhaps the temptation had been too much for a man with a growing family. She hoped not. Their unloving widowed stepmother did not help them, living instead off her inheritance from their father's testament. Jordi and Belina were suspicious of this document, which had been drawn up by their stepmother's cousin, a notary from Montréal. As a result, the mill had become under-funded so that it had been difficult to avoid getting behind with the rent.

Catalina Moulié came from farming stock and had been considered a good, safe match for a miller like Jordi. But her family's farm upstream of Condom had been badly flooded twice, and many of its crops were ruined. Their landlord, the Abbot of Flaran, had graciously cancelled their rent for the last two years, but had told all his tenants that rents would need to be paid again as from the next Martinmas, whatever the harvest and vintage situation was by then. November 11th was not far off. Belina wondered whether the Abbot too had been forced to send money to this grasping foreign count in Brittany. She must ask Guillaume. He would know.

Belina unlocked the door leading to the cathedral's staff residence. She walked into the courtyard and waved to Sir John and his valet resting in the shade. She climbed the steep stairs up to her chamber and unlocked the heavy front door, wondering why Guillaume had insisted on having such a solid door put there. His long reports? His mysterious travels for the bishop? His secret nationality? His part in the plans for the English King Edward to re-conquer Gascony? Plans that she supposed the new King Richard would use.

She felt too tired to puzzle it out. Instead, she carried inside the two wooden buckets of water which the residence porter had left by the door. Then she stripped off her clothes and had a quick wash, using very little water. She hung her tunic on the hook beside the chest, put on her house dress and uncoiled her long black hair. Deep in thought, it was some time before she realized that someone was knocking at the door.

"Who is it?" she called out.

"It's Alain, Dame Belina. Sir John's waiting for his game of chess."

She had forgotten Guillaume's instructions about the Sunday routine of playing chess with their English neighbour, Sir John Keyham.

"Sorry, Alain," she called through the door. "Please tell him I will be down in a moment."

She fastened her hair up again and put on her head-cloth, stroked the cat, unbolted the door and went downstairs to Sir John's corner of the courtyard where he was sitting on his special chair, setting out the chess pieces with his left hand. He smiled at her without speaking.

Belina touched his left arm lightly. "I'm very sorry, Sir John, I've been so busy that I forgot the sun was already behind the river."

He stared at her sadly.

"Perhaps Dame Belina was resting, Sir John," said his valet.

"Oh no, I wasn't," she retorted more sharply than she intended.

Sir John smiled and moved his king's pawn forward two spaces. Alain slipped away and Belina concentrated on her game, hoping Sir John would forgive her poor play this afternoon. Perhaps he would think it was because of the hot thundery weather, but since he could not speak it was always difficult to know his thoughts.

In due course he knocked over her king with his queen. "Aaahh," he gloated.

"Sorry I haven't given you a very good game," Belina apologized.

Sir John made the sign 'G' with his left hand.

"Guillaume?" she guessed.

"Aaahh."

"He's gone on a journey for the bishop," she said quietly. Sir John could not give away Guillaume's secrets, but who else was listening? Seven people lived in the residence, plus servants and grooms. Discretion was never easy.

Sir John called out for Alain and mimed having a drink. They drank a cup of hypocras and ate some little honeycakes as the shadows lengthened across the courtyard.

Belina bade farewell to Sir John and crossed the courtyard to the staircase. To her surprise someone was coming down it. The stranger bowed a greeting to her and then smiled, looking straight at her face. Behind him came the hated Rocca, thin and pale. No smile from him. It was common knowledge in the cathedral that Rocca did not like women – although his busy and suspicious assistant, Loupmont, certainly did. Belina wondered whether his accusation of her brother's dishonesty was somehow her fault. Since March, Loupmont had been living in the same staff residence and she always tried to avoid him and his insolent smirks. Some of the cathedral staff maintained that Loupmont hated Rocca as much as everyone else did, and that he was waiting to replace him. Other staff said that Loupmont resented Rocca's superior education. In the inns and the streets the men made more lewd accusations about the two of them.

She pushed past the stranger with difficulty because he did not stand to one side to let her pass without her clothes touching his. She was so close to him that she could smell the rosemary oil on his face. Rocca, on the other hand, flattened his skinny body against the banister and looked the other way. She hurried along the corridor and let herself into her chamber.

Minet was waiting for her, and went straight to her empty bowl near the sink. Belina sniffed the jug of sheep's milk and wrinkled her nose. In spite of keeping it inside the large cooler crock (which she used in winter for preserving duck) the milk had gone off. She tried to tempt Minet with a few drops, but they were spurned with an angry meow, although the cat lapped more eagerly at the fresh water from the covered bucket.

Belina was well aware that she had eaten nothing since breakfast apart from the two honeycakes with Sir John. But she felt much too hot and tired to cook anything. She sighed, thinking wistfully of the planned Sunday dinner at the Pont Barlet inn which Guillaume had cancelled for the second time. With her thoughts on the pilgrim and his unexplained death, she ate up the last of the cheese and most of the loaf which her brother had given her. Its superior quality revived her and she tried to make a note of what she knew already and what she needed to find out.

She made her pebble points: first, the doubt that the corpse belonged to a genuine pilgrim returning from Compostela; second, the enormous number of coins he was secretly carrying; third, how and when he was poisoned if he had not eaten the meal in the hospice; fourth, why did he not fill up his gourd on arrival at the hospice even though it was empty; and lastly, the unexplained assortment of possessions in his satchel. Her to-do list started with questioning the guard on the Barlet Bridge about pilgrims entering Condom from the west bank, and then the cathedral staff about what the pilgrim had done in the cathedral because presumably he had gone there on arrival in the town to give thanks to God for his safe journey, and to give money to the cathedral for his indulgences.

That led her to wonder what crimes he might have committed that he needed to walk all the way to Compostela and back. And she also wondered where his pilgrimage – if that's what it was – had begun.

Belina looked through the contents of the satchel again, trying to get a better picture of its owner in her mind. The satchel itself was of fairly good quality, but worn and grubby. It smelt of musty fruit. She emptied out the contents, which included a needle, thread and scissors and some small coins which she put to one side of the table. At the bottom of the satchel were crumbs and some bits of cheese. She sniffed the breadcrumbs and sorted them. Some were not Gascon wheat bread. More likely they were rye bread and therefore from an upland region. The bigger crumbs were from a cake but with a funny colour and with a faint salty smell. A few of the crumbs were almost white. Or perhaps they too were cake crumbs? She thought of swallowing a couple of crumbs but Minet interrupted her by meowing to go outside. Belina unbolted the door.

Forgetting the crumbs, she turned her attention to the shirt which had been screwed up on top of them. Judging from the stains it looked as if it had been worn inside-out for as many weeks as the right way. It stank of stale sweat. She made a face and examined the shirt he had worn when he died. This also looked and smelled horrible, but from the poison, not from having been worn. She estimated that the pilgrim had only worn it for a few days. She touched a clean area of it and found a lump in the sleeve seam. She unpicked this, with difficulty because it was getting dark, and extracted a tiny piece of cloth inside which was a silver token. Belina examined this as carefully as she could in the fading light. It contrasted with the scruffy, very ordinary homespun clothes and had a quality feel to it. She put it in her jewel box, next to the medal which she had received at her baptism twenty-two years ago. Then she changed her mind and hid the silk-wrapped token underneath her Sunday head-cloth.

Belina felt the other sleeve seam and found a slightly smaller lump, but by now it was too dark to unpick. She folded the shirt so that the lump was uppermost and put it in Guillaume's chest. Then she unbolted the door and locked it behind her even though she would only be outside the chamber for a few minutes while she used the communal latrine. She hoped to avoid the other neighbours by using the latrine just before complete darkness fell.

When she reached her door again the cat was pawing it. They went in together. Belina bolted the door top and bottom and turned the heavy key in the lock. Minet slept better that night than Belina did. Weird and terrifying dreams of corpses kept waking her up.

CHAPTER NINE

It was a brighter, fresher morning and Belina wished she felt brighter and fresher to match it. She washed her hands and her face, and slipped into her tunic. She needed to buy some eggs so she put on her shoes and her head-cloth and went to the poultry shop in the Place Lion d'Or. On her way back she bought some more cheese, had her milk jug filled up and bought a fresh supply of fruit. She climbed the stairs carefully whilst watching the milk jug. So intent was she on not spilling its contents that she did not notice that someone was coming down the stairs.

"Oh!" she tried to keep the jug and herself upright while holding on to the eggs, the cheese and the fruit. But one pear slipped through her fingers and rolled down to the stairs.

"Dame Lansac," said a voice very close to her, "stay very still and I will fetch your pear for you."

It was the stranger who had been with Rocca the previous afternoon. He sidled past her, retrieved the pear and gently took the eggs, cheese and other fruit from her. He led the way upstairs.

"Which is your door?" he asked. A very pleasant voice, musical and with a slight accent which she could not place.

"At the end of the corridor," she replied automatically. They walked towards it.

She wondered what to do next. Would he slip into the

room and prove difficult to push out? She had already had that problem twice with Loupmont. And would he notice the extra strength of the door and the hefty key? Worse still, would he notice her husband's absence?

She put the jug down and went to the edge of the corridor, where she leant against the railing and gazed at the courtyard below. "Are you staying with Messire Rocca?" she asked him. He came very close to her and stared at her head-cloth, gradually lowering his gaze till he was looking at her feet.

Belina had got used to looks like that when she'd been living at the mill. The reputation of millers' wives and daughters had accustomed her to insolent stares. She repeated her question.

"Yes, I arrived last Friday from Paris. I live in Paris," he explained, thrusting out his chest. But meeting a Parisian did not excite her. She had met many in the shop, pushing other shoppers out of the way, jumping the payment line and talking loudly. To her, Parisians were just foreigners, and bad-mannered foreigners at that.

"But are you Parisian?" she asked.

"What makes you doubt that I am?" he smiled at her and touched her arm.

"You don't speak fast enough to be a Parisian," she replied, still not looking at him.

He laughed. "You are right, Dame Lansac. I am Flemish, from Bruges."

Belina remembered that someone had mentioned the Flemings to her not long ago. She frowned. She tried to remember who it had been - and where, and why.

"Do you get many Flemings in Condom?" he interrupted her train of thought.

"I don't know. We don't ask people's nationality, only where they started their pilgrimages."

Belina picked up the milk jug and took the eggs and fruit from him. She turned to the door. "*Adischatz*", she said, dismissing him. She hoped he would take the hint.

Luckily, at that moment her neighbour the choirmaster emerged from his chamber and called out to her, "did you like the new chant yesterday?"

"It was not as new as all that," she replied. "I have been hearing you practise it all month."

"I hope I haven't disturbed you, Dame Belina," he said in his usual gentle way.

"No, no, not at all."

"You see," he continued, "I don't like to think my music-making disturbs your husband."

"Not usually. He is concentrating at present on a long report for my Lord Bishop." Belina hoped neither man would see through her lie. "He's so busy writing that he hasn't even waited for me to fetch some eggs for breakfast." She wondered where Guillaume was by now in his journey to Bordeaux.

The stranger had not moved and was staring at her. He gave Belina a radiant smile, while she studied his appearance. In spite of herself, she liked what she saw: medium height and muscular; black, curly hair worn rather long; dark eyes with heavy eyelids, and eyebrows which nearly met; a strong, cleft chin and full lips. He was very smartly dressed in a rather short dark green doublet with a neat, stiffened collar and an elegant leather belt. His hose and hat were russet-coloured. He was standing so close to her now that she could smell the scent of rosemary oil on his face. She wondered if his looks were typical of Flemish men. He certainly looked very different from Guillaume.

Feeling slightly guilty, she turned her attention to the elderly choirmaster. "Brother Charles," she said, "please could you help me for a moment with my purchases?"

She pushed the eggs, cheese and fruit into his arms before the Flemish stranger could hold them again, put down the jug and took the door key from her belt. Her hands shook whilst she turned the key in the lock. The choirmaster's eyesight was not very good but the other man might have noticed.

She removed the key, picked up the jug and ushered Brother Charles inside, much to his surprise.

"Where is Messire Guillaume?" he asked, looking around anxiously.

"In the other room, among all his papers." She put the jug on the table and took the eggs, cheese and fruit from him. "Thank you so much Brother Charles. That new person makes me nervous."

"Why, Dame Belina?"

"I had the impression that he wanted to come in here."

"Messire Guillaume would not have liked such an interruption," he said.

"No, he hates interruptions. Not even the cat is allowed to disturb him." She smiled at her kind neighbour. "I hope I haven't delayed you."

"Not really. But I must make haste now." He slipped out and she bolted the door behind him immediately.

Belina poured out some milk into Minet's bowl and cut a slice of bread from the loaf her brother had given her the day before. She stared at the bread, trying to remember why bread was important for her at this moment.

What she remembered instead was the second lump in the pilgrim's sleeve seam. She unpicked the seam carefully and took out a piece of silk inside which was a gold medallion. She gasped at its beauty. It was much more delicate than the ones the cathedral shop sold. She decided to show it to Messire Benasse, the goldsmith who had taught her how to make metal objects for the shop.

Belina put the gold medallion back inside the silk cover, wrapped that in a thick piece of cloth and placed it into her purse. She added the silver medallion she had found the night before. Then she fastened the purse to her belt and went downstairs to the shop where she told Quiteira that she was going to the apothecary.

Quiteira pouted and continued putting out the trays of

carvings and *babioles*. Imitation keys of various sizes glinted in the sunshine. The tray of pewter medallions of Saint Peter carrying keys she placed further from the street, to discourage pilfering. The shop's large statue of a seated Saint Peter presided over all the merchandise, out of reach of people walking past.

Belina watched the throngs of passers-by in case something was stolen. But everyone seemed intent on walking towards the cathedral, walking with their heads bent. Belina noticed most of them were weeping. The cathedral bell started tolling. Another funeral perhaps? She joined the crowd.

The cemetery behind the cathedral was already crowded and she could hardly see the cart bearing the shrouded corpse. Belina crossed herself. "God rest his soul and release him from Purgatory," she whispered while she watched the disconsolate mourners make their way to the newly dug grave inside the cemetery wall.

"Who has died?" she asked one of the mourners, putting her arm round his shoulders.

"My neighbour, Jehan Duffour, the pastry-cook. He took his own life on Saturday because he couldn't cope with being evicted on Rocca's orders. He was already very depressed with the death of his baby son last week and his wife has been too ill to help in the shop. They have so many debts. "

"Did Rocca know of these circumstances?" asked Belina.

"Maybe he did, maybe he didn't. Doesn't make any difference now that Jehan's dead. And Rocca will seize his shop even sooner than he had intended. It's in a good location and he will get higher rent for it. And Loupmont will get a special payment from Rocca for having got rid of Jehan and his family."

It was depressingly similar to what had happened to the cobbler and his family in the same street last month. Rocca had 'stolen' his workshop and home on the pretext of shoddy workmanship, although everyone knew the cobbler was skilled and conscientious. His problem was that he had too many children to feed and clothe. He had become too poor and too desperate to prepare the leather correctly.

Belina wondered whether his eyesight had deteriorated too. With people eating less, their abilities and strengths were diminishing. Masons repairing the cathedral had been working more slowly than the master builder had envisaged and Rocca had fined all of them for delays in their work.

"He's a thief," said a voice behind her.

Belina spun round. How had someone guessed her thoughts? It was the seamstress who repaired the cathedral vestments. "Who is a thief?" Belina asked her, looking at her wrinkled face and tired eyes.

"That foreigner, Rocca. All Parisians are thieves. They talk so fast that I can't understand them. I hate them and their pushy attitudes. The best pastry-cook in Condom has been killed by Rocca."

"He killed himself," said Belina.

"No, Dame Lansac. He is dead because of the evil Rocca. We are saying that he died of a heart attack, so that he can be given a proper funeral and burial in the cemetery."

Belina realised the logic of this remark. "Where will his widow live now?" she asked.

"They say she will try to go to the Pradau hospice and help in the kitchens there."

"But they already have far too many kitchen staff," Belina objected, aware that Brother Pierre tried to employ as many unfortunate people as he could. It did not make the hospice efficient but his kindness was more important than money-making. At least, Belina hoped that God judged it to be so. What was efficiency if everyone suffered?

"One more deserving person won't harm the hospice," said the seamstress, interrupting Belina's thoughts again.

"No, but perhaps the cathedral could employ the pastry-cook's widow," she suggested.

"Last year, the Steward would have taken her on. But Rocca refuses to employ any more staff. We are all having to work harder and longer." She sighed. "And we have been moved to a cramped, dark building so that he could let our big airy sewing-room to his new Chief Accountant from Paris. Rocca said he needed the light to study the accounts better."

"It doesn't make sense to me," said Belina. "How do you manage to sew in a dark room?"

"I don't."

"But what can you do about it?" Belina asked her.

The woman looked around her. No one was very near so she whispered in Belina's ear, "my husband wants to kill Rocca. He and a group of his *copains* are going to waylay him in a dark alley and bludgeon him to death. Or near-death."

Belina looked at her, startled. "That would be murder."

"Not if it was only near-death."

Belina was amazed. The seamstress was a gentle, middle-aged woman, careful and talented. She must be desperate. But why? "You could insist on being given a better work room," she suggested.

"I've tried that."

"Well, try again. Why don't you all go to the Steward after Mass and ask him?"

"We wouldn't dare."

"It would be a lot safer than having Rocca murdered," said Belina.

"Not murdered, Dame Lansac. Just beaten senseless."

"If he died of his wounds, it would be murder."

"No one would know."

"Why not?"

"Because they would throw him over a wall.Into a building site, for example. My husband and his *copains* are masons. They could manage that easily."

Belina was not convinced, but decided to say no more. If Guillaume were at home, she could have asked for his advice.

She touched the seamstress lightly on her arm and left her standing in the middle of the cemetery as weeping mourners trudged past her.

Belina did not wait to see the pall-bearers lift the shrouded corpse off the cart and carry it to the grave. Funerals always brought back to her the misery of her mother's death long ago. In some ways, she had never got over it, and the arrival a year later of the young stepmother had upset her enormously.

She edged towards the cemetery wall, only half hearing the angry comments around her blaming Rocca and Loupmont for yet another death. Someone put an arm round her shoulder, and she presumed it was a relative or a school-friend trying to comfort her, mindful of her distress at funerals.

She turned round and found she was staring at Rocca's Flemish friend. She stepped back at once, colliding with a weeping mourner.

"Everyone seems very upset," said the Fleming. "Who has died?"

"The pastry-cook whom Rocca evicted for not paying his rent."

"How did he die?"

Belina hesitated for a moment and then said that people thought he must have had a heart attack.

"Perhaps he was poisoned by one of his bad pies," the Fleming suggested.

"Definitely not," she retorted. "He was an excellent pastry-cook."

"Even so, his pies could have gone off in hot weather like this," persisted the Fleming.

"Nonsense. It's not particularly hot today. Just normal Gascon summer weather."

"If he had become so poor, he may have neglected hygiene," the Fleming continued. "Perhaps it was one of his bad pies which poisoned that dead pilgrim."

"What dead pilgrim?" She snapped.

"The one whose death you are investigating," he replied.

"I don't know what you mean."

"Yes you do. I have already heard from six different people that you are personally investigating the death of a pilgrim in the Pradau hospice." Belina was silent. How could so many people know, and so soon? "Dame Lansac," he said, "I am an inquirer. I can help you. I offer you my services." She said nothing. "I am having to spend a few days in Condom, waiting for a colleague to arrive from Lleida. I can easily help you. Indeed, I think you need my help."

"Messire," she replied, "it is my husband who is doing the investigation, not myself. He is the Bishop's Rapporteur and very experienced in these matters."

"And yet, it is you who went to the hospice yesterday and questioned everyone," he replied.

"People talk more easily to me than they would to my husband," she said.

"Especially if the husband is not there of course." He smiled at her, fixing his large dark eyes on her face and coming closer to her.

She backed away and explained she needed to return to the shop.

Quiteira assumed that Belina had already visited the apothecary's store and she was churlish at learning that Belina needed to leave her again to run the cathedral shop.

"In your absence I've had lots and lots of pilgrims," she muttered, banging three pots of foot balm on the counter. "If you had been here we would have sold much more."

"Sorry, Quiteira. I was on my way to the apothecary's shop but I was delayed by a funeral."

"Yet another funeral. Whose?"

"Jehan Duffour, the pastry-cook in rue Jean-Baptiste, God rest his soul."

They crossed themselves.

"That will bring more trade to the Castanéa brothers' pastry-shop in rue Cadéot," said Quiteira.

"It's an ill wind that blows no good," said Belina.

"It's not a wind that'll help the Castanéa brothers," said Quiteira. "Loupmont has already forced them to give their shop to Rocca, in return for not denouncing them for breaking the curfew last month."

"More fool them," said Belina.

"Yes, of course. But they were at a cock-fight and they got drunk on their winnings."

"A fine would have been cheaper than surrendering their shop," said Belina.

"Loupmont told them that if they did not give up their shop they would be imprisoned for five years and each would have his right hand cut off."

Belina gasped. "And they believed him? Amputation has been forbidden for years and years."

"Of course they believed him. Loupmont made the same threat to Jiroma Corrent at La Bouquerie last July. And he was a good apprentice butcher. Just too outspoken for Loupmont's delicate ears."

Belina wondered if the Corrent family too had plans to waylay Rocca, or Loupmont, in an alley and inflict a severe death. But instead she repeated that mutilating for theft did not happen anymore.

CHAPTER TEN

Belina walked halfway down rue des Argentiers and called at the goldsmith's house. He was surprised, and delighted, to see her. "Good morning, Belina, my dear, come in. What a pleasure to see you."

She gave a little curtsey. "How are you today Messire Benasse?"

"Not too bad. I forget my aches and pains now that I have my new spectacles. They make me feel ten years younger."

She smiled. "I hope that your new spectacles will help you identify two medallions for me." She showed him what she had found in the pilgrim's shirt.

He was very appreciative of the gold one. "Very fine, very fine, very fine indeed." He turned it over and over in his gloved hands. "Burgundian maybe, or perhaps from Lorraine." He peered at it again. "Or perhaps Italian."

The silver medallion did not elicit the same degree of admiration. On one side was an engraving of a female saint. The other side had a large coat of arms with the letters E L Y underneath it. They wondered what E L Y stood for.

"May I venture to ask you how you found these objects?"

Belina told him about the investigation she was doing in Guillaume's absence and also that she had found many gold and silver coins inside the lining of the pilgrim's cloak. In order to examine them in daylight she needed to borrow the cathedral shop's foreign exchange coin chart. But she and Quiteira used it in the shop every day with customers of so many different nationalities paying with coins produced in various government mints. Quiteira would soon notice if the coin chart was absent from its normal place.

The goldsmith got up slowly and rubbed his back. "How is your rheumatism these days?" Belina asked him.

"Worse when it rains. That means most days this year."

"Oh dear. But I thought you said that your new spectacles helped you."

"Yes indeed. I did say that. But my suffering is nothing compared to what the farmers have had to put up with. Ruined crops, seeds gone mouldy, and so on. The last two years have been so very difficult for them."

"I know. This year's wheat harvest has been very poor," said Belina.

"How is your brother's mill coping with reduced business?"

"He gets by, but he's worried. And there's another child on the way." Belina tried to steer the conversation away from her brother's financial worries, but the goldsmith was not to be distracted.

"Did you know he has been borrowing money?" he asked. Belina shook her head. "Of course, many folk have had to borrow money this year," he continued, "not just the country people. Many of the town's shopkeepers and stallholders are in debt too."

"And Rocca is making things even worse," said Belina, "along with his assistant Loupmont."

"Is Loupmont bothering you in the residence?"

She shook her head again. "Not yet, anyway." She tried not to think about what her brother had told her about the dreaded Loupmont.

The goldsmith shuffled some papers about, picked out a large chart and handed it to her. Belina looked at the drawings of various coins. "Take it away with you and check what your dead pilgrim's coins are."

"Thank you very much, Messire. I will take good care of this and let you have it back as soon as possible of course."

"Keep it as long as you need it, my dear. And take care. Don't tell anyone that you have found some coins. And put them in a really safe place, somewhere no one will find them. In these difficult times, people might be tempted to steal them."

"Rocca would find a pretext to demand them, I'm sure," she replied.

He rolled up the chart and wrapped it in a piece of cloth. "Best that no one sees this chart." He re-wrapped the two medallions in their bits of silk. "Put these in your purse and keep it well fastened to your belt. I have a feeling that the gold one could be valuable. It has the appearance of a Saint Mihiel quality gold medallion."

"Saint Mihiel?"

"Yes, a town in the Barrois famous for its goldsmiths."

"But that is where Rocca and Loupmont come from. At least that is what my brother says."

"I thought they came from Paris," said the goldsmith.

"So did I, but Jordi insists they originally came from Saint Mihiel. Where is it, by the way?"

He explained that it was in the east, near Lorraine, and had Italian trading connections, that often brought gold.

Belina asked him if that meant Rocca might be connected with the dead pilgrim.

"It is possible," he replied. "I have some drawings of Saint Mihiel gold-work somewhere." He looked round his cluttered room. "Trouble is, my wife insists on tidying my papers. It might take me some time to lay my hands on those drawings. I will send you a message in a few days to come and see me."

"A few *days*?" she queried.

"Are you in a hurry?"

"I am not sure really. Guillaume always gives priority to his investigations and so I thought I should do so too."

"When will he be back?"

"No idea. He didn't know either. And after all this rain the roads will be slow and muddy of course." She paused. "Please don't tell anyone that Guillaume has gone away," she pleaded.

"Still worried about Loupmont?"

Belina nodded, thinking also of the Flemish stranger. "Guillaume insisted I tell no one about his absence."

"Perhaps he is carrying money to Bordeaux?" suggested the goldsmith.

Belina thought the hasty journey was more likely to be connected with Guillaume's clandestine activities regarding the planned English re-conquest of Gascony. But she kept silent about Guillaume's secret plotting. Instead, she said, "if he is, he didn't tell me. He just talked about a message from the archdeacon of Condom to the archbishop of Bordeaux."

"Perhaps there's more to it than that?"

"Very likely, but I don't wish to know," she replied.

He smiled and got up. *"Adiu*, my dear Belina. Take care. Take care."

She curtsied and went downstairs with him. "Don't forget," he said as he unbolted his front door. "Keep *your* door locked always, always."

"I promise you. I keep it locked anyway."

She heard him pushing the bolts home behind her as she crossed the street and walked towards the town hall. From the corner of her eye she noticed a groom whose large cap hid his fair hair. He shrugged himself from the wall he'd been leaning against and followed in the same direction. Two well-dressed men pushed past Belina and went into the building, talking irritably about the Senclar family. Belina decided to follow them inside and listen in on the Monday meeting of the consuls of Condom. Guillaume sometimes had to attend this, listen to their comments about Bishop Montbrun and then inform the bishop of the consuls' attitudes. She wondered what they would say in public about the demonstration on Saturday.

She stood in a corner and tried to look inconspicuous. Much of the time the discussion was boring, and she felt a strong sense of disappointment. The night watch rota needed to be modified again, the stench from the Bouquerie tanneries bothered everyone. The Barlet Bridge was falling into a dangerous state because of the bad weather and the consuls wondered where they would find the money to fund the bridge repairs. It would be very difficult. King Louis' taxes were enormous by now and the consuls disapproved of them being used to pay Swiss mercenaries at Pont-de-l'Arche near Rouen. Citizens of Condom were still complaining about having to contribute to the rebuilding of the neighbouring town of Lectoure, sacked by the king's troops ten years earlier. Would taxes decrease once the king died? Did anyone know the latest news about his health?

Belina wondered if she was wasting her time. Then she heard angry voices raised about the bishop.

"The bishop is never here, but his Treasurer is never absent. Not one possibility of payment evades him. It is high time the bishop stopped this preying on our wealth."

"I wouldn't mind so much if the money stayed in this town. But it doesn't. It is rushed off to Paris. I hate Paris."

There were grunts of agreement. "Parisians never bother to learn Gascon," said an old consul. "They expect us to make an effort, but they don't even know how to say hello or goodbye."

"Bishop Montbrun is no better. He receives an enormous amount of wealth from Condom, and he cannot even say *thank you* in Gascon."

"Some of that wealth comes from the *dime*, the tithes," said Henri Senclar, "and that stays here in Condom."

"How can you be sure of that?" asked one of the men who had pushed past Belina at the entrance.

"Of course I am sure," replied Henri Senclar. "I assure you I take care that the *dime* remains here."

"What does 'here' mean? The town treasury or in your personal treasure chest?" someone asked.

"Apologize for that remark this instant!" shouted the Consul Senclar.

"All right, all right, I apologize – for upsetting you – but nevertheless I request that the accounts be shown to us right now."

Senclar ordered a clerk to bring the accounts. Whilst waiting he fiddled with the collar of his purple doublet.

"I trust they will also show that Rocca and Loupmont do not receive any monies personally," drawled the notary.

"Of course they don't," Senclar snapped.

They decided to wait and see. As they waited for the ledgers to arrive they listened to the town clerk droning on about the census that year, how some people had less land than the previous year and how he had seen that only a very few had more than a page of items in the census parchment.

The accounts register arrived and they crowded round it, perusing the figures, snarling about the heavy handwriting and scrutinising the statement at the foot of each page verifying the accuracy of the figures.

Belina took the opportunity to slip away and return to the cathedral shop, still trailed by the unknown groom. It was quiet in the shop so she left, taking no notice of Quiteira's protests. She crossed the courtyard, went down the lane to the cathedral stables and from there to the Barlet Bridge. The gatekeeper was talking to a Jewish couple travelling with a heavy chest strapped their mule. The wife slumped on a donkey appeared pregnant, and Belina watched the gatekeeper charge them double for the pregnant Jewess.

"Why double for my wife?" asked the Jew.

"Because it is the rules, Messire," replied the gatekeeper.

"We are refugees from Castilla and the Inquisition, and we have very little money."

"I'm sorry to hear that, Messire, but I have to apply the rules." He held out his hand for the toll.

"How recent are these rules?"

"We have had them for hundreds of years," replied the gatekeeper. He pushed his hand nearer the Jews. They paid the toll and the gatekeeper noted it in the register. The man led the heavily laden mule passed through the gate and into Condom followed by his wife on the donkey.

Belina went up to the gatekeeper and smiled at him. "You have a difficult job," she said.

"It's getting worse and worse," he replied. "The takings are split between the bishop and the consuls, and they're both as greedy as Hell." Belina touched his arm in sympathy. "They don't thank me for collecting their taxes, and the travellers moan about paying the tolls. People no longer have money to spare, what with two years of bad harvests and the high taxes for King Louis."

"Perhaps it will be better when the king dies," Belina suggested.

"Not if it brings the English troops back here again," he replied. "It's only thanks to King Louis that the English have not tried to re-conquer Gascony."

"Of course," said Belina, "the pilgrims don't pay any toll."

"No, more's the pity," he growled. "Personally, I think that all sorts of rogues and cheats dress as pilgrims, just to avoid them."

"The hospice staff have that trouble too," she said, "trying to get pilgrims to pay something for their board and lodging." The gatekeeper made no reply, so she tried again. "Some pilgrims - or so-called pilgrims - don't seem tired enough to have walked a full day's pilgrimage. For example, Brother Martin was telling me that one arrived mid-afternoon two days ago from Mouchan, saying that he was really tired and could not go any further than the Pradau hospice."

"I can check that up easily enough," said the gatekeeper. "Come and look at my register of incoming travellers."

She followed him into his booth and waited while he picked up his ledger. "Two days ago," he said, turning the pages back. "That's Saturday." He peered at his scribbles. "No pilgrim from Mouchan that day. They were all from further away, from Cazeneuve usually or Eauze."

She looked over his shoulder and pointed out an entry for Mouchan.

"That's not a pilgrim. You see he paid a toll. That is a youth coming to work as a mason."

"Oh."

"Though I'm not sure how much work there is nowadays for building labourers." He pointed to a group of unfinished warehouses beside rue Barlet. "He could work on that site, the old timber yard, but it is plagued with troubles. The masons are always moaning about it."

"He could try repairing the cathedral," Belina suggested.

"Not likely. Rocca has already stolen the building repair fund."

"So I've heard," said Belina. "People say he is giving it to an English count in Brittany."

"Damn all English counts." The gatekeeper spat out of his doorway.

"So you're sure, really sure, that there were no pilgrims from Mouchan through your gate on Saturday?" Belina insisted.

"Yes, Dame Lansac, I am completely sure." He showed her his ledger again. "See for yourself."

"Thank you so much," said Belina," I'll tell Brother Martin as soon as I can. He will be very interested."

She gave him her smallest coin, and slipped away while he dealt with some peasants leading six goats. She walked along the wharf deep in thought. Why had the dead pilgrim told a lie? After all, the hospice staff did not care whether their visitors were going to Compostela or coming back from it. In any case, most people who stayed in the hospice - and in the other hospices in Condom - were not pilgrims. The establishments were mostly for the ill, the crippled, the aged with no family, and various other unfortunates down on their luck.

So why pretend to be a pilgrim? She realized that one reason would be to get away with paying next to nothing for a night's accommodation. But surely that did not apply to 'her' pilgrim with his cloak weighed down with many coins?

CHAPTER ELEVEN

Belina continued along the wharf upstream from the Barlet Bridge. The river still flowed fast after the previous week's thunderstorms and rowing looked difficult, dangerous even. She stood aside to let a draught horse come past and saw that it was being led by Tomas.

"Good morning, Dame Belina." He stopped the horse. "How are your investigations going?"

"A bit slow, I am afraid. I wasted too much time listening to the consuls moaning at their Monday public meeting."

"Does Messire Senclar lead them all by the nose?" Tomas asked.

"He would like to, I'm sure," Belina replied, "but they were all against him. It did me good to hear them."

"It would do me good to hear them too," said Tomas. "The family is rich and pretentious, but they are bad masters to their servants. Bad mistresses, too. We all know of past colleagues who have died unexpectedly, and in ghastly pain. Dame Senclar is ruthless, completely ruthless." He glanced over his shoulder to check if anyone was listening. "They say that she has even had children poisoned, including one of her own grandchildren."

"No," Belina gasped.

"Yes, one of her granddaughters was a bit simple and she died mysteriously aged about three."

"Tomas, how dreadful!"

"The little girl died in terrible agony, they said."

Belina thought about the ghastly face of the dead pilgrim in the hospice. "Has Dame Senclar poisoned any pilgrims?"

Tomas glanced at her in surprise and shuffled his feet. "Not that I know of. The people who interest her are tenants, and landowners in debt. She can purchase their lands and possessions cheaply."

"What about Dame Jeanne?" asked Belina. "I have the impression that she's interested in pilgrims. At any rate, she is always talking about the Chemin de Saint Jacques."

"She has been to Compostela herself, that's why," replied Tomas. "But she didn't get farther than Condom on her way back."

"Why not?"

"Oldest trick in the book. She got herself pregnant and could prove that Messire Senclar was the father. Very artful woman is Dame Jeanne."

"Did her parents approve?"

"Of course they did. Meant they got rid of a domineering, disdainful shrew." He smiled. "They were delighted, even if they pretended to be furious. Dame Jeanne's mother stayed here until the baby was born, then she went back to Aubrac."

"Does Dame Jeanne visit the hospices?" Belina asked.

"All the time.Likes to order the tired pilgrims about, and the aged poor living there too."

"I saw her at the Pradau hospice yesterday afternoon," said Belina. "I wondered if she was there on Saturday afternoon too."

"Don't know," replied Tomas,"but I know someone who will be able to answer that question." He turned the horse round. "Come to the stables and I will introduce you to Arnaud. He's her groom and will know where she went andwhen."

"But he might think I am checking up on his mistress," Belina objected, fingering her head-cloth.

"Dame Belina, it is your job to check up what everyone was doing on Saturday afternoon. You have already asked all of us. All except Arnaud who was on duty to Dame Jeanne. The family were having lunch with the consul's uncle in La Romieu when you were doing that."

They went into the stable courtyard. "Don't make it obvious to Arnaud that you think Dame Jeanne poisoned the pilgrim."

"I shall be discreet."

It turned out that Dame Jeanne had visited all the hospices on Saturday morning, ending up at the Pradau. She had taken foodstuffs to each one, carried by Arnaud. He could not remember what was in the baskets, but he gave Belina the empty one which had contained the gifts to the Pradau hospice.

"How do you know this is the right basket?" Belina asked him. Arnaud pointed to the three parallel knives on the Saint Bartholomew badge fastened to the basket. "Ah yes, the tanners' knives that commemorate Saint Bartholomew's death. Can I take this away with me please?"

"Of course you can, Dame Lansac. Maybe it will help your investigations." He smiled. "But bring it back before next Saturday."

"Does she only donate food on Saturdays?"

He nodded. "Dame Jeanne is as niggardly as a Hollander. I should know."

Belina walked upstream to the Moulié mill at Gauge. She doubted if the basket would provide any clues about the poison used on the dead pilgrim, but it was worth asking her brother to examine the crumbs in the bottom of it. He might be able to identify poisonous ones. She wondered if Dame Jeanne was learning from her heartless mother-in-law and had started to poison people as some kind of experimental project. Or perhaps she gave away food that had gone bad in the hot, thundery weather? In which case, the Senclar kitchen staff might have poisoned the pilgrim. But if that had been the case, other pilgrims would have suffered too.

She showed the basket to Jordi and Catalina Moulié, though ensuring that Catalina did not touch it. Jordi sniffed at it.

"Stale bread, overripe fruit."

"Would anyone get food poisoning from them?" asked Belina.

"Don't think so. In any case, a pilgrim who had gone to Compostela and back would have developed a strong stomach from the Spanish food."

"Yes indeed. I've heard customers in the shop talking about the dreaded *auberges espagnoles*," said Belina. "Apparently, everyone brings their own food into Spanish inns. If they don't, they starve."

"It must be terrible travelling in Spain," said Catalina, "what with bandits and bad inns and poisoned water, a stranger in Spain risks death, or near-death."

Belina remembered the seamstress using the same expression that morning. 'Near death'. She asked her brother if Loupmont had threatened him again.

"Not yet, too busy celebrating the death of the pastry-cook."

"Celebrating? Why?" said Belina.

"They say Loupmont intends to put debtors to work in his kitchen, cooking food for the clergy. That way, he could dismiss some of the cathedral cooks, and replace them with badly paid poor folk desperate for work."

"No Gascon would do something so cruel and dishonest," said Catalina. "But of course Parisians like Loupmont would be used to treating workers badly."

"Jordi," said Belina, "I thought you said Loupmont, and Rocca too, come from Saint Somewhere-in-the-East."

"Saint Mihiel, near the Château de Koers," he replied, "where Queen Marguerite d'Anjou lived in exile until seven years ago."

"Where did she move to?"

"Back to Anjou. She died penniless in Saumur last year and went to her grave unlamented."

Catalina ladled the *garbure* into bowls and handed round bread to dip into the thick, steaming soup. She insisted they started eating before it grew cold.

Jordi repeated his request of yesterday morning that Belina should get her husband to help him. Guillaume knew the cathedral administrative and budget staff. Best of all, he knew Bishop Montbrun. Guillaume would know how to escape from Loupmont's avaricious clutches. Or should Jordi escort Belina back to Guillaume's chamber after dinner and plead his case himself with Guillaume?

Belina shook her head. "My husband insists on being left alone all day whilst he writes his report."

"Then, you'll have to persuade him to get Loupmont off my back,"Jordi replied. "To help you I will give you a good *big* loaf of bread." He picked one up from the basket near the window and wrapped it in a bit of cloth.

"This, Belina, is bargain bread. As the saying goes, 'the way to a man's heart is through his stomach'." He hesitated. "But it is up to you to get Guillaume to rescue us."

"If you put it like that, Guillaume might think you have indeed been cheating the bishop over flour quantities."

"You know very well I have done no such thing." He stood up, knocking his stool over.

"So what does Loupmont base his accusation on?" she asked.

"Absolutely nothing. He is horribly greedy. He will stop at nothing to make money."

"Same as Rocca, in other words."

"Possibly worse than Rocca. Their deaths would be welcome, they really would."

Catalina and Belina crossed themselves hurriedly. "Don't talk like that," they said together. "Please don't."

"No need to be worried," replied Jordi. "Half the town wishes them dead. And so do all the peasants whose land belongs to the bishop. They talk of nothing else when they visit the mill. And now, if you two will excuse me, I need to check that the water wheel is not clogged up by floating branches or dead ducks."

"Don't forget to bring back any dead fish caught up in the fish baskets," Catalina called out. But he was already gone.

Belina thanked Catalina for the lunch, said her goodbyes to the two children playing near the door, grabbing the Pradau hospice basket and the loaf Jordi had given her, hurried out into the scorching afternoon sunshine.

CHAPTER TWELVE

Belina trudged along the river bank as far as the Gaichou Gate. The river was full of branches and sodden plants hurtling downstream. Normally so clear, the water was rich and muddy and moving very fast. Ducks sheltered in the reeds beside the bank. She turned right and walked uphill and through the Gaichou Gate. Sheep crowded together in the shade of an oak tree, guarded by a boy and his dog. Belina turned away from them and walked along rue Latournerie to the cathedral, trying to keep in the shade of the tall houses and at the same time avoiding all the mess passing animals had left. It was not easy. Flies buzzed inside the apparently empty basket. She wondered how the dead pilgrim had managed to walk into Condom on Saturday in the thunderstorm. It was odd that his clothes and boots were not soaked, but perhaps they had dried out in the hospice dormitory.

She had eliminated most of the poisons in Guillaume's chart from causing the pilgrim's death as they acted immediately. Of course, he might have committed suicide, but surely not by such unbearably painful means? In any case, suicide was ungodly, a heresy. No one chose to commit suicide – especially not on a religious pilgrimage. And then she remembered the pastry-cook who had been buried that very morning. Gossiphad it that *he* had taken his own life and that the announced cause of death from a heart attack was just a way to ensure his Christian burial.

Belina felt she was making very little progress in her investigations. Guillaume would have solved the mystery by now, she was sure. Still lost in thought, she collided with Dame Edith Senclar who was walking towards the cathedral.

Belina backed away. "I beg your pardon, Dame Senclar," she said, curtseying.

The tiny woman glared at her. "Look where you are going, girl," she shouted.

Everyone around them stopped and stared at Belina. An old clergyman said that youth nowadays had no manners or consideration for their elders. The physician accompanying Dame Senclar said the same, but even more severely.

"I beg your pardon, Dame Senclar," Belina repeated her apology.

"Humph." Then Dame Senclar noticed the Senclar medallion next to the St Bartholomew badge on the Senclar basket used to take food to the Pradau hospice. "What's this?" she snarled, trying to snatch the basket.

Belina held on to it tightly and tried to think up a plausible excuse for possessing Senclar property without the permission of its angry owner.

"Just because you are a miller's daughter, and therefore a thief, doesn't mean you can steal my property," said Dame Senclar hissed.

"Dame Senclar, I am not a thief," replied Belina, still holding the basket too tightly for its owner to wrest it from her.

"You must be, you jade. How else do you come to be holding my basket?"

"But it is not your personal basket. It is the basket used to bring food alms from Dame Jeanne to the Pradau hospice."

"So why it is in your possession, girl?" Dame Senclar demanded.

Out of the corner of her eye Belina noticed Jeannot. She

called out to him, asking him to take the Pradau basket to Brother Martin 'who had requested it'.

Dame Edith scowled at her. "Why would a friar want my basket?"

"To check it, Dame Senclar. All the containers of food received by the Pradau hospice on Saturday are being checked for possible poisons." Someone behind Belina gasped. "A pilgrim died in the hospice on Saturday and it is of course essential to find out why he died and who supplied the poison. It is beyond doubt that he died of poisoning."

Dame Edith seemed to shrivel even smaller. "I trust you are not daring to accuse me of poisoning," she said icily.

"I am not accusing you of anything," replied Belina. "At least, not yet."

"On the other hand," said Dame Senclar, "I am accusing you of many sins: theft and rudeness for a start, followed by being employed unsuitably in the cathedral shop and by living illegally in the cathedral staff residence."

Belina was astonished at this malignant accusation. "I can assure you, Dame Senclar, that I live legally in the staff residence, in my husband's chamber, and that I am employed legally in the shop."

"I doubt it, girl. A miller's daughter should never be given a position where she can steal from the money box and, worse still, the shop's stock of holy carvings and medallions. I shall speak to the Lord Bishop as soon as possible and request him to cancel your appointment in the shop and turn you out of the residence. Your husband can remain there, if the Lord Bishop absolutely insists, but you will leave it." She tilted her face upwards, gloating at Belina's discomfiture.

Belina turned round and left Dame Senclar standing beside the cathedral door surrounded by her friends and enemies. An ironmonger who had been demonstrating on Saturday against Rocca took Belina's arm and congratulated her on her courage.

"Thanks. But I am really worried. That rich hell-hag has enormous power. I feel doomed."

"Don't worry, Dame Lansac, there's many more people in this town who would support you than would support that nasty old wretch." He guided her towards the cathedral shop. "You rest in here. This is where you belong. Dame Senclar is a foreigner, she's from Lectoure. Rumour has it that her family helped the invaders in the Sack of Lectoure ten years ago. That's why their mansion was one of the very few to be spared. And then they made piles of money buying up derelict land and property very cheaply and reselling it at enormous profit."

Belina squeezed his arm. "It's a pity that her family survived. I don't mind that someone killed the Comte d'Armagnac, but in the confusion surely some Lectourois could have killed Dame Senclar."

"Maybe they would have done. But she was already living in Condom, married to Henri Senclar's father." He paused. "He was a bad person too, marrying Dame Senclar when she was only twelve and getting her pregnant immediately."

The ironmonger left Belina sitting at the back of the shop, her head in her hands.

Eventually she looked up to see Quiteira brusquely selling foot balm pots. She was obviously irritated, and pilgrims were hesitating to buy anything from her. Belina realised that it was high time that she employed her own sales negotiating strategies. She hoped that Dame Senclar would not force her out of the shop. That threat made it all the more important that she paid attention to the shop's success and profits.

Belina got up and went to greet a group of pilgrims who had stopped beside the medallions counter and had begun to finger the seals showing the tower of the Barlet Bridge.

"Ooh, look at this, the Pont Valentré," said the fattest pilgrim, picking up a pewter medallion showing a bridge with a high tower.

"No," said Belina," it is the bridge over the river Baïse, here in Condom." She looked at his scallop shell. "You must have crossed it yourself."

"If I did I was too tired to notice," he replied. "Anyway, the Pont Valentré is much longer than this bridge," he said, pointing to the pewter medallion and sniffing. "What else have you got to show me?"

Belina took out another box of medallions and brooches of Condom cathedral, but kept it near her just in case any of the pilgrims grabbed one and rushed off. They looked too well-nourished and well-clothed for that, but she had learnt the hard way to be careful.

"How much for this small one of St Peter and his keys?"

"Two *sous*."

"May I take three of them for five *sous*."

"I am sorry, Messire, but I am not allowed to reduce the prices," Belina said.

"Who owns this shop?"

"The Lord Bishop of Condom."

"Take me to him."

"I cannot do that," replied Belina.

"And why not, young woman?"

"Because he is not here," she explained.

"I can see that. I mean, take me to his palace."

Belina put the box back in its drawer, went round the counter and told the impatient pilgrim to follow her. She wondered if she had misunderstood his request. His accent was difficult to follow and in any case her own accent was very Gascon, or so Dame Jeanne Senclar told her, with that sneering air of superiority which so exasperated Belina.

She showed her irritable customer into the bishop's ante-chamber. "This pilgrim wishes to speak to my Lord Bishop," she told the footman, winking at him.

"Come this way, Messire." The footman indicated a door to his right.

Belina scuttled away before the pilgrim could realize that he had walked into a trap. No one saw the bishop without either a proper letter of introduction or a messenger's identity token, and all cathedral staff obeyed his orders. They would abandon tiresome visitors in an ante-room for at least an hour.

In Belina's absence Quiteira had managed to sell various medallions and *babioles* to the other pilgrims and was wrapping them in bits of cloth. She glared at Belina. "Someone came in looking for you," she told Belina in Gascon.

"Who?"

"No idea. A foreigner from Paris perhaps, judging from his accent. Good looking."

Belina shrugged her shoulders. "Would you like to buy some of our foot balm, Messires?" she asked the pilgrims standing uncertainly in front of her. She put some small pots on the counter. "Or perhaps some of our *aygue ardente* if you are in pain after such a long journey. They say that Compostela to Condom is two hundred leagues. That is a very long journey by foot or even on horseback." She eyed them carefully. They did not look particularly tired. "Have you got many more leagues to travel?"

"Indeed we have. We are returning to our homes in Luxembourg. We've been away nearly five months."

"Your families will be pleased to see you back," said Belina and Quiteira together, automatically, although they knew that some pilgrims went to Compostela to get away from their wives and in-laws. The more Belina saw of the Senclar family, the more she understood pilgrims.

"I hope my wife will have recovered from her sickness by now," said one of the pilgrims.

Belina pushed a flask of *aygue ardente* towards him. "This medicine might help her," she said.

He removed the stopper and sniffed it. "Hmm." He licked the base of the stopper. "Not bad."

"Five *sous*," said Belina.

He counted them out and put the re-stoppered flask in his satchel. "What's it made of?"

"Distilled wine, heated in an alembic," she told him.

"How long ago?"

"Last December."

"I'll have some too," said one of his companions. He examined his coins and put down nine *sous*. "Do I get two flasks?" he asked.

"No, but you get a bigger flask." She put one on the counter, "and it is from two years ago."

He put it into his satchel. "Can you recommend a place to eat this evening?"

"The Lion d'Or has a very good reputation," said Quiteira, "but of course you could dine where you are staying the night if you want to avoid curfew problems."

"We are staying in the Senclar mansion, but we prefer to eat by ourselves."

Belina smiled at them. "They say the Senclar mansion is very comfortable, but expensive."

"The furnishings are comfortable, but the conversation is too inquisitive for us."

"And too dogmatic," said the youngest pilgrim. "I mentioned that the story of Adelard founding the hospice of Aubrac was a myth, and that the tale had been made up as a way of getting out of paying taxes."

The others laughed. "The young Dame Senclar was furious with him," they told Belina. "She seemed to take it very personally."

"She comes from Aubrac," Belina explained. "Dame Jeanne Senclar was the daughter of the Chief Steward of Aubrac Hospice."

"She has married above herself in that case," came the crisp reply. The pilgrims said their goodbyes and walked along the street towards the Place Lion d'Or.

Belina felt pleased with having sold the *aygue ardente* flasks and even more pleased with their criticism of Dame Jeanne Senclar. It was only after they had gone that she remembered that she should have asked them about Luxembourg, and also that she should have shown them the dead pilgrim's carving of the little boy peeing, in case they recognised who its owner had been.

However, she remembered to do this with the next pilgrim to visit the shop, but he was travelling westwards towards Mouchan. After him came three women from Gondrin, but Belina did not like to show them such an embarrassing carving. Nevertheless, at this time of the year most Compostela pilgrims were returning home and therefore reaching Condom from the Mouchan road. She tried the carving on several other visitors to the shop. They stared at her in astonishment. No one had seen the carving's owner. It was disappointing.

Disconsolately, Belina looked at the street outside. The bell had begun to toll and people were walking slowly towards the cemetery behind the cathedral, accompanying yet another corpse. She decided to join the mourners and to try to discover the cause of death in case it too was poison. She did not know whether she hoped it was poison – although that would have been terrible for the dead person – and whether she hoped it was someone she knew, in which case it would be easier to question the grieving family.

But when she reached the cemetery she learned that the dead man was yet another victim of Rocca. He had been one of the ringleaders of the angry demonstration on Saturday and Rocca had sent the cathedral guards to arrest him for inciting rebellion. In trying to escape over the rooftops he had fallen and broken his neck. Death had not been instantaneous and the mourners were filled with hatred and venom against Rocca. Vengeance was being discussed by several men, while the weeping women pleaded with everyone to calm down and not make things worse than they were. Some spoke of the permanent state of war in their parents' and grandparents' time when the country was left without men to till the land and to herd the animals, when cultivated land became fallow and reverted to waste and to overgrown forests. Belina overheard many anxious voices saying "don't do it."

A hand stroked her left shoulder. "Oh!" She jumped and turned round, expecting to see a friend or a relative.

"Dame Belina, I am so sorry to startle you." It was the new-comer from Bruges. Belina tried to step back but his hand was still on her shoulder, pulling her tunic slightly and keeping her close to him. She hoped that no one had overheard the Fleming's over-familiar greeting.

"Indeed, Messire, you did startle me."

"I have been looking for you everywhere," he said.

"Why?"

"You are investigating the death of a pilgrim. As I have already mentioned to you, I am an inquirer trained in Liège, and I put my experience and knowledge at your disposal."

"Thank you, Messire," Belina replied. She wondered what to say next. People were staring at her and she felt embarrassed. "Thank you, Messire," she repeated, "but it is my husband who is doing the investigation and he has plenty of experience and knowledge about solving crimes."

"Is this death a crime, Dame Belina?"

"Poisoning. Probably deliberate."

"It could just be food poisoning, especially in this weather. Are summers always hot like this here?"

"Yes of course they are. In fact it's not as hot now as it was in July, as I have already told you," she replied, still wondering how to get away from him. "If you think the death was not a crime then why would your inquirer's experience be helpful?"

Her rude, abrupt speech only made him smile and stand even closer to her. Belina was relieved that people all around them were getting agitated about Rocca's harshness and ava-rice and paying little attention to her.

"The best way to find out if it was merely food poisoning and not something more deliberate will be to check out all the street pastry-cooks and food shops," said the Fleming.

Belina was unenthusiastic, and turned away to leave the noisy cemetery and return to the cathedral shop. But the crowd was in her way and she had to make for the cemetery's east gateway into the Place du Marché au Bled. She hoped the Fleming was not following her.

At the other side of the open wicket gate she walked into the market *halle*, going round the groups of shoppers. Soon her way was blocked by a street pastry-cook arguing with an old peasant woman who was sniffing one of his pies. "It smells off to me," the woman was shouting. "It must have been cooked yesterday. I won't buy it."

"Suit yourself. Someone else will buy it instead. And of course it wasn't made yesterday. Your memory is going. Yesterday was Sunday and I don't bake on the Lord's Day."

"In that case you baked it on Saturday," she retorted.

The people around her smiled. "Maybe you are right," said one of them, "little mutton pies will go off in this weather quicker than that anyway."

"It's not a mutton pie," said the angry pastry-cook. "It is a bacon pie."

Someone picked up a pie and sniffed it. "Smells like chicken to me."

"Chicken and bacon, Messire."

"Whatever it is, I am not buying it." He put the pie back on the tray hanging from the pastry-cook's shoulders.

Belina moved away, and found her way blocked by a cheese seller. The same sort of conversation was taking place, and the goat's cheese especially was so smelly that she wondered if someone had trodden in some dogdirt. However, she was sure that the pilgrim's satchel had not contained goat's cheese because Minet would not have snatched it up and eaten it.

With her mind on the contents of the dead pilgrim's satchel, she had not noticed that the Fleming was standing beside her again.

"You see what I mean, Dame Belina," he said, holding her

elbow, "food bought in the street here is not always safe to eat."

"Maybe it is, maybe it isn't," she replied, "but even if it is off it would not kill. You may not know this, but this town is always full of pilgrims going to and from Compostela and they are used to dubious food. They need to be because the food in Castilla has a really bad reputation."

He laughed, a trilling laugh which made people turn round and stare at him. And at Belina. She hoped nobody recognized her.

"Come with me, Dame Belina," he said, holding her elbow again," and I will enquire in shops about food safety and whether anyone saw the pilgrim." He steered her down rue Royale. "Which day did he die?"

"Saturday."

"Perhaps that was when he was found dead," he suggested.

"No, poisons act quicker than that, as you – an inquirer – would presumably know."

He laughed again, the attractive laugh of a confident man with a pretty girl on his arm. He led her in and out of shops, enquiring on her behalf about the pilgrim and the food and wine which the pilgrim might have bought and consumed. No one said anything useful to Belina, but it took them a lot of time. People who knew her looked very disapproving and she was asked several times why her husband was not doing the investigation 'like he usually does'. In the end, she made an excuse that she needed to see Sir John about some new medicine and she hurried back home.

She hobbled across the residence courtyard. Her feet had swollen in the heat and from walking in and out of all the shops. Several people had recognized her and had looked astonished. She expected that being escorted into shops by an unknown elegant foreigner would have done her reputation no good. She had tried to be unfriendly to the Fleming but had found that very difficult. The old problem of the reputation of millers' wives and daughters did not help. Someone was bound to talk to Guillaume about his wife's apparent friendship with a man in his absence and Guillaume would not like what they said.

Quiteira would be bound to confirm the gossip. She had been married to an old soldier who had never really recovered from his last battle. Her children were grown up and living in La Romieu. Gossip was her way of avoiding loneliness and Belina suspected that Quiteira had discovered that Guillaume might not be completely French. She was always asking questions about their relationship, hinting that it was time Belina had babies, that Guillaume was absent far too often, that marriage to an outsider such as Guillaume was risky and would end in tears. Belina rebuffed these hints every time, saying that she had a very happy marriage, that she loved her husband very much, and that she enjoyed their life in the cathedral staff residence.

She glanced up at the door to Guillaume's chamber and then saw that Sir John was trying to tell her something, waving his left arm in the air. She tried to decipher the capital letter he was signing swiftly in front of her. He was determined to tell her something important, but since he could not speak or write any 'conversation' with him took ages. His agitation and perseverance made it worse. That the letters were backwards to her eyes did not help either.

She made out the letter 'R' easily enough, though. "Rocca?"

"Aaahh," he nodded. But the signs following that were more puzzling. He repeated 'B' several times.

"Bordeaux?"

Sir John put his forefinger downwards. That meant "no".

Belina tried again. "Burgundy?"

He thought for a moment and tentatively pointed his forefinger to the sky. Then came 'RIII'.

"Rocca has arrested three people?"

Apparently it was not that. It was 'R' and the number '3',

but not people.Belina could not make it out. Next came an 'EIV'. Incomprehensible.

Then an 'HT'. Belina could not think of a word beginning with 'H' which was so important for Sir John. *Hibou?*she suggested, but thought it was unlikely he was thinking about an owl. *Homme?*she suggested in case he was talking about a man.

Sir John pointed his forefinger to the stone floor. He gave up on signs in the air and pointed to a table and two stools near his bedroom. His valet, Alain, explained to Belina that Sir John had listened to the conversation during the last three evenings between Rocca and his Flemish guest, and at breakfast too, and perhaps that was what he wanted to tell Belina about.

Sir John pointed straight at the sky. "Aaahh."

Belina was worried. Was he criticising her for talking to the Fleming? Had Alain seen her in Condom that afternoon going in and out of shops? Would he tell Guillaume about her inappropriate escort? She hoped that Guillaume would not believe him, or at least pretend not to believe him. But if Sir John somehow managed to convey to Guillaume that she had been accompanied for hours by the Fleming Guillaume would be furious. He had disapproved of her friendliness towards the soldiers in Geraud's troop and had made it very clear that he was glad when they all marched south to the Pyrenees and into Spain.

Sir John pointed to the table again and then to his left ear. Belina gathered that he had listened to something, but what? It could only be about her being with the Fleming because he was so insistent and anxious.

He pointed at her and then again at his ear. Belina felt more and more uncomfortable and embarrassed. She liked the old English gentleman and she did not want his disapproval. She looked at Alain to see if he too appeared disapproving, but he had a jar of hippocras in his hand and was pouring some into a cup for Belina. He handed it to her with his usual deferential politeness. At least, she thought so. However, it was not Alain's place to rebuke her for apparent friendship with a strange man in Guillaume's absence.

Belina stared at Sir John as she sipped her hippocras. She felt very uneasy. "I am very sorry, Sir John," she said, "I am so tired from walking around Condom all day that I am too slow-witted now to understand you. Tomorrow I will be better, I promise."

She said her farewell *bonne nuit* and climbed the stairs to her chamber, wondering why Sir John had not waited until Guillaume came back from Bordeaux. Why was it so urgent? What, or who, were 'R', 'B', 'EIV', and 'HT'? Why was 'R' trebled? Was the urgency because Sir John feared he would have another attack of apoplexy and die? She was so tired that she had forgotten all about the death in far away England of King Edward and the coronation of his successor, King Richard.

Minet was waiting for her at the door, meowing irritably.

"All right, all right, you'll get your supper in a moment." Belina took the second largest key from her belt and let the cat and herself into the chamber. She shut and bolted the heavy door behind her. The thick stone walls had kept the room cool in spite of the hot day. There were several advantages in living in the cathedral staff residence and dwelling in a stone building was certainly one of them. Belina unhooked the matting from the windows, took off her head-cloth and washed her face.

She sniffed the milk in the stone jug. It seemed all right, so she gave the cat some, narrowly avoiding tripping over her. She broke off a bit of crust from the loaf Jordi had given her and gave that to the cat too. She cut a slice of bread for herself and ate a chunk of cheese with it. She wondered whether to investigate the crumbs in the pilgrim's satchel but decided to study the coin chart first while there was still enough light. She went into the inner room and unlocked her winter clothes chest. She pulled out the *chausse* containing the coins and tipped them on to Guillaume's work table. Minet immediately jumped on top of them but Belina scolded her so fiercely that the offended cat ran into the main room, jumped on to the window sill and looked at birds flying outside, her tail lashing. Belina sighed and began to sort the coins.

CHAPTER THIRTEEN

There was a loud knock at the front door. It brought back memories of Jeannot the previous Saturday. Belina hoped that it was not the bold Fleming. "Who is it?" she called.

To her relief it was Alain with a message from Sir John. "Dame Belina, Sir John insists that you come down straight away and mend his clothes. He is getting very anxious about it, so please do come at once." Bellina made no reply as she tried to think up a suitable excuse. "I'm sure you are tired, Dame Belina, and normally I would have told Sir John that, but he really is insistent. I think he wants you to be sitting in his room before Rocca and the Fleming come into the courtyard. I am sure something in the conversation could help your investigations."

"That is unlikely," Belina called through the door.

"Please come down, Dame Belina, with your sewing basket. It's true, there are lots of things to mend, and I will light one of the best candles for you when it gets too dark."

"All right, Alain, I'll come down as Sir John wishes it so much. But first I must put my head-cloth on. Go down now and tell Sir John I am coming."

She gathered up all the coins, stuffed them back into the *chausse,* put them back into the bottom of Guillaume's big chest of winter clothes and locked it. Then she picked up the rectangular piece of white lawn which formed her head-cloth, and wound it round her head, fastening the ends neatly. Doing this at the end of a very tiring day made her arms ache, but she could not emerge from her chamber without wearing a head-cloth. Only Guillaume saw her without it. She collected her sewing basket, and made sure that Minet did not slip out of the front door.

When she reached the courtyard Sir John was still having his supper, helped by his valet. She stood a little distance away as she knew Sir John was embarrassed that he needed so much help when eating meals because of his paralysed right arm. However, as soon as he saw her, he put down his spoon and waved his left hand in her direction.

Belina went over to his chair and curtseyed. Sir John pointed to the carafe of wine and mimed a question mark in the air.

"Yes please," she replied, "but only a little. I need to concentrate not only on my sewing but also on this conversation you want me to memorize." Alain poured some wine into a goblet. "Your health, Sir John," said Belina, raising her goblet, "but please don't let me interrupt your supper."

She drank the good wine, appreciating the absence of water in it, and handed the goblet back to Alain who told her that he would show her where to sit in Sir John's room so that Rocca and Barvaux could not possibly see her.

"Who is Barvaux?" she asked.

"Rocca's Flemish friend. The one you met on the staircase." And the one who had escorted her in and out of many shops. Belina wondered if Alain had already heard about that.

She found herself in a large room, with sunlight still coming through a tall window facing west. Alain had placed a stool for her sewing basket, a table laden with an assortment of clothes, and a large chair for her so that she was very near the open door leading to the courtyard but out of sight of Rocca and Barvaux.

Belina settled into the big chair and began mending the first shirt. As often with his clothes, there was a hole in the left elbow where he had scraped the arm of his chair, trying to lever himself when he stood up. She started to darn the fraying cloth. Alain had disappeared to wash up Sir John's soup bowl. From where she sat she could just see Sir John reclining on his couch, staring at a bat which was darting around the courtyard.

Footsteps echoed in the courtyard, and soon Belina heard Rocca's voice quite close to her. "Philippe, let's drink to the success of our plan. May France conquer England and bring wealth to us both."

"How will Tudor's invasion bring you wealth, Claude?"

Belina heard Rocca's thin hard voice replying, "Archbishop Cato will see that I get my reward for providing so much money from Condom for the Count of Richmond. We Italians stick together, you know."

"The Earl of Richmond, or the Count as you call him, is not Italian. He's half Welsh, half English."

"I know, I know. I also know that he is a young man with no experience of government so that when he does become king – if he does – he will have to rely on his supporters, and pay them generously."

"Including me," said Barvaux, pouring some liquid into his goblet. Belina wondered what it was, and whether it would make him drunk.

"Including you, Philippe." They clinked goblets. "Tell me how the Count's mother has managed to progress so far with her invasion plans."

Belina listened to Barvaux explaining that when King Edward died unexpectedly – possibly poisoned – the Earl of Richmond's mother, Lady Margaret Beaufort, had put into action a plan which she and Bishop Morton had already established. Lady Margaret needed to get rid of King Edward's younger brother (the Duke of Gloucester), King Edward's two sons, and the Duke of Buckingham who was another heir to the throne and her nephew by a former marriage.

Belina gathered that Buckingham had, on Lady Margaret's instructions, falsely befriended the Duke of Gloucester and persuaded him to arrest the step-brother and the uncle of the new king, Edward V, on the grounds that their servants had tried to kill the Duke of Gloucester in Northampton. But in reality the assassins were Beaufort's soldiers, who had been ordered to kill the Duke of Gloucester, if possible. Belina wondered just how much of this story Guillaume already knew. Did the archdeacon know it too?

Barvaux was explaining to Rocca that since the assassination attempt had failed, the Beaufort-Morton Plan B had come into action. The two dukes had escorted the boy king to London while his mother went into sanctuary with the younger prince and all her daughters. Then Bishop Morton, the Duke of Buckingham and Lord Hastings had put it about that the two princes were illegitimate and therefore the Duke of Gloucester should be crowned king instead of just being Protector.

Rocca hissed at this suggestion. "Surely, that's very risky. A crafty, ambitious duke would keep a tight hold on his throne for ever and put all his enemies to death."

"That is exactly what the Earl of Richmond will do when he becomes King of England," replied Barvaux, "but the Duke of Gloucester is a great champion of justice and fairness, of helping the weak and poor. He's far too Christian and religious for his own good. He will not believe that a lady and a bishop could have such deadly ambitions."

"Go on with your story then," said Rocca. Belina heard the two goblets being refilled.

"Lady Margaret's husband, Lord Stanley, has made sure that he is the main adviser to the Protector-become-King, on the grounds that he was King Edward's main adviser. In fact, King Edward distrusted Lord Stanley and much preferred Lord Hastings. But the plotters needed Hastings to be in Calais to see how he could set free the Earl of Oxford imprisoned in Hammes Castle there so that they could make use of Oxford's military expertise to lead the invasion of England. Unfortunately, freeing the Earl of Oxford and his troops is going to require a tremendous amount of money, and that is what I am here to collect."

Rocca interrupted. "I thought I was providing funds for the Count in Brittany."

"Yes, yes, you are," replied Barvaux. "What I am waiting here for is a treasure chest from a Catalan merchant called Daniel Berga who should be arriving here any day. Then I will travel to Calais with him to hand over the money."

"I trust you'll keep some for yourself," said Rocca.

"Of course I shall. So will the Catalan. That's why he will be bringing a very big chest."

Both men laughed.

"Where will he be staying?" Rocca asked.

"In the Senclar mansion with his own servants guarding the chest day and night. After that we plan to go to Bordeaux and take a ship to Calais. Quicker and easier than going overland such a long distance with a heavy chest."

"What happens if Lord Hastings cannot release the Earl of Oxford?"

"He has already failed to do so," replied Barvaux. "Most unfortunately, the Protector sent for him, bribing him with the appointment of Master of the Mint."

Rocca drew in his breath. "Some bribe."

"Yes indeed, but Hastings was foolish to return to London in order to take it."

"Why?"

"Because part of the Beaufort-Morton plan was to denounce the Hastings Plot to the Protector once he had been crowned king and thus get Hastings arrested."

"How, and why?" asked Rocca.

"We needed to eliminate Hastings so that his vast numbers of Midlands retainers and troops could transfer to the Duke of

Buckingham, and in due course be used in a rebellion against King Richard."

"I find all this plotting difficult to follow," muttered Rocca. Belina almost agreed with them out loud. She began darning yet another garment.

Rocca continued, "and how was Hastings to be denounced?"

"By my own personal skill," replied Barvaux. Belina heard him refilling his goblet, and Rocca declining to have another drink.

"In what way?" Rocca persisted.

"I forged documents in Hastings' own handwriting and with his seal as Lieutenant of Calais, addressed to the dowager queen, Elizabeth Woodville, saying he was invading England to put her elder son back on the throne."

Rocca asked how the documents had reached the Protector.

"Via his new clerk, Catesby, who transferred from Hastings' staff to the Protector's staff. He is very ambitious."

"Like you and me," Rocca replied.

"Yes."

"Was Catesby aware that the documents were forged?"

"I don't know, actually."

"So what happened next?"

Barvaux continued his tale, saying that the Protector, predictably, was furious with Hastings, but also with himself, for having been fooled. Hastings was arrested, tried a week later, and then beheaded. The protector let Hastings' widow off without further financial penalties. "The Earl of Richmond wouldn't have been so soft-hearted. He will punish all the families of people against him. Lots of money to be made that way," Barvaux remarked, helping himself to yet another drink.

Belina shuddered and gave a little sigh.

"Can that old man over there understand our conversation?" Barvaux asked Rocca.

"No. He's a senile sergeant, badly crippled and very deaf. Too old to talk. No need to worry yourself about him."

"And his servant?" Barvaux persisted.

"He was leaving the courtyard as we came in here," said Rocca.

Belina jumped. Alain had come stealthily into the room holding a brightly lit candle. He put it down silently on the stool beside Belina, keeping a finger to his lips. She smiled her thanks. She hoped she had not missed too much of the extraordinary conversation taking place the other side of the wall. By now she had realised that Sir John wanted her to tell Guillaume about this terrible, wicked plot when he came back. It would occupy his thoughts – which could be very useful. The less Guillaume heard about her and Barvaux the better. She frowned at her sewing and concentrated on the discussion in the courtyard.

Rocca was commenting on the Protector's extraordinary clemency to the plotters. "Surely they should have been be-headed, even the bishop? Especially the bishop."

"As I told you," Barvaux said," the Duke of Gloucester is very religious. He is a pious and good man. He's not cunning, he's a military man from the north of England. He doesn't understand greed and plotting."

"Unusual," said Rocca. "Are you sure?"

"It's what Bishop Morton says," replied Barvaux. "He says it often. I should know. I am one of his confidential staff."

"Forger, clerk; spy too perhaps?" asked Rocca.

"I do whatever my Lord Bishop asks me to do," replied Barvaux.

"And he pays you well, I hope," said Rocca.

"He has to pay me very well indeed."

"Why?" Rocca demanded.

"Because long ago when he was living in St Mihiel with Queen Marguerite d'Anjou I used to carry out rough tasks for him as well as bringing him money from the Grand Duke of the West. Lots of bribes for him personally from the Duke of Burgundy."

Rocca wanted to know why the Duke of Burgundy had bribed an English bishop.

"It suited him to have an alternative potential ruler of England. He knew, as I know myself, that Bishop Morton has always planned to rule England. And even though a lot of time has passed, that is still his ambition."

"I trust his health is better than his ethics," said Rocca.

"And who are you, Claude, to talk about ethics?" replied Barvaux.

No reply to that bold comment. Belina heard Barvaux pouring more liquidinto his goblet.

"What is the unethical bishop going to do next?" asked Rocca.

"Simple, but expensive," replied Barvaux. "He is fomenting a rebellion against the king – who is progressing around England with his queen. Lady Margaret is financing that rebellion while my Lord Bishop stays in the Duke of Buckingham's castle in Brecon reminding the duke of his grievances and that he should be king instead of the newly crowned King Richard. The rebellion is set for the 18th of October and it will be called the Duke of Buckingham's Rebellion. That way, when it fails – as it will – the duke will be beheaded by the victorious King Richard."

"I don't quite understand the need to get rid of this duke," said Rocca.

"Next in line to the throne," replied Barvaux.

"What about King Edward IV's sons? And does King Richard have sons?" asked Rocca.

Barvaux explained that part of the plot had centred round declaring the Woodville princes illegitimate but that they would continue to live in the Tower of London instead of being sent northwards to Yorkshire to live with their cousin at Sheriff Hutton. Lady Margaret had spread rumours that King Richard had ordered them to be murdered. However, she herself had arranged for their murder. King Richard had only one son, quite young, living at Sheriff Hutton. Lady Margaret would send some of her so-called minstrels there to poison him.

"Ruthless," said Rocca, "and definitely unethical."

"Maybe, but that way the path to the throne is cleared for her son Henry Tudor, the Earl of Richmond, to become King, and for herself to be styled the King's Mother."

"I see. And how does a failed rebellion damage the victorious King Richard?"

"All the gentry of the south and the Midlands will be found guilty and have to flee penniless to Brittany. Northerners will be appointed in their place and the peasants will hate that, same as they hated Queen Marguerite d'Anjou's northern English troops. Uncouth behaviour, uncouth speech."

"The costs of supporting all those exiles in Brittany will be huge," said Rocca.

"Indeed. That is where your contributions will be so valuable."

Belina gritted her teeth. So, all the financial sufferings endured in Condom were to finance English rebels against a just, good Christian king. She tried to blame Rocca for all this, but Barvaux's bishop sounded wicked.

She heard stools being scraped on the courtyard paving stones and the exchange of "*bonne nuit*". Alain came into the room and whispered that in a little while he would escort her back upstairs to Messire Guillaume's chamber. Belina wondered if he suspected that Guillaume was not there, but many leagues away riding towards Bordeaux.

Sir John was still reclining on his couch. By the light of Alain's lantern Belina could see his face, grim and frowning. The plot for the usurpation by the young Henry Tudor to overthrow a good king must be agony for Sir John. For his sake, as well as for King Richard himself, Belina hoped the plotters would fail and be hanged. Surely, God would not allow such wickedness to prevail? She crossed herself, touched Sir John's left arm and whispered *bonne nuit*. Alain escorted her back up the staircase in the dark, and held a candle very close to the keyhole of her front door as she tried to unlock it without making a noise. Minet rushed out, but Alain caught her and pushed her inside again, shutting the door quickly. Belina felt her way towards the shelf where she kept her tinderbox and candle. She lit it with great difficulty because her hands were shaking with emotion engendered by the terrible conversation she had overheard.

Her hands were still shaking as she ate some cheese with two slices of bread. She poured out some wine from the pitcher, but most of it missed her goblet and landed on the bread and cheese instead. It was a messy supper.

She removed her head-cloth and her clothes, put on her nightcap and climbed into bed. Sleep was a long time coming.

CHAPTER FOURTEEN

The following morning dawned fair and bright. The birds were singing in the courtyard trees and Minet was anxious to get near them. The cat was no music-lover, but hunting birds was a joyful pastime for her, much to Belina's dismay. Against her better judgment, she unlocked the heavy door and let Minet out.

"Please, Virgin Mary, don't let my cat kill any birds. Mice, if you permit it, but not birds," she whispered.

She washed her hands and face, got dressed, ate two pears and a slice of bread, all the while thinking of the secrets she had overheard the evening before. What wickedness, what horror. She shuddered at the thought that she had been so attracted to Barvaux. What other evil things had he done? Why was he so interested in the pies sold by the dead pastry-cook? Why was he so certain that the pilgrim had died from food poisoning?

She decided to put such thoughts at the back of her mind. Instead, she should concentrate on writing down a summary of what she had heard. She put her tablets and stylus on the table and methodically set down the details of the Barvaux-Rocca conversation. She took care, though, to hide any of her own feelings about Barvaux and made sure never to mention his Christian name, Philippe. She scratched away with her stylus concentrating on facts, carefully concealing any connection between herself and her Flemish suitor. But was he really a suitor? In reality, he was just an unscrupulous Flemish clerk, forger and spy. At least, that was what Rocca had suggested. She hesitated to believe that. He was too helpful and attractive, not only to look at but also to listen to. She wondered if he was musical. She hoped that the Catalan merchant would arrive very soon and that the two of them would be on their way to Bordeaux and Calais before Guillaume returned to Condom. But suppose they met each other on the way? She shook her head and picked up another tablet. Her writing became rather wobbly with emotion, but she persevered.

There was a thump and a scratch at the door. She got up and let the cat back in. Minet immediately jumped on to the table and began to wash herself on top of one of the tablets. Belina transferred the cat to the unmade bed, went into the other room and put the inscribed tablets in Guillaume's investigation bag. She put the bag back in the corner beside the pilgrim's staff, hitting her head on the empty gourd dangling on the hook near the top of the staff. Then she put a cloth on the table with Messire Benasse's coin chart and retrieved the *chausse* full of coins from Guillaume's winter clothes chest in the inner room. She slid the coins out one at a time and divided them into two groups: gold and silver. Next, she sorted out the gold coins, starting with the ones she knew best, the *ecus au soleil* and the *ecus à la couronne* and the half *ecus* issued by King Louis. She was surprised to see an earlier version among them dating from King Charles's reign, and even more surprised to see an *angelot* gold coin. She turned these last two coins over and over in her hands, admiring their beautiful engraving. And then she began sorting out the rest of the gold coins into piles.

The largest pile contained many gold coins of a design she had never seen before, with a complicated circle of lilies, crowns and leopards around a sun on one side and an engraving of a crowned king standing on a ship on the other side. She bent over Messire Benasse's coin chart, looking at his drawings of *maravedis*, *kreuzer*, florins and many other coins. She turned the chart over and saw a rather wobbly drawing of a king on a ship and a drawing beside it looking approximately like a circle of lilies and leopards surrounding a sun with a rose in the middle.

Taking the chart to the window and peering at it, she could see the similarity of the central rose with that on the middle of the ship engraved on the other side of the coin. Messire Benasse identified this complicated coin as a *noble d'or à la rose*, issued by King Edward IV in London. English coins! No wonder she had never seen one before. Few English pilgrims or traders travelled through Condom. They went by sea usually, to Bayonne or Bordeaux. Belina wondered how far Guillaume had reached on his journey to Bordeaux. She stopped searching the coin chart and gazed out of the window for a few minutes. Then she sighed, pulled herself together and sat down again at the table heaped with coins.

There were several Italian gold florins with portraits of St John the Baptist with the name S.JOHANNES.B engraved around the edge, and a couple of gold ducats issued by Pope Sixtus IV. Belina had seen some of these before, but the dozen gold florins issued in Liege by the Prince-Bishop Louis de Bourbon were new to her. An even more surprising coin was an ancient royal Hungarian florin with an engraving of St Ladislas on one side.

She picked up her stylus and listed the gold coins on a wax tablet, and then returned them to the *chausse*. Now for the smaller pile of silver coins. She separated the French coins from the rest on the table and listed them on a different wax tablet: nineteen *gros de roi*, sixteen *grands blancs de la couronne*, twenty-eight *grands blancs au soleil*. There did not seem to be any *petits blancs*. She peered again at the heap of silver coins and compared them with Messire Benasse's chart. Three coins looked like *grands blancs* but turned out to be from Provence, territory newly acquired by King Louis. She added them to the pile and to the French tablet list.

Most of the other silver coins were portraits. According to Messire Benasse's chart they were Italian. A dozen coins of the Venetian *Doge*, Nicolas Tron, with an engraving of St Mark's lion on the other side; seven coins of St Constantius on horseback on one side and an unattractive portrait on the other; four coins of another Venetian *doge* with St Mark on one side and Christ on His throne on the other.

Belina examined all these portraits and wondered what the coins were worth. The chart made no mention of values. Then she noticed two more portrait coins, with a Sforza on one side and a different Sforza on the other. Both of them wore armour. These too were new to her. Below the Sforza drawing on the chart was a sketch of what Messire Benasse had identified as a seven-headed hydra. She searched for something resembling it among the remaining coins and was sorry not to find anything.

Belina reached for another tablet and listed the three *maravedis* coins issued by both Fernando and Isabel of Spain, together with their half and quarter *reales*. But there was no sign of a silver four *reales* coin. Perhaps the dead pilgrim had changed the rest of his Spanish coins when crossing into Navarra on his way back from Compostela? If so, why had he kept so many valuable gold coins, especially all the English ones? She shook her head. Another puzzle was the existence of ten Aragonese coins on which King Fernando was described as Count of Barcelona. Belina frowned as she turned the heavy coins over in her hands.

The rest of the silver coins were easier to deal with because she was familiar with them from the cathedral shop. Methodically she listed each *kreuzer*, *double gros*, *jager* and *double briquette*. She noted the absence of *groschen*, *escalin* and *stuben*, but that there werea dozen *demi-ardants*.

Finally, she fetched the pilgrim's satchel from the other

room and extracted the copper coins from it. Or were they nickel? By now she did not care, and just made a brief list of *pugesas* from Gerona, *señales* from Tarragona, *double tournois* (should she put these in her money-box?), eight coins showing a bear, and four showing a knight in armour. According to Messire Benasse's coin chart, these came from the Tyrol. Belina wondered where that was and whether the engraving was a real portrait of someone named by Messire Benasse as Erzherzog Sigismund.

She surveyed her tablets. Should she remove some of the gold coins and re-write that tablet? Or should she remove the copper coins and erase their tablet list? Where would she put these 'procured' coins? She stared at the empty cloth and touched the *chausse*, uncertain whether to be conscientious or practical. She swallowed nervously. In the end, she decided to be honest and to put the coin-filled *chausse* at the bottom of Guillaume's other clothes chest, underneath his winter travelling clothes and sheepskin cap. She walked into his workroom, stowed the heavy *chausse* under his clothes at the bottom of the chest near the far wall and put the key back in its usual place hanging from a nail in the rafters above a framed drawing of Bordeaux.

What had she learned? Why were most of the gold coins English *nobles*? Where had the pilgrim travelled, and for how long? She did not think she was much further forward in her investigation in spite of her careful identifications and tablet lists.

She wrapped the coin chart in the cloth provided by Messire Benasse and added it to her newly inscribed wax tablets, which she placed in her winter clothes wooden box under the bed. She put her head-cloth on, stroked Minet, put some more tablets in her satchel and hurried outside. Brother Charles was going down the wooden stairs, gripping the handrail because his arthritic knees made descending staircases difficult and painful.

Belina caught him up, and then went into the shop's storeroom to find some *babioles* she had promised to give to Françoise, the widow who looked after the stall at the cathedral entrance. She caught Brother Charles up again and they walked slowly together towards the cathedral. He was bothered that morning by the worsening situation inside the cathedral itself.

"Dame Belina," he told her, "it's becoming dangerous for the pilgrims to sleep overnight in the side chapels. Recently one pilgrim even had his cloak, hat, and staff stolen. He was particularly sad to lose his scallop shell bought in Compostela for more money than he could really afford."

"If he is still in Condom, he could come to the cathedral shop and I will give him one of ours. But he will need to prove somehow that he really is the victim of theft," said Belina.

"That is kind of you, Dame Belina, but I don't understand how it is you have scallop shells for sale. Surely these are only available in Santiago de Compostela?"

"Theoretically, yes," replied Belina, "but in practice they are a very lucrative object to sell, and now that the members of the Cathedral Chapter are so keen on making money we have been told to stock real shells, and metal ones too."

"Where do you get them from?"

"The real shells come from the coast, near Bayonne. The metal ones come from our own workshops. I have made some myself, but not particularly well."

"That I find hard to believe, Dame Belina. Everything you do is very well done."

"You are too generous, Brother Charles." She smiled. "Did the pilgrim lose any money?"

"Fortunately not. What little he had was inside a purse fastened securely to his belt and he was wearing his satchel. Luckily, its strap is too thick to be cut off by a thief. But he was very sorry to lose his especially large gourd which he had refilled with wine. Stealing in the house of God is wicked, so wicked."

"Yes indeed it is," replied Belina. But she thought it was trivial in comparison to the English plot she had heard about the evening before. "Greed leads to wickedness," she said.

"Greed and ambition are evil. In my young days I think we had less of both sins," he replied. "But of course the soldiers caused havoc. My parents' manor house was burnt down by the troops of King Charles. They even regretted having called me Charles," he smiled at Belina.

"Does that mean that your parents supported the English in Gascony?" Belina asked.

"Of course they did, my dear. Most people did. The English and the Gascons were more cultured than the French invaders, and everyone wrote in Gascon in the good old days before France conquered Gascony."

Belina knew that already, because it explained why Guillaume had such a good mastery of written and spoken Gascon. They always spoke it together in public. However, very secretly he had taught her English – mostly words of endearment at first – and by now she knew his mother tongue fairly well.

CHAPTER FIFTEEN

Belina and Brother Charles found themselves in the midst of an angry crowd shouting insults about Rocca. The choirmaster hurried into the cathedral to take the Tuesday morning choir practice. Belina handed some imitation St Peter's keys to Françoise for her stall beside the cathedral door.

"Thank you Belina. I've hardly sold anything since these demonstrations against Rocca started, but perhaps that's more because no one has much money. Except that rogue Rocca himself of course." She put the imitation keys at the back of her table. "Talk of the Devil – and he is a devil – here he is."

Belina looked up and saw the thin, grim figure of the hated Treasurer advancing towards them. She stepped back and turned to face Françoise. But out of the corner of her eye she saw Jeanne Senclar coming out of the cathedral having heard the morning Mass as usual.

Rocca greeted Dame Jeanne curtly, but did not receive a reply. He continued by saying he hoped she had given a substantial donation to the cathedral rebuilding fund since she was the parishioner who used the cathedral the most.

Dame Jeanne was not amused. "I offer what I consider a correct amount of money, as well as fruit and vegetables from my garden for poor parishioners."

"Surely, the produce comes from Dame Edith's garden, not yours?" asked Rocca.

"That's the same thing," she replied.

"I don't think Dame Edith would agree with that remark. Moreover, she is very generous in her donations," Rocca commented.

Jeanne Senclar shrugged her almost bare shoulders. Rocca, embarrassed, looked the other way.

"Dame Senclar, maybe you would like to buy something from the medallion stall," said Françoise, moving the St Peter's keys to the centre of her table.

"No thank you." Jeanne Senclar tried to find her way through the crowd, but the angry butchers from La Bouquerie were barring her way, and leering at her ample bosom at the same time. Rocca had turned his back on her and was talking to Chezelle, Edith Senclar's physician, who had just emerged from the cathedral.

Belina had the impression that when he was not accompanying Dame Edith, Chezelle could be found keeping an eye on Jeanne Senclar, and sometimes on Henri Senclar too. He did not appear to look after anyone's health except occasionally the decaying teeth inside Dame Edith's thin mouth.

Chezelle was asking Rocca if it was true that the Hôpital Dômerie d'Aubrac had not been founded by Adalard, Vicomte de Flandres, but as a strategically sited tax evasion investment on the frontier of three dioceses. Belina realised that he must have been present at the argument between Jeanne Senclar and the pilgrims from Luxembourg.

"Yes, Messire Chezelle, the Dômerie was very rich and therefore was plundered by the Albigeois in 1210, coveted by the Order of St John of Jerusalem in 1297, by the Knights Templar in 1310, and by the English in the last war. It has only been operating as a hospice for pilgrims for about a dozen years. It doesn't compare with Le Puy, Vezelay or Conques. The Compostela tradition here in Condom is much more authentic. That story about a Flemish Viscount called Adalard founding the Dômerie d'Albrac on his return from Compostela is just a myth."

Jeanne Senclar swung round angrily, her bosom heaving. Rocca averted his eyes. "You lie," she accused him. "You are a liar."

"Dame Jeanne," said the physician, "you should not speak to the Treasurer in such a way."

"I will speak to him in whatever way I wish," she retorted, "and I will not accept any suggestion that Aubrac's foundation by Viscount Adalard is a myth."

"But Dame Jeanne," said Rocca in his very iciest tone, normally reserved for debtors, "much about the Way of St James to Compostela is a myth, especially the tradition that his bones are there in Galicia instead of in Jerusalem where he was beheaded."

"How dare you?" Jeanne Senclar shouted at him. "How dare you, a cleric, question the belief in St James?"

"Of course I believe in the existence of St James as one of the Apostles. But I do not believe his body was taken from Jerusalem to Galicia."

"Then pray tell me whose bones were found in the Field of Stars?" Chezelle asked, before Jeanne Senclar could spit out a denial of Rocca's firm statement.

"Probably no one's," Rocca replied. "It was theologically and politically convenient to say that St James's relics had been found in Galicia." He paused while the gathering crowd gasped. "And the tradition that they were found in a Campo de Estrellas – the Field of Stars, in other words – is rubbish. If *any* bones were found, they would have been unearthed in a *compostum*, the Latin word for cemetery. Thus came the term Compostela."

By now it was not just Jeanne Senclar who was disbelieving and angry. Everyone was hissing criticism at Rocca. Belina, too, was very uneasy. Why was she working in a cathedral shop for Compostela pilgrims if St James had never been in Galicia? Her livelihood depended on people's devotion to relics and medallions. Moreover, Condom Cathedral made a handsome profit from pilgrims, and Rocca had helped himself to much of it. She tried to compose a suitable sentence to tell him so.

Before Belina had decided on a clear, but safe, reply to Rocca's astonishing statement a well-clad merchant holding a fine horse said that in Trier, where he came from, there was a tradition that the bones found in the *compostum* at Santiago were those of Bishop Prisciliano, a Spaniard who was beheaded in Trier over a thousand years ago and whose body was taken back by river and sea to Galicia to be interred there.

"Interesting suggestion, Messire," said Rocca, "but do many people in Trier believe it?"

The merchant began to reply but was interrupted by Dame Jeanne effusively greeting Barvaux who was walking towards her, holding a letter with an impressive red seal. He took no notice of Dame Jeanne and continued walking so that he almost collided with the German merchant's horse which stamped its hooves on the cobbles.

"Look where you go, you fool," shouted the German.

The crowd drew away a little, wary of the big horse's hooves. Rocca slipped back into the cathedral. The merchant grabbed Barvaux's curly locks and pulled them upwards.

"Nasty scar have you here," he announced in his rather basic French.

"Leave my hair alone," snarled Barvaux.

The merchant displayed Barvaux's neck, and its scar, to some soldiers standing nearby. Everyone else craned their necks, and oohed and aahed.

"I repeat, leave my hair alone."

The merchant laughed and let go. "You very angry."

Chezelle grasped Dame Jeanne's arm and steered her across the square to the apothecary's store opposite the tower at the north end of rue Cadeot. A couple of butchers followed her whistling and calling out lewd remarks about her appearance, and someone shouted "Aubrac tax-avoider!"

Meanwhile Barvaux had seen Belina and, pushing two

people aside, came towards her, his eyes glinting. She looked away.

"Good morning, Dame Belina," he greeted her with a brilliant smile. Several people turned round to find out what foreigner knew Belina well enough not to address her as Dame Lansac. Five women frowned at her, women who knew her as the *molièrota* (the miller's daughter).

Belina felt annoyed and embarrassed. She took a deep breath and replied, "good morning, Messire", hoping that Barvaux would take the hint.

He did not. On the contrary, he put his hand on her arm and announced he would take her into shops and inns. This suggestion was too much for the glovemaker's wife standing nearby. She reminded Belina that wives do not go into inns with strange men.

"Dame Lansac," she continued, even more loudly, "what would your husband say?"

Belina was waiting for that. "He would approve, as a matter of fact. A pilgrim has died in the Pradau hospice. He was poisoned, and my husband has asked me to check up where he was before he reached the hospice, so I do need to go into shops and inns."

"Why can't Messire Guillaume do that?" asked a cathedral groom.

"Because he is writing a very important report for the bishop." The stock reply came out immediately. Belina hoped the groom had not seen Guillaume ride out of the cathedral stables early on Sunday morning. He was certainly looking puzzled. It was high time she escaped from the crowd.

Barvaux took her into the cobbler's shop, but the cobbler could not remember that particular pilgrim. So many pilgrims limped into his shop to have their boots mended. In any case, Belina remembered that the dead pilgrim's boots, and his feet, had been in good condition. The owner of the cloth shop told her sadly that pilgrims never bought anything from her in summer.

The apothecary's store was very crowded. Jeanne Senclar was monopolising the attention of the owner and his assistant whilst other customers waited impatiently and grumbled. Belina left without questioning anybody, hoping that the apothecary had not seen her with the elegant Fleming. She went in and out of all the other shops near the cathedral. Some people were more helpful than others, but no one remembered anything definite or useful to her.

Plucking up courage, she went into the Lion d'Or. There at least the presence of Barvaux prevented the owner from pushing her out immediately, as had happened in the Cheval Blanc. Nevertheless, she felt very uncomfortable in such a place and left as soon as she could.

She had an easier time in the Compagnons' *auberge* next door, talking to the *Mère*. But no newcomer had arrived for several weeks and her cooks made all the food served to the young workmen and artisans lodging there. The *Mère* was vehement that her *auberge* never sold bad pies.

Belina and Barvaux walked back down the street leading to the cathedral. The narrow street was crowded and Barvaux held Belina very close to him. She prised his hand away but not before a woman selling herbs had stared at her and muttered "*molièrota*". A mule laden with furniture jostled her, giving Barvaux the excuse to pull her towards him again.

She sighed with relief when the street opened out into the cathedral square, but just outside the Serpent tavern they were almost crushed by an enormous cart drawn by two straining horses. Barvaux gripped Belina's arm protectively, pulling her close to him yet again. To her horror, she saw that Brother Martin was coming towards her, but talking to Jeannot trotting beside him. She turned away, hoping they had not seen her yet, and tried to enter the tavern.

Barvaux pulled her back. "You cannot go in there, Dame Belina".

"Why not?"

"It is a dark and dirty tavern. No place for someone like yourself." He gripped her arm more tightly.

"Let go of my arm please. I am perfectly capable of standing without assistance."

He stared at her, clearly surprised by her forthright remarks, and released her arm. She pushed past two soldiers coming out of the tavern and went into it, not caring to decide which was worse: meeting Brother Martin and the chatty Jeannot, or entering a place which she knew she ought to avoid.

It took her a few minutes to become accustomed to the dim lighting and, especially, to the smell of sour wine and stale urine. The rush matting on the floor was humming with insects. Dogs were scratching. Two cock linnets were singing away, presumably oblivious of the angry quarrel taking place beneath them. Belina did not wish to sit down in such surroundings.

The taverner strolled round the edge of his counter and approached Barvaux and Belina. He greeted them brusquely in Gascon. Belina explained that she was investigating the death by poison of the pilgrim in the Pradau hospice.

"Let me think. Perhaps there was a pilgrim here last Saturday afternoon who drank my wine and ate some cakes. And now I come to think of it, there was something odd about that pilgrim." He paused and scratched his head.

"This chap does not seem to know anything," Barvaux said to Belina, in French. "I think we are wasting our time here. And certainly you should not be in such an establishment." He tried to steer her towards the door.

"Wait a moment," she replied, removing Barvaux's hand from her arm, "he's thinking."

The taverner continued his conversation with Belina, but in French this time. "There were two customers for those cakes, but they didn't eat them all, only one each. And the man who paid the bill placed the remaining cakes in the pilgrim's satchel. There was something odd about those cakes." He paused and looked directly at Barvaux for the first time. "And the customer looked very much like you, Messire."

"Don't be so absurd," Barvaux shouted, as he seized Belina's elbow and edged her towards the door. "As I said, Dame Belina, you are wasting your time with this oaf."

"But he is not an oaf," she protested. "He is answering my questions with politeness and respect."

"Maybe so, but I repeat that this tavern is no place for a woman. Surely, you know that?" He dragged her out of the tavern. Fortunately, Brother Martin and Jeannot had their backs to her and were walking towards the cathedral door.

"That tavern was a very dubious place," said Barvaux, "you should not have entered it. I told you not to do so."

"Well then, to retrieve my reputation – as you are implying that entering that tavern has damaged it – I will strike up a conversation with a friend of mine over there." She pointed to the cathedral seamstress who was going into the cloth shop. "Wait here for me. I won't be long."

Belina followed the seamstress into the shop, explained her problem to the owner and asked if she could leave the shop by the back door.

"Of course you can, Dame Lansac. What a nasty Parisian! I didn't like the look of him when you were here a little while ago. If he comes in here searching for you I will keep him here, wasting his time. I might even try to sell him some cloth to give to you."

"Please don't do that. I hardly know him. But he's trying to help me in my investigations and that's useful for going into inns and taverns and questioning their staff."

"I can well understand that. My husband would never let me go into a tavern by myself."

The seamstress said her husband would not do so either.

Belina was keen to escape before they asked about her husband's opinion of her going into taverns. What would Guillaume say if he heard where she had been going with

Barvaux? Or rather, *when* he heard. She swallowed nervously. Guillaume would lose his temper. She had not forgotten his fury at seeing a merchant in the cathedral shop put his arm tightly round her waist. Guillaume had pulled him away and punched his face so fiercely that he had fallen down, breaking the urn behind him. However, once the merchant had picked himself up and stumbled outside the shop, Guillaume had hugged Belina, apologised for his anger, kissed her forehead and begged her forgiveness.

"You had better hurry, Dame Lansac," said the seamstress. "I will hold the fort here, whilst Suzana shows you out the back way."

Belina smiled her thanks and rushed to the door behind the enormous counter. She followed Suzana through a narrow corridor which opened out into a large store room full of corded bales of cloth with lead identity seals. Belina looked at a cat feeding her kittens.

"I suppose mice are a problem for you here," she said to Suzana.

"Not only mice, but rats too. Even spiders eat cloth. I get my sons to remove all the webs, block up the mouseholes, and put poison down for the rats. It's hard work protecting one's property here in Condom."

"What sort of poison do you use?" Belina asked her.

"I buy the arsenic from the apothecary and then I put on my thickest gloves and mix the arsenic powder with a quarter of pig's fat, a pound of wheaten meal and four eggs. I bake that mixture in the oven in this courtyard so that the fumes don't get into the house or the shop. Then I cut the arsenic bread into strips and nail them down where I think the rats are living. That kills them off. It's very effective."

They emerged into a courtyard dominated by a lime tree. An old woman was sitting in its shade sewing a cotte.

Suzana went up to her, bent down and kissed her. "Is Papà feeling better now?"

"Only a little. He was sick again twice this morning. It's very messy."

"Was it food poisoning, do you think?" asked Suzana, "or maybe he ate or drank something bad in a tavern?"

To Belina's regret Suzana did not really wait to hear her mother's reply, but took a key from her belt, unlocked the door at the far side of the courtyard and told Belina that it led into the rue de la Monnaie.

CHAPTER SIXTEEN

Belina walked as far as the old fortified gate guarding the Place Lion d'Or, turned left into the busy rue Latournerie, crossed the narrow entrance to rue des Argentiers and picked her way carefully round the mules and packhorses and their mess. She was glad to reach rue Sainte Luce and the imposing entrance to the Senclar mansion.

She did not presume to enter the mansion by the front door, past the footman and the stable lad posted ready to take visitors' horses down to the stables beside the river. Instead, she went further down the shady street to the kitchen entrance. That too was guarded, not only by a member of Henri Senclar's security staff but also by two Pyrenean sheepdogs. It was common knowledge in Condom that those two animals ate more meat and eggs every week than most citizens ate in a month. She eyed them anxiously.

Fortunately, Belina knew the security guard because he used to bring cartloads of Senclar wheat to the Moulié mill at Gauge. She explained that she needed to question the kitchen staff in case they had seen the pilgrim. She stressed that Dame Senclar was famous for her gifts to pilgrims.

"You mean that Dame Senclar might have poisoned him?" the guard replied.

"No, not at all. I need to know what he was like, if he was

ill, if he was rich or poor, if he limped... Things like that," she hastened to explain.

"Dame Belina, if you want to say it, say it," he replied.

"Say what?"

"That Dame Senclar is famous for poisoning people."

Belina hesitated and then said, "I have heard that perhaps she poisoned people long ago in Lectoure when she was a child, but naturally I am sure that she does not do that now."

"Never say never," was the cryptic reply.

Belina could not resist the temptation to probe further about the dreaded lady's reputed abilities. "Do you think she might have poisoned someone in Condom?"

"No 'might have' about it. Five years ago she poisoned a pilgrim in the Cardinal Teste hospice in La Bouquerie. The bishop and his staff received a large donation to protect her from prosecution. But that was before your husband arrived here of course. She would, I hope, not repeat that murder now."

Belina was careful not to be side-tracked into discussing Guillaume and his work. She knew that quite a lot of it was secret. The guard was already exhibiting the typical Gascon loquaciousness, and she had to be careful to curb her own tongue.

Fortunately, the guard enjoyed gossiping about Dame Senclar. "They say that she poisoned her eldest sister, or rather half-sister. Maybe poisoning is in the blood. After all, Dame Senclar's father committed suicide when she was aged two."

"I had no idea," said Belina. "Why did he do such a terrible thing?"

"He was a complete failure in the war against the English. Maybe that's what made Dame Senclar hate the English and favour the French so much."

At this moment a cart drew up with a load of furniture, and Belina's helpful witness had to turn his attention to seeing to its unloading. Belina slipped through the wide open doorway whilst he was not looking and the dogs were growling at the furniture deliverers.

Inside there was a delicious smell of chicken cooking. Belina followed it and arrived at the kitchen, a spacious, airy room where a row of assistant cooks were occupied one side, chopping onions, shelling peas and scraping carrots. On the other side a girl picked peaches from a bowl of hot water, removing their skin and cutting them up. A cook was stirring a small pan on the smallest hotplate, carefully adding cinnamon to it.

The master cook was watching this. "You need more almond milk in that cameline sauce," he scolded.

"I know, Messire, but Dame Jeanne's nurse has stolen half of the almonds which I had just pounded."

"Don't let that happen again."

"No Messire. I am so sorry about it. I didn't expect her to do that."

"That's no excuse. We all know that nurse is a thief on Dame Jeanne's behalf," replied the master cook. "On her own behalf too, for that matter."

That was news to Belina. She decided to get them to tell her more about their opinions of Jeanne Senclar, even if they were busy. For a moment she wondered if they would offer her dinner, but that seemed very unlikely and she had no desire to be poisoned.

She went round the kitchen questioning each person about the dead pilgrim and whether any food had been delivered recently to the Pradau hospice. She gathered that the kitchen leftovers were divided into three: one for the pigs in a Senclar farm near Sempuy, one for the Cardinal Teste hospice on the other side of the river Baïse and the last one for the Pradau hospice.

"You mean, you make three equal piles?" she asked.

"No, Dame Lansac. We sort it into pigswill for the farm, food that's easily transportable by boat for the Teste hospice, and the rest for the Pradau one," was the condescending reply.

Belina wondered how he knew her name, but she carried on questioning. "Why not take food for the Teste hospice by cart over the Barlet Bridge?" she asked.

"To avoid the toll of course, and the queuing to get out and then back into Condom again."

"Gives Consul Senclar's boatmen something to do, and an excuse to cross over to La Bouquerie," someone added. "Especially Troubat, the head boatman. He somehow has a frequent need to visit the house of a head-cloth maker."

Several people sniggered.

Belina remembered Jordi's scorn for the head boatman. "Suppose the boat overturns in the river?" she suggested, "especially when the river is flowing fast like now."

"Even when the river is sluggish in July that stupid head boatman could overturn a boat. He's not much good at steering a boat, let alone rowing one."

"Then why is he employed?" Belina asked, although she already knew the reason. There was an embarrassed silence so Belina persisted and asked what other work he did for Consul Senclar.

"A special task which is nothing to do with boating."

Belina waited and wondered if she should provide a coin. But she decided against that because it was probably not important for her investigation.

The two servants looked at each other and came to a decision. "The head boatman's main task, which apparently he carries out to the great satisfaction of the Consul, is to procure pretty young women for his pleasure."

It was as Belina had guessed. "You mean, these girls are entertained here, in this house?" she asked them, keeping her voice low.

"Usually, yes. That is, in Dame Edith's part of the mansion, not in Dame Jeanne's."

The master cook came up to them, directed his staff to

concentrate on their work, and glared at Belina. She interrogated him about the dead pilgrim. Did pilgrims come to the kitchen door perhaps for food and drink?

"They do indeed, but the security guards have orders to turn them away. They lower the tone of the house. All these beggars are given a coin or two, and directions to the nearest hospice for their onward journey."

"You talk as if pilgrims and beggars are the same people," said Belina.

"Very often they are," he replied," almost always in my opinion."

"Does Dame Jeanne think that?" Belina asked. "She is always talking about helping pilgrims in the Aubrac hospice."

He corrected her, "the Dômerie d'Aubrac," and continued, "personally, I don't care much what Dame Jeanne thinks, or even if she thinks of anything other than herself and making money."

Belina was tempted to agree with him out loud, but the cellarman came up to them and began to question the master cook, so she walked to the far side of the kitchen and watched the pans bubbling on the long wide cooking range. They smelt delicious. Again, she wondered if she would be invited to lunch. Meanwhile, she had an excellent opportunity to watch professional cooks at work. Before her fascinated eyes, she watched an elderly cook remove six bundles of linen from an earthenware pot of wine and vinegar and unwrap them on a marble slab. He skinned and filleted the six trout and returned the skin, bones and heads to the poaching liquid while one of the kitchen boys worked the bellows to increase the fire under the pot. The cook lined a small strainer with two layers of linen cloth and put pinches of ground cinnamon, cloves, pepper and grains of paradise into the cloth. Holding the strainer above the pot, he ladled some of the stock over the spices. Then he added three bay leaves to the cloth and tied it into a small bundle. He plunged the bundle into the broth and told the boy to heat it until it was reduced by two-thirds. "And when that happens," he instructed, "add half a spoonful of lavender blossoms from this little plate."

Belina asked the cook if this deliciously scented broth was for a soup.

"No, Dame Lansac, it's for pouring over the fish when it has cooked, to make an aspic. My secret to success with this dish is to keep back three spoonfuls of broth, and when it begins to gel I brush it over the trout to give them a lustrous coating of aspic. Dame Senclar is very fond of this dish."

Belina thanked him and walked to the other side of the kitchen where she watched a much younger cook draining some peas and beating them into a purée. Then he peeled and chopped two large onions and cooked them gently in some walnut oil.

She asked him about Dame Jeanne Senclar.

"A bad mistress," he muttered. He heated two spoonsful of wine in a little pan and poured it over his pea purée, topping that with the browned onions. Belina realized that she could easily copy this 'secret to success'.

She tried to question another young cook about Dame Jeanne but he was concentrating on making his *leyt bulida*. So she watched him in silence as he infused a pinch each of cinnamon, ginger and salt in some drops of cold milk and then beat four egg yolks in a bowl. Then he brought a pint of milk to the boil. Immediately after that he added the hot milk a little at a time to the egg yolks, stirring the mixture constantly. Frowning, he added the infused spices and put the pan back on to a very low heat, still stirring with his long wooden spoon.

The master cook strode across the kitchen and told Belina to stop interrupting his staff's work.

"I am certainly not interrupting them," she protested. "I am observing them with admiration." She smiled at him. "I will not disturb anyone making sauces, but I do need to question the group of cooks over there," she pointed to the vegetable cooks, hoping to find out more gossip concerning Dame Jeanne. She hoped the stern master cook would not guess her intentions.

He turned his back on her and bustled away to supervise the final stages of cooking chickens with a *moxerich* sauce. The aroma delighted Belina and made her feel hungrier than ever.

She watched an apprentice preparing *lletugat*, while chatting to his colleague making *porrada* out of leeks and bacon. The apprentice boiled five lettuce hearts with three onions, and after he had recited six *paternosters* he drained them through a cloth. He added the vegetables to an earthenware pot of hot almond milk. Belina hoped it had not been spoilt by Dame Jeanne's thieving nurse.

She asked the cook when he would add the slices of cheese which were sitting in a dish near him.

"When I have drained the vegetables again, crushed them in my mortar, and put them into bowls. Then I add my cheese slices, sprinkle nutmeg over them and give them to Tionot over there," he pointed to a cook without a shirtwho was standing sweating beside a roaring fire and holding a hot sheet of iron over food presented to him by other cooks.

While Belina was looking at Tionot and pitying him for such hot work on such a hot day a parlour-maid came in with a copper pitcher to be refilled with wine. She looked at Belina and whispered to the servant handing her the refilled pitcher. Belina overheard the reply, "Dame Lansac, wife of the bishop's messenger."

"What's she doing in here?"

"Asking each and every one of us lots of questions."

"What about?"

"Pilgrims and poisons. She is very thorough."

The parlour-maid stared at Belina and hurried out of the kitchen. Belina hoped not to see her again. She turned her attention back to the food waiting to be cooked. One of the vegetables was unknown to her. It had a shiny purple skin, and was about six *pouces* long and pear-shaped. She watched it being sliced and fried in a large amount of olive oil, and asked the cook what it was.

"*Alberginie*," he said and went back to shaking the frying pan.

"Where does it come from?"

"From the garden of course. Where else would it have come from?"

"Then why have I never seen one before?" Belina asked.

"Because they aren't normally grown in Gascony. The young plants come from Cataluña, delivered especially to Dame Senclar each April."

"Is the plant small, tall, wide or what?" Belina asked, mostly to keep the conversation flowing.

"Don't know. Never seen it myself. The vegetables arrive in the kitchen without any leaves or flowers attached."

"Why?" Belina asked.

The cook shrugged, but his assistant on the other side of Belina supplied an answer. "Because the leaves can be poisonous. We have been told never even to touch the leaves of *alberginies*. They would give a really nasty bellyache."

"On top of the danger of working for Dame Senclar, you mean," said Belina boldly.

"As you say."

Belina longed to pursue this tricky line of conversation but decided to be prudent. She went back to observing the activity in the kitchen and walked towards the corner furthest from the roaring fire and Tionot's grills. She was puzzled by five conical blocks of an unknown foodstuff sitting on a marble slab, and she touched the tip of the biggest cone. No one seemed to be looking so she licked her fingers, her curiosity making her forget the danger of being poisoned in the Senclar mansion. Much to her surprise her fingers tasted of honey. But even when honey had become solidified it was not hard like a stone.

A woman pushed Belina aside and nipped off the top of

the smallest cone with some outsize scissors. She placed the lump into a mortar and ground the lump with a pestle. It looked hard work and Belina offered to help.

"No thanks. It's a lot more difficult to do properly than you think. It took me a month to learn the technique."

Belina accepted the snub politely and asked what the 'rock' was and where it came from.

"They are cones of white sugar being used for confectionery, bought in Toulouse, not from any Condom apothecary. It's made from sugar cane grown in Valencia, shipped to Narbonne and refined there before being taken to Toulouse." She picked up her sugar nippers and removed another lump from the cone. This lump she chopped with a knife and then broke up the pieces with the end of a rolling pin, being careful not to grind any of the sugar into powder.

Belina asked her which was the better way to prepare sugar.

"Using the pestle and mortar is easier, or at least it is less difficult, but for special effects like sprinkling the sugar on sweet pastries Dame Senclar insists that I prepare the sugar with a knife and a rolling pin." She sighed. "And then I have to sift it through three colanders." She sighed again. "And finally through this hair sieve." She picked it up and frowned.

Belina asked her if she nipped and pounded sugar all day long.

"No, Dame Lansac, I spend most of my time making it into sweets for Dame Senclar. She has a sour character, everyone of us here is well aware of that, but she is very fond of eating sugary food."

"Perhaps it can disguise poison?" Belina suggested.

"Hot spices do that better," was the laconic reply, "but poisoning wine is safer still because it works more quickly than a poisoned sugary cake, even a poisoned hot spiced one."

Suddenly, every member of the kitchen staff stopped chatting, stiffened and set to work very earnestly. The Steward had entered the kitchen. The master cook greeted him respectfully.

Belina hoped her presence was undetected, but the hawk-eyed senior servant had seen her. He pointed at her, saying "young woman, leave this kitchen immediately. Do not come back in here again."

Belina caught a glimpse of the parlour-maid standing behind him, smirking. She retraced her steps to the door of the kitchen building. There was a different security guard on duty. The dogs were sniffing a dead rat on the other side of the street. She ran down rue Sainte Luce to the Senclar stables beside the wharf.

CHAPTER SEVENTEEN

Tomas was busy cleaning tack, but he greeted her enthusiastically. Belina asked him if she could visit the Senclar garden again.

"Of course you can, Dame Belina, no problem. And when you have seen enough stay with us here in the stables and share our dinner."

"That's very kind of you, Tomas, but will the head groom allow me to do that?"

"He won't know. The senior domestics have a separate dining room."

"Are there so many of them?" Belina asked.

"Sometimes. Depends on what sort of servants visitors have brought with them."

Tomas showed Belina into the garden. She walked to the trees on the south side, looking for a yew tree because Guillaume's poison chart had indicated that yew bark or yew needles were the most likely cause of poisoning after about an hour and would result in vomiting and diarrhœa. There had been ample amounts of both those smelly substances around the dead pilgrim. She noticed several cypresses, but no yew trees.

It was disappointing. Belina consoled herself that yew trees could grow on any of the Senclar country properties, and no one would ever know about them unless or until a branch was used during a funeral. But even then, she realised, a Senclar funeral could have included a branch of a cypress tree rather than a yew sprig or branch. She pulled a tablet from her satchel and read through the list she had compiled from Guillaume's poison chart. Another tree with vegetation which could cause death after about an hour was juniper. But that was terribly bitter, even when turned into savin oil or with the needle tops dried. That was why it was considered the best repellent for deer.

She saw on the list that an alternative poison could have come from a bush called daphne. This not only caused vomiting and bloody diarrhœa but also convulsions and severe burning of the lips, mouth and throat. She could see some shrubs not far away, the leaves of which looked like daphne. She was not so sure about the pink flowers.

She turned her attention to the second column on the poison chart, showing immediate symptoms for oleander, symptoms after three minutes for mandrake, after twenty minutes for false hellebore and after thirty minutes for black hellebore. But the pilgrim was unlikely to have been poisoned by false hellebore, because according to Guillaume's chart it only grew in moist soil, something which was rare in Gascony.

Belina realised that the pilgrim could have arrived with the poisoned food already in his satchel, more than the piece of cheese which Minet had stolen and gobbled up. A pie for example. He had arrived at the hospice mid-afternoon and had gone straight up to the dormitory. He could have eaten his pie, or whatever, and then died at once. No one would have known until the next group of pilgrims had gone upstairs to the dormitory after having their feet washed and eating their supper in the refectory. What if someone had been in the dormitory earlier but had not raised the alarm? Or had not noticed that the pilgrim was dead? Or of course had said nothing because he was himself the murderer?

All this meant that she needed to visit the hospice again. However, when she did that Brother Pierre would insist that the corpse be buried in this hot weather. Belina knew that Guillaume had a habit of attending funerals of pilgrims whose death was unexplained just in case a possibly guilty person revealed his (or her) connection. Disgruntled servant girls deprived of being paid for favours had been known to poison pilgrims, as a variant of the oft-repeated story of the Pendu Dependu of Santo Domingo de la Calzada.

Belina decided to postpone visiting the hospice and instead concentrate on identifying the poisonous plants in the Senclar garden. Presumably there were several. Whilst she had been turning over all these problems in her mind she had not noticed that Dame Senclar and a gardener were quite close. Belina positioned herself to overhear their conversation, but kept out of their sight. It reminded her of eavesdropping on the appalling Rocca-Barvaux discussion the previous evening.

"Dame Senclar," the gardener was saying," I know that this daphne bush is getting too large for its area. In theory, I could take some seed, but it would be better to use semi-ripe cuttings so late in the summer. In any case, I cannot transplant the bush. Daphnes resent being moved."

"I know that," the lady snapped. "However, I told you that I want you to take seed and that is what you are going to do. And you are going to do that now."

"No, not this very moment."

"Now means now."

"Begging your pardon, Dame Senclar, but I must fetch my gloves first. Daphne seeds are poisonous."

"I haven't time to wait for that," she said icily.

The gardener tried another tack. "Dame Senclar, now that the head gardener is sick, it is very important that in his absence I keep in good health, so that in turn your garden is in good health."

"Don't be such a coward, man."

Silence. Belina wondered who would win the argument. She began to say a quick prayer for the gardener, but two squirrels squeaking and squabbling in the tree above her interrupted her *Salve Regina*.

"Don't let those squirrels bury walnuts in the garden this year," Dame Senclar said.

Belina kept very still and hunched, praying this time that she would not be discovered.

"No. I have told the new gardening boy to search for all the walnut saplings and heave them out with an iron bar. I will show you what he has managed to do in the east rose bed."

Belina breathed a sigh of relief. The Virgin Mary had answered her prayer, saving both Belina and the gardener.

Belina was curious to know what Dame Senclar wanted the daphne seeds for. She thought again about when and what the pilgrim had eaten before he had reached the hospice. Or had he taken food out of his satchel when he had settled himself into the dormitory? She had not noticed any food remnants when she examined his body and its filthy surroundings, although she had searched thoroughly. She would need to examine the satchel again, with gloves on. Definitely, with gloves on.

"*Adizchatz.*"

Belina jumped and feared the worst. But it was Aralha, the young kitchen maid who had been so helpful during her first visit to the garden.

"*Adischatz,*" replied Belina.

"Would you like to see the kitchen garden perhaps?"

"Oh yes, indeed I would. Thank you," Belina replied. "Could I see it now please, and after that those flower beds where there are oleanders and hellebores?"

"Of course you can see whatever you want. Stay as long as you need to. Everyone is about to have dinner. You will not be disturbed." She led the way to a vast *potager*, bigger than the one Belina had seen before, which was mostly a herb garden. The girl gave her a guided tour and was impressively knowledgeable. Moreover, she picked several plants and flowers for Belina.

In due course they came to a row of rather tall plants with large leaves, small pale mauve flowers and long shiny pear-shaped purple vegetables hanging heavily. They were the Catalan vegetables which she had watched being fried in the Senclar kitchen.

"Please could I have a leaf and a flower of one of these extraordinary plants. I have never seen them before."

"Oh no, Dame. Don't touch the *alberginies*. They're very poisonous."

Belina stepped back, surprised. "If they are poisonous, why are they cultivated in this kitchen garden?"

"For the vegetable. The rest is poisonous. Only the shiny purple pear can be eaten safely."

"What does it taste like?" Belina asked.

"Difficult to describe. It tastes sort of dry and yet squishy." The maid unclipped the scissors from her belt and cut an *alberginie* for Belina.

"Thank you very much, that's very kind of you. Can I eat this shiny purple skin safely? It won't poison me?" Belina asked.

"The skin is perfectly safe. Just cut the *alberginie* into slices and fry it in lots of olive oil, or walnut oil if you prefer. After that add several slices of onion to the pan, with some garlic and spice."

"I'm afraid I can't afford spice, except for pepper, and sometimes a pinch of cinnamon for special dishes which need a cameline sauce," said Belina sadly. It sounded very tasty to her, but difficult in the cooking area of Guillaume's chamber. Perhaps being a kitchen maid in the Senclar mansion had the advantage of an interesting, varied diet.

"Does the Cheval Blanc inn cook them that way too?" she asked.

The maid laughed. "Yes and no. Yes, the kitchen staff cook *alberginies* for themselves, but no, never for the customers." Belina looked surprised. "Did you visit the inn like I suggested?" asked the maid.

"I tried to, but the landlord shooed me out, which was a pity because I needed to interview everyone there."

The maid cut two more *alberginies* and gave them to Belina. "These two are for the inn," she told Belina. "Go round to the kitchen entrance and ask for Ramon. Give these to him personally and say they're from me and that in exchange he is to answer your questions and introduce you to everyone else."

"Are you sure?" asked Belina.

"Of course I'm sure. Ramon will do anything for me. We're in love."

Belina returned to the stables. The horsey smell was mixed with an aroma of *garbure*. Tomas was waiting for her and ushered her through the stables to the vine-covered terrace beyond. The rest of the stables staff were already seated on benches beside the long trestle table, busily scooping up their vegetable soup.

"I'm sorry to have made you late, Tomas," Belina apologised.

"No problem. There's plenty of *garbure* to go round."

They sat down on the end of a bench, where an elderly groom ladled some *garbure* into a bowl for Belina. "It will be a bit tepid by now," he told her.

"Doesn't matter," she replied, helping herself to some bread. She examined this with interest. Its poor quality surprised her.

"Dame *molieròta*," said the person opposite her, "don't you like the bread?"

Belina bit into the chunk. "It's all right, but I would have supposed that the Senclar budget could have provided better quality bread."

Tomas poured some wine into a goblet for Belina. "Try this. It's not bad for wine in early September."

She sipped it. He was right. It was quite good quality Colombard. She listened to the conversation around her. Everyone sounded very angry with Rocca. Several of the men had participated in the demonstration last Saturday. Even though they were probably safe from eviction or fines by Loupmont, they were uneasy for friends and relatives in a precarious situation.

"When I was a lad," said the groom beside her, "life was less ferocious in Condom. Gascons ran it better without French interference, especially without supercilious, grasping Parisians like Rocca. And in my grandfather's time the English ran it even better, or so he always used to say."

"The nuns who taught in my school told me that the English destroyed the crops and the farms," said Belina. She was anxious not to let this group of unknown people discover that Guillaume was half-English.

"Those nuns exaggerated. That was a hundred years ago when Edward of Woodstock, the Prince of Aquitaine, pillaged from Arouille to Narbonne and back in order to punish the Comte d'Armagnac for his treason. Before the time of even your oldest nun." The groom drank the rest of his wine. "Anyway, the worst troops were not English, they were Welsh. They got drunk and disorderly even before they had reached the territory of the Comte d'Armagnac at Arouille, which was where all the troops were ordered to start pillaging and setting fire to villages and small towns."

"The troops of King Charles were much worse," said the head groom, "and ten years ago the Bishop of Albi's troops destroyed everything in Lectoure. Only the house of Dame Senclar's mother and stepfather was spared."

"Why were they so lucky?" Belina asked.

"Most likely, they bribed the soldiers with more drink than they could hold."

"Same as King Louis did at Amiens two years later when he sent three hundred cartloads of good wine to the English soldiers," said the saddlery-keeper. Belina knew about that. But what had annoyed Guillaume even more was that King Edward had accepted an enormous bribe from the French king's negotiators. Or, rather, his diplomats had done so. Guillaume had cursed them for it. She tried to remember their names, but the only name that stuck in her mind was the Duke of Gloucester, the king's brother, who was now King Richard of England and who was planning to regain Gascony (according to Guillaume). He had been furious with the cowardice and greed of the English diplomats. Belina wondered if they had kept their positions when the Duke of Gloucester had become king, and if Bishop Morton had been one of the diplomats. She picked an apple from the bowl on the table and looked at it.

"A *denier* for your thoughts, Dame Lansac," said the head groom.

"Oh, sorry, I was thinking about the investigation I am pursuing into the death of a pilgrim last Saturday," she lied.

Tomas reminded them of what she was doing, and that the pilgrim had been poisoned. Various suggestions were put forward: food poisoning from pies brought in the street, sour wine that had been tampered with, toadstools, mouldy rye bread, licking leaden paint by mistake.....

"How old was he?"

"Mid twenties, I think," Belina replied. "Why do you ask?"

"An angry, cuckolded husband could have poisoned him." Belina had not thought of that. "Or an angry father," someone suggested. "Pilgrims travel in groups. Young men have plenty of opportunity to chat up a girl on the journey, either in a group or in an inn."

"You sound as if you know," said Tomas.

"Not myself, I don't. I have never been to Monsieur Saint Jacques in Galicia," came the very quick reply. "You know I haven't."

"I meant that you might know someone who has done so, or at least have gone as far as Sainte Quiteira in Aire," Tomas said smoothly.

There was a clatter of hooves outside and some of the men got up hurriedly and left the terrace.

Belina sat very still, trying to work out where in Condom

the pilgrim had chosen to sit to darn his clean shirt. And where had he sewn the gold and silver medallions into it? In a side chapel of the cathedral perhaps, or even in the hospice dormitory. And where had he sewn all those gold and silver coins inside the hem of the cloak? She was still not convinced that the dormitory had been unoccupied all the time since his arrival. If he had sewn his hoard of coins into the cloak on Saturday afternoonthat meant that either he had stolen them from the hospice or that he had acquired them not long before his arrival there. The hospice would certainly keep their funds very safely. Rocca insisted on that. So, was the pilgrim a thief? Had he stolen from another pilgrim? If so, why had nobody discovered the loss of so much treasure and reported the loss?

She wondered whether he was a soldier who had been wounded too often. Perhaps he was remorseful at having killed people? Perhaps his victims had been innocent villagers somewhere, victims of an army tramping through their farms? She thought about Brother Pierre's remark that pilgrims went to Compostela to atone for their sins. So maybe 'her' pilgrim was fleeing from his victims? She wished she knew more about him and why he had travelled alone.

"Dame Belina," Tomas interrupted her thoughts, "excuse me, but I am needed to look after a new arrival."

"Oh, I'm so sorry Tomas," she replied, getting up from the bench. "I was thinking about the dead pilgrim." She thanked him for the dinner and followed him out of the stables into the courtyard.

Grooms were bustling about the new arrival. Belina stood in the shade and watched a swarthy, middle-aged man wearing a close-fitting buttoned green doublet giving orders for his servants to take a treasure chest off his hackney. The head groom was explaining that it would be placed in a locker in the safe room in the stables and only the merchant would have the key. His servants would be expected to sleep in the safe room. If he wished, his servants could have their meals there too.

The conversation was a bit awkward because the head groom was speaking in Gascon whereas the merchant was speaking in Catalan. Belina could follow his speech fairly well because she was used to Catalans coming into the cathedral shop.

The merchant was asking the head groom if a Flemish lawyer was staying in the Senclar mansion.

"What name, Messire?"

"Barvaux, Philippe Barvaux, from Bruges."

"No Messire, there's no one of that name here at present."

The merchant tried again. "We have a firm arrangement to meet in Condom and to stay at the very best lodgings."

"These are the very best lodgings. They are well known to be the very best lodgings. Perhaps the Flemish lawyer has been delayed on his way from Bruges? The weather has been very bad this summer, with many storms making the roads slow-going," the head groom said in his most deferential voice.

"I know the roads are slow. I have myself been delayed in crossing the Pyrenees near Velha because of violent storms and swollen rivers."

So, thought Belina, the merchant is not from Perpignan, but from the middle of the Kingdom of Aragon. He must be the 'colleague from Lleida' for whose arrival in Condom Barvaux had delayed his own journey. She wondered what the treasure chest contained. It was obviously very heavy. She stared at the two Catalan servants carrying it into the safe room. She decided not to tell the merchant where Barvaux was staying, and she slipped unobtrusively out of the stables and walked towards the wharf.

CHAPTER EIGHTEEN

Belina stood on the wharf and watched the people struggling to tie up their boats securely against the fast-flowing current. The latest thunderstorms in the Pyrenees would have been worse than those in Gascony and the river Baïse was coming perilously close to bursting its banks as a result.

She decided against walking up rue Sainte Luce past the Senclar mansion. It would be safer, although longer and hotter, to walk upstream along the wharf and then turned left up the steep hill leading to the Gaichou Gate. After that she kept to the south side of the common which now filled the original moat of Condom – which Guillaume had told her had been developed by the English when they first occupied the town long ago. She trudged eastwards in the shade of the high walls of the Cordeliers convent and just before she reached the Sainte Claire Gate she crossed the common and went through the narrow entrance of the rue des Bouchers. Then she turned immediately right into the rue des Trois Eperons and walked slowly along the narrow street in the shade of tall houses belonging to equestrian trades: the makers of spurs, saddles, harnesses, a blacksmith shoeing a *destrier,* a wheelwright. . .

She kept well away from the nailmaker's shop where she had hurt her hand the last time she had struggled along the crowded street.

At last she reached the Cheval Blanc inn. She pushed open

the kitchen door of the inn and was almost knocked backwards by the stench and the heat. It took her a while to recover, and she was tempted to abandon her search for Ramon, Aralha's betrothed.

"What do you want?" someone asked her roughly.

"I am looking for Ramon. His betrothed has asked me to give him something," Belina replied.

"Who are you?"

"Dame Lansac of the cathedral shop."

"Oh, *la molieròta*."

"Yes, I am the miller's daughter," Belina replied. She wondered if the traditional reputation of millers' daughters would remain with her for ever for some people.

"If you give me a kiss, *molieròta*, I will take you to Ramon."

"You save your kisses for women without a husband," she retorted, pushing past him.

She asked a sweaty waiter laden with empty dishes where she could find Ramon. He jerked his head towards the door leading to the noisy dining-room. A thickset man was telling two waiters to hurry up with the fig and honeycakes ordered by the army sergeants.

Belina smiled at him. "Are you Ramon, the betrothed of Aralha of the Senclar mansion?" He nodded. "Aralha has asked me to give you these," said Belina, holding up two *alberginies*. "She says that in return for these precious vegetables you will answer my questions."

He took the *alberginies* and examined the purple skins carefully. "Very nice. But they are not vegetables, they are fruit."

"I find that surprising," said Belina, "for I saw them growing in the Senclar *potager* among the cucumbers. The fruit was in the orchard."

"Yes, I understand what you mean, but from a cooking and preserving point of view these *alberginies* are treated as fruit."

"Like carrots?" Belina suggested.

"Sort of," he replied. "What other questions do I need to answer?"

Belina explained about her investigation and how she needed to question everyone in every inn and tavern to find out about the pilgrim.

"Pilgrims are never allowed in this kitchen," Ramon declared.

"Of course not," she replied, "but I suppose some of the better-off ones stay in the inn or at least eat here."

"Pilgrims who ride mules or horses do, but not the poor sort shuffling into Condom, wincing at their blisters and full of fleas and lice. We try to keep those types out of our inn."

"I understand you,' she said. "Some of the pilgrims who visit the cathedral shop are full of fleas and lice. I make sure that they keep to the street side."

Belina remembered that there were no fleas on the dead pilgrim, nor lice burrowing in his hair or inside the back of his neck. "I think this particular pilgrim was free from fleas and lice, so perhaps he was here for dinner last Saturday. I would be extremely grateful if you could remember if there was such a pilgrim."

"A lone pilgrim?" he asked.

"Possibly. The hospice staff are certain that he arrived there alone on Saturday afternoon."

"I don't remember any lone pilgrims," he replied. "They usually travel in groups, for safety."

"I know," replied Belina. "I think the hospice staff were surprised to see a pilgrim arriving by himself."

"Might have quarrelled with the others of a group. Might have stolen from them. Might have got left behind with sore feet, or something."

"I would be very grateful if you could let me question everyone here in this kitchen," said Belina, taking back control of the conversation.

"Go ahead."

He went with her, making sure she was as quick as possible in her questioning. Most people shook their heads and continued in their tasks, but a pantry-boy refused to be rushed in spite of Ramon's rebuke at his hesitations.

"Yes, I remember a pilgrim in here a few days ago. Don't remember which day it was, but it was in the afternoon, just as a storm was finishing."

"Then it must have been Saturday," said Belina. She waited for more information, not liking to produce a coin with Ramon still beside her.

"Funny thing was," continued the pantry-boy," he hadn't been dressed as a pilgrim when he went out after breakfast and he didn't have a stick with him."

He paused and scratched his head. Belina hoped he did not have fleas or lice.

"That's right. I remember now. The chap left a bundle of clothes – clean clothes – in the pantry." He glanced at Ramon, and continued, "having asked my permission first of course. He said he was going into the cathedral and didn't want to carry a bulging satchel."

"But he took his satchel with him," asked Belina, "even if it was nearly empty?"

"Yes, but that's natural. There might have been something valuable in the bottom of it that he wouldn't want to leave in the pantry."

"Of course."

"And yet, when he came back into the inn that afternoon and asked for me, he was dressed as a pilgrim, complete with cloak, gourd, staff and big-brimmed hat."

"Did he still have his satchel?" Belina asked.

"Yes. And it looked at least half full and rather heavy."

"He'd probably bought food and saved his money from eating here," Ramon suggested. "I remember him now, but I certainly did not know that he left his belongings in the pantry." He grasped the pantry boy's shoulder. "You should have asked my permission first."

"I wanted to, but you were in the landlord's office looking at accounts with him. I could not interrupt."

Belina decided to support the pantry-boy, so she asked him what was in the satchel. "I didn't see what he had in his *besace*," the pantry-boy told her. "He stuffed his bundle of clean clothes inside it, thanked me very politely and went back into the dining-room, walked straight through it and out into the street. And that's the last I saw of him."

"I trust he didn't waste your time too much," said Ramon. "Did you check his name?"

"Yes, of course. He was called Robert Penge. He had written it in the register on his arrival."

"Thank you so much," Belina whispered, slipping a coin into the pantry-boy's hand. "You have been very helpful."

"You know," she said to the surly Ramon, "his observations are really useful. Colleagues who pay attention to customers and remember things well are to be cherished."

"I agree, he's good at his work," Ramon replied, "but I had no idea he was so observant. Nevertheless, he should not have agreed to let the pilgrim – or pretend-pilgrim – leave anything in the pantry. It's completely against the rules. If the landlord had discovered it there would have been a terrible fuss."

"I can well imagine that," said Belina. She told him of her unsuccessful attempt to enter the inn on Sunday. To her relief, Ramon's face relaxed and he invited her to accompany him into the dining-room where he made her sit down near a *notaire* studying a long document.

The room was full of soldiers chatting over their wine goblets, whilst the waiters finished clearing away the dishes and soggy trenchers. Peach stones and apple cores littered the tiled floor and two dogs were quarrelling over a fallen trencher. A waiter kicked them out of his way. A cat seized the opportunity to steal a bit of the trencher and jumped on top of the sideboard with it. No one noticed Belina among all the noise and bustle.

She tried to concentrate on the conversation, and learnt that the soldiers were on their way to southern Spain to join King Fernando's army attacking the Moors in the Kingdom of Granada. They had heard of the wealth and the women of Granada, but they had also heard of the magnificent fighting qualities of the Moors. However, they had received positive reports too of the Aragonese king's military abilities. It sounded a good opportunity for them to switch armies. It was six years since the Duke of Burgundy had been killed in the Battle of Nancy and their fighting careers had seemed over. King Louis' Swiss mercenaries' camp at Pont-de-l'Arche had attracted some of them, training the French on how to invade England and deal with the famed English longbowmen. But now that King Louis was dying the camp might be disbanded by his likely successor, his daughter, Madame de Beaujeu. Women hated war. So did taxpayers.

"But surely it would be easier to invade England than to conquer the Moors?" someone suggested.

"Definitely not. The new English king is an excellent general and very experienced. He beat the Scots easily last year."

Belina remembered Sir John's enthusiasm about this victory.

"If the French had an equally good general, could an invasion succeed?" the unseen voice continued his questioning.

The voice sounded familiar to Belina. Not Swiss or German like a few of the other accents, but more like Barvaux's soft and musical tones. Belina peered cautiously at the group near the front door of the Cheval Blanc. A soldier came in and the shaft of afternoon sunlight lit up the group near the door. Belina realised that it was indeed Barvaux who was chatting to them. He was insisting on knowing who could best lead an invasion of England.

"Philibert de Chandée," was the considered opinion.

"Where is he at the moment?" Barvaux asked.

"No idea."

"Could he be attacking Granada perhaps?" Barvaux asked in his silky, sexy voice.

They shook their heads. He could just as easily be in Italy. There were battles there all the time, in the war between Venice and the Pope for the control of Ferrara, for example.

Barvaux asked if Chandée could be at Pont-de-l'Arche.

"Unlikely. But the Sieur d'Aurigny is probably still there. He's Scottish. He would jump at the chance of invading England."

"He could use the blinding by sunlight tactic."

"What's that?" asked Barvaux.

"Manoeuvre one's own troops so that the attacking cavalry has the sun in their eyes, and in their horses' eyes. That stratagem would beat even a first-rate commander like the English King Richard."

The conversation switched back to King Fernando and Spain. They looked forward to the distribution of excellent Moorish weapons and other objects and, especially, to acquiring Saracen slaves. Their descriptions of what they would do to these Moorish women made Belina very uneasy. She wondered if her younger brother Geraud talked like that too. Had he acquired slaves? Worse, had he fathered Moorish children? If so, would he return to Condom someday bringing a Saracen woman - or women - with him, along with their children?

By the time she listened to the conversation again it had switched to the Spanish Inquisition and how it was gradually moving north. The soldiers had heard that an inquisitor called Tomas de Torquemada had turned his attention to Jews called *conversos* who had become baptised Christians, and to *moriscos* who were Moslems who had converted to Christianity. The inquisitor was confiscating their property, presumably to finance the war against Granada. Andalusian taxpayers approved of the inquisitor's activities and the fact that Jews were being expelled.

"I've heard that King Fernando's army captured the young

leader of Granada after the battle of Lucena but that Queen Isabel had him liberated."

"That means she would have bribed him to turn traitor. Hence the need for money extorted from the Jews."

Belina lost interest in this conversation. She returned to the noisy, smelly kitchen and slipped out of the back door of the Cheval Blanc inn where she found herself in the alley leading to the rue des Trois Eperons.

She walked along rue Royale on her way back to the cathedral shop and reached rue Cadeot. She glanced inside the apothecary's store and debated whether to buy some foot balm for herself. Her feet were very sore from trudging across town in search of answers. She wondered how the pilgrims managed to walk all day, every day, and she watched two pilgrims coming out of a tavern nearby. They stopped for a moment and looked back at the tavern. Belina realised that it was the Serpent, where Barvaux had cut short her discussion with the tavern-keeper, insinuating that the tavern was a dubious place for her. She hesitated. Should she go in? Who, or what, would she find there which she should not see?

Belina looked around the cathedral square, hoping that nobody was watching her. People were bustling about, a donkey was peeing on the cobbles close by, an old woman walked past carrying a duck in a basket. Belina held her nose at the stench coming from both the basket and the mess dropping from it on to the ground. She made up her mind, and entered the tavern.

Late afternoon seemed to be a quiet time. Two old men were playing dominoes in one corner. A third old man was snoring beside them. One of the cock linnets was asleep with a leg tucked under its wing. The other linnet was pecking at some seeds and trying not to notice the cat, which was twitching its tail and staring at it.

"*Adishatz,*" Belina greeted the tavern-keeper polishing a pewter cup behind the counter.

"*Adishatz.*" He smiled and put the cup down. "Got rid of your aggressive companion?"

"What do you mean?" Belina asked.

"You were in here this morning asking me questions about a dead pilgrim, and your companion pushed you outside. I don't forget faces. I don't forget bad behaviour."

Belina seized her opportunity. "If that is so," she said, "perhaps you can tell me if you had seen the person accompanying me – and who is certainly *not* a companion, merely an acquaintance – before, either in your tavern or anywhere else."

"I am sure that I have seen that forcible foreigner before. Here in this tavern." He paused, and began polishing another pewter cup. "He came in here on Saturday morning at the same time as several other men. He wasn't nearly as aggressive then as he was this morning when he was here with you."

He put the cup down and leaned over the counter. "A ladies' man."

"I do not care whether he is, or not," said Belina. "What interests me, and my husband Messire Lansac, is to find out about the activities of the poisoned pilgrim on the day he died."

"Ah, my apologies, Dame Lansac."

"Don't mention it." Belina smiled and asked his name.

"Pourcet."

Belina thanked him and explained about her investigations on Guillaume's behalf.

"The foreigner came in here, as I was saying to you just now, and sat down in that dark corner," he pointed at the corner opposite the domino players. "One of the other men who had arrived at the same time followed him there and sat down with his back to the wall. Difficult to describe him because it's the darkest part of this dark room. But I think he was a pilgrim."

"Did he drink from his pilgrim's gourd, or did he buy a drink from you?" Belina asked. The tavern-keeper hesitated for a long time. "You said that you don't forget bad behaviour," Belina prompted him, "so I suppose that means he did not buy a drink." Pourcet was still hesitating. "Or perhaps the forcible foreigner, as you call him, bought the drinks?"

"Yes, that's right, he did," said Pourcet. "But the other man didn't look like a pilgrim then. No big-brimmed hat, no cloak and no staff with a gourd."

"Oh," said Belina.

"Are you sure that the dead man was a pilgrim?" Pourcet asked her.

"No, not really," she replied, "but I am very sure that when he died he was dressed as one, wearing and carrying all the usual pilgrim things, including a satchel, a staff and a gourd."

"I remember his satchel," said Pourcet, "and the way he kept it near him."

"That's natural," said Belina.

"Of course, but when he left the room to go to the latrine he took the satchel with him. He walked as if it was very heavy." Pourcet frowned. "And he was away a long time, so long in fact that I thought he had slipped out by the back gate, abandoning the foreigner."

"But he did come back in the end?" Belina asked.

Pourcet frowned again and scratched his ear. "That's it, that's it," he said excitedly, "that's why I remembered them. Before he came back from the latrine the foreigner had ordered some cakes and more wine for them both."

Pourcet leaned even further over the counter and said excitedly, "and when I had placed the bowl of cakes in front of him and gone back to behind the counter the foreigner sprinkled salt on top of the cakes."

"How do you know it was salt?" Belina asked sharply.

"Because out of the corner of my eye I saw that he helped himself to the salt on a nearby table."

"Did he eat any of the cakes?" Belina asked more gently.

Pourcet thought for a long time whilst she managed not to

show her impatience. "He pressed the salt into the top of each cake and then waited till the other man came back and put his satchel down with a thud."

"And then?"

"They each ate a cake."

"You are sure?"

"Why don't you believe me, Dame Lansac? I'm not a liar." Pourcet banged a cup on the counter and glared at her.

"I need to tell my husband very precisely what happened," she said quickly. "The salt would have made the men thirsty. Did they drink a lot more wine?"

"All the wine in the pitcher." Pourcet frowned while Belina waited, still trying not to show her impatience. "That's right," he continued at long last, "they drank up their wine very quickly – because of the salty cakes, I suppose – but they didn't eat the remaining cakes. The foreigner pushed all of them across the table and the other man put them in his satchel."

"And then they paid up and left?" Belina suggested.

"Yes."

"Who paid? Or did they share the bill, like Hollanders?"

"The forcible foreigner paid for them both. Didn't query the amount.Didn't wait for his change.Just told me to keep it."

"Did they leave by the front door or the back," Belina asked, hoping he could remember something more useful than a heavy satchel and some salty cakes.

"The front door." He frowned again.

"I suppose they took care not to leave the satchel behind," said Belina.

"No, the pilgrim took it."

"You told me he was not dressed as a pilgrim," Belina reminded Pourcet.

"Not when he came in, he wasn't."

"What about when he came back from the latrine?" she asked.

"No, still wearing normal clothes. But when he left he was wearing a pilgrim's cloak and the hat with a scallop shell."

"And carrying a pilgrim's staff?" she asked.

"Yes, he carried the staff in one hand with the heavy gourd swinging from the hook at the top of it. The staff was getting in the way of his satchel. Perhaps the full gourd unbalanced the staff." Belina suggested that perhaps he had found the cloak and the other pilgrim things in the latrine. "No, it's much too small and filthy for that. Besides, I am sure I would have noticed."

"Absolutely sure?" she asked.

The taverner assured her that he would definitely have noticed if the man had come back from the latrine dressed as a pilgrim.

"Then he must have found the stuff here in this room," said Belina. "Perhaps some pilgrim had left it here?"

"Maybe. I had only just arrived myself. The apprentice taverner on duty before me wouldn't have noticed half a dozen pilgrims' cloaks, hats and staffs. Nor if the gourd was still full, even though he's supposed to fill up pilgrims' empty gourds with wine. We make a nice little profit on that."

"Are the pilgrims fussy about wine for their gourds?" Belina asked.

Pourcet laughed. "Not at all. All gourds make any wine taste sharp."

Belina smiled. She thanked him, walked out of the dark room into the bright sunlight of the Place Saint Pierre and collided with a pilgrim.

"I'm so sorry," she said picking up his staff and handing it back to him with her best smile.

He took it from her and walked towards the cathedral door. Belina noticed that his staff did not get in the way of his satchel. So why had the poisoned pilgrim – if he was a pilgrim – in the Serpent tavern have difficulty in walking with his staff and satchel?

CHAPTER NINETEEN

Belina walked back to the cathedral shop deep in thought. The long conversation with the taverner had not told her much. Perhaps he'd just been chatting her up? And yet, Barvaux was involved in the story, or so Pourcet had said. She was puzzled by the idea that a customer could come in wearing ordinary clothes and leave the tavern sometime later dressed as a pilgrim. How and where had he found pilgrim's clothes and a staff? She regretted not having asked Pourcet more about the man's original appearance. But most of the customers in her shop wore homespun shirts with a varying amount of stains and dirt on them. Nothing memorable, except their smell.

She entered the shop, fearing a scolding from Quiteira.

"Belina, wherever have you been all day?" Quiteira shouted at her. "You've missed lots of customers."

Belina explained how and why she had filled her day.

"Why don't you tell Guillaume to do his own work?" Quiteira snarled. "If you did that, I wouldn't have to do yours." She banged a drawer shut.

"Did you remember to show the customers the pilgrim's carving?" Belina asked, trying to keep calm.

"No, I did not. I don't show lewd carvings to customers. I take care about what people think of me. Not like you. And does Guillaume allow you to shove such a disgraceful carving under people's noses?"

"Yes," said Belina. She picked the carving out of the top drawer and approached some pilgrims. But it did not mean anything to them, and they limped out of the shop without buying anything.

"See what I mean," Quiteira said. "If I were you I would keep that thing hidden." She banged another drawer shut and nearly tripped over an enormous urn in her haste to serve a new group of pilgrims.

Belina managed to sell plenty of *babioles* and medallions during the next half hour, each time asking her customers if they had come across a pilgrim called Robert Penge, travelling back from Compostela carrying the weird carving with a wine-stained head. Everyone shook their heads, the women glaring at her, the men looking at her up and down, eyes glinting. Quiteira glowered in disapproval.

It was nearly dusk when a well-dressed group entered the shop and started looking around. Belina eyed them hopefully. They behaved as if they meant to buy something but intended to take their time. She pulled out a tray of St Peter's keys and medallions.

"You may already have bought something similar on your entry into the cathedral," Belina told them, "but we have a bigger selection than there is on the entrance table."

"Is the stallholder at the cathedral door your competitor?"

"Not really. We are both employed by the cathedral," Belina replied. "Or perhaps you would like to buy an extra silver scallop shell?" She brought out another drawer. "Are you on your way back from Compostela?"

They laughed and told her they were merchants, not pilgrims, and they were on their way west into Spain, only not nearly as far as Santiago. They were investigating cloth trade possibilities in Medina del Campo, but they weren't in a hurry because it was still too hot to travel across the *Meseta*, and there would probably be no fodder available for their horses.

"And no food for yourselves in Spanish inns," said Belina.

"What do you mean?"

"*Auberges espagnoles* don't serve food. You have to bring your own. Quite different from Gascony."

"What about inns in Béarn and Navarra?" asked one merchant, patting his substantial stomach.

"Oh, they're all right. It's in Spain where you and your horses risk starvation."

"What do all the pilgrims do, then?"

"Stay in hospices, or in people's houses," Belina replied. "Spaniards are friendly people, so I am told, but their inns have no food."

"Oh dear." The merchants discussed this unwelcome news among themselves, or at least that was what Belina supposed they were talking about in their own language.

"Have you travelled far?" she asked.

"From Bruges, in Flanders."

"Aahh," said Belina, "so you are Flemish?"

They nodded, and turned their attention to the trays of souvenirs and medallions. Belina picked up the pilgrim's lewd carving unobtrusively and waited until they had chosen and paid for several items. As she was wrapping these up carefully in pieces of cloth she began her speech about the pilgrim's carving. She remembered too late that they were travelling west towards Mouchan and therefore could not have met the pilgrim coming the other way last Saturday.

They fingered the carving, but without the habitual lewd comments or embarrassment. "It's the *Manneken Pis*," the man with the stomach said.

"It's the what?" she asked, bewildered.

"Little man having a piss."

"Yes, I can see that's what he's doing," Belina muttered.

"He's called the *Manneken Pis*."

"By whom?" Belina asked.

"By everyone in Brussels."

"Why?" she asked.

"It's a carving of a famous old statue near the Grote Markt. It's the Brussels equivalent of your St Peter's keys."

"Whatever do you mean?" she asked in amazement.

"It's what all the *babioles* shops in Brussels sell and what all travellers passing through Brussels buy," they explained.

Belina tried to work out what they were saying. Their French was not very good, not nearly as fluent as Barvaux's.

They repeated their explanations and continued to examine the carving, frowning at the wine stain on its head. Belina pointed to it. "I think that might be wine."

"Yes, indeed it is."

Then followed a long story in broken French about how on their journey from Flanders they had often come across the owner of a carving of the *Manneken Pis* and a carving of St Roch. At first they had thought he was an English soldier travelling by himself to Spain to join in the *Reconquista* battles to conquer the Kingdom of Granada. In due course they had discovered that he was called Robert Penge.

"Surely, soldiers would travel in a group, the same as pilgrims do?" Belina asked. Her heart thumped, her hands felt moist. The man who had left the Cheval Blanc inn dressed as a pilgrim on Saturday was called Robert Penge. The pantry-boy had been clear about that. Could it be the same person? She almost missed the merchants' reply to her question.

"This one was not really alone. He seemed to be trailing someone else, someone who tried to keep out of his way, someone who pretended to be a botanist and who collected poisonous plant cuttings such as bits of yew twigs."

Between them, the merchants described this person in considerable detail. Although they did not, and could not, know it, it was clear to Belina that they were describing Barvaux. His nationality, his height and build, his curly black hair, his attractive way of speaking, his delightful laugh, his vitality, his mannerisms, his elegant clothes, and his confident attitude, were all familiar to Belina. She hoped the merchants did not notice her embarrassment. And there were plenty of reasons to feel embarrassed because she learned that in almost every inn they stopped at Barvaux managed to persuade a chamber maid to sleep with him. Twice, he had even brought a prostitute with him into an inn.

"We are all married men, and we don't do that sort of thing, but this Fleming – this compatriot of ours – he was an accomplished womaniser."

Belina accepted their remarks about themselves with a few grains of salt, but took care not to indicate that. Besides, she was feeling very confused and embarrassed. She brought the conversation back to the two carvings and asked if the carvings were always wine-stained?

"No, that happened quite recently, in Moissac. There was an argument between the soldier and a Bavarian drunkard who had realised that the soldier had lost his sense of taste. He teased the soldier about that and made him eat something rotten. The soldier punched him, and then the Bavarian spilled wine on to the heads of the carvings. The soldier knocked him to the ground and would have injured him badly if we hadn't pulled him away. The innkeeper got his servants to carry the drunk outside, and we bought the soldier some more wine and some food."

"Was that wise?" Belina asked.

"Yes. He wasn't drunk, just touchy about his possessions. Not just the two carvings but also a couple of medallions he had sewn very carefully into a clean shirt when he thought we weren't looking. We made the soldier travel slowly with us the next two days as far as Lectoure. After that he hurried on. Presumably he wanted to catch up with the womaniser."

"And you are sure the soldier was trailing him?" Belina asked.

"Yes." They told her a dozen anecdotes which supported their opinion. At first, they had wondered whether the soldier was threatening to expose the womaniser for some misdeed in the past, something about a woman perhaps. But gradually they pieced together the background to the soldier. Since the age of sixteen he had been a professional soldier and had joined the army of the Duke of Burgundy. After the Duke had been killed in the Battle of Nancy the soldier had gone to London and become a member of the security staff of an English landowner called Welles. Some weeks ago Welles had ordered him to remove two boys from the Tower of London at night and take them downstream to the sea. His particular job had been to get them quietly into the boat. He had refused to tell the Flemish merchants how exactly he had managed that. Belina swallowed nervously as she imagined the rough way the boys would have been treated.

"We didn't press him too hard for details about how he made them get into the boat. But what we did learn one evening after the soldier had drunk a lot of wine, was that when the boat reached its destination, the Fleming who was in charge of taking the boys from the Tower ordered the soldier to fetch something from the bows while the seamen were furling the sails. When he returned to the stern the boys had vanished."

"You mean, the Fleming had thrown them overboard?" said Belina.

"That's what the soldier thought. And presumably that is why he was trailing him, trying to extort money from the murderer."

Belina wanted to hear more about Robert Penge, but Quiteira was making a great show of shutting up the shop, banging things about and trying to fold down the upper shutter. The merchants took the hints, picked up their packages and asked Belina how to reach the Place Lion d'Or. Belina said that she supposed they were staying at the Lion d'Or inn.

"Yes, we have already reserved a private room there. It seemed a quieter place than the Cheval Blanc inn."

"Too full of noisy soldiers," said one of the merchants.

"Yes, much too full" replied Belina automatically.

They looked at her in surprise. So did Quiteira. Belina pulled the lower shutter upwards, fastened it hastily and bid Quiteira "*Adiu.*"

CHAPTER TWENTY

Belina went into the storeroom to finish her accounts for Loupmont the next day. She lit two candles and set up the checkered cloth and the tokens. So, the dead pilgrim was not really a pilgrim, but someone who had travelled through Brussels. One of the Flemish merchants thought he was an English soldier. But if he was English, why did he speak French so well? Was Robert Penge a French name or an English one? Guillaume had once mentioned that some English troops were so angry at King Edward's refusal to fight the French that they had switched to the Duke of Burgundy's army and had gone to help him attack Nancy. But Belina could not remember when that had happened, and she was unsure where Nancy was anyway. Intruding into these vague memories came the upsetting descriptions of someone who could only be Barvaux. Quiteira had made it very obvious that she thought that too, and her sneers had embarrassed Belina.

She manoeuvred her tokens about the cloth, and wrote down the various totals in the ledger. It was a task that took a lot of concentration even when she was not tired, as she was now. The two candles had almost burnt out and it was dark in the storeroom. She got up to fetch the lantern from the shop. When she came back she was surprised to hear voices outside the narrow window slit of the storeroom.

"... and I was shown into the Lanthern Tower by the replacement guards," came Barvaux's voice.

"What do you mean, replacement guards?" came the thin, sharp voice of Rocca.

Belina stood near the *meurtrière*window slit. She extinguished the lantern and put it on the floor very quietly. For a moment the only sound was the beating of her heart. Then she heard Barvaux's confident reply. "The Duke of Buckingham as Constable of the Tower of London had replaced the original guards with his own men."

Belina wondered if Rocca was satisfied with this reply. Guillaume would have been suspicious, she was sure. Barvaux continued his story of breaking into the Tower of London and reaching what he called the boys' chamber.

"What boys?" asked Rocca.

"The princes, of course, the sons of King Edward."

"I thought that the elder boy was the king," said Rocca.

"Not really. He was illegitimate, like his father," said Barvaux. "Everyone knew that."

"Whatever do you mean?" asked Rocca, amazed.

"King Edward had been officially betrothed to Lady Eleanor someone, daughter of the loser of the battle of Castillon. King Edward's marriage to the widow Grey was considered bigamous."

"By whom?" asked Rocca.

"By lawyers and bishops."

"And you have just told me that the king too was illegitimate?" Rocca said.

"So it is believed. The Rose of Raby slept with an archer when her husband was fighting in France. King Edward was the result."

"So why did he become king?" asked Rocca.

Belina noticed his unbelieving tone. She wondered if Guillaume knew about this story. He was so supportive of the late King Edward. She could not believe he would have been so loyal had he known the truth of his birth. If indeed it was the truth.

"He won his crown in battle and ruled England very well," replied Barvaux. "Unfortunately."

"Why do you say that?"

"Because he was a Yorkist, and Bishop Morton is a Lancastrian, a supporter of Queen Marguerite d'Anjou (King Henry's widow) and of the Earl of Richmond."

"How closely did this bishop support King Henry's queen?" asked Rocca.

"Very, very closely. You understand what I mean?"

"Hmphh." Rocca's grunt was non-committal.

"But surely, Claude, you remember them living together in St Mihiel when you lived there with your parents?" asked Barvaux.

"Not really. In any case, they were not in the town of St Mihiel. They were in the Château de Koers, a few leagues away."

"True," Barvaux admitted. "That's where I first got to know Dr Morton, because I brought him money from the Duke of Burgundy. After I delivered the funds, I travelled on to St Mihiel to see you, and the others, and enjoy myself."

Rocca gave another non-committal grunt.

Belina's thoughts strayed back to the conversation in the cathedral shop with the Flemish merchants. When she concentrated again on Barvaux's story of breaking into the Lanthern Tower, he was telling Rocca about escorting the princes into the waiting boat. The younger boy had resisted this loudly and vigorously, and Barvaux had to clasp his hand over the boy's mouth. A soldier had carried the older boy into the boat and gagged him with a piece of cloth. Then he had snatched the younger boy from Barvaux in such a way that the lad could not make any noise. Barvaux had thrown a blanket over the boy's head.

"How old are the princes?" asked Rocca.

"They were twelve and nine."

"Were?" Rocca queried. "Have they just had birthdays?"

Barvaux laughed. "No. They are dead. Drowned."

"But *you* did not drown," Rocca pointed out. "You stayed on land, I take it, on the wharf of the Tower of London."

"No. Far too dangerous. Of course I went in the boat with them. We went down the Thames as far as Queenborough."

"And then?" Rocca asked in a taut voice.

"When all the sailors were occupied furling the sails I pushed the boys overboard."

Rocca gasped. "No! How could you do such a thing?"

"I was obeying orders."

"Whose orders?" Rocca's tone was very clipped by now.

"Lady Margaret Beaufort's."

"Surely Bishop Morton would have disapproved?"

"They were illegitimate Yorkists. They were no loss," Barvaux explained.

"They were children. Killing innocent boys is a dastardly murder."

Barvaux offered an impatient explanation of the Beaufort-Morton plan to publicise the illegitimacy of the princes, thereby removing the danger of the dowager Queen Elizabeth and her large family ruling England. The Duke of Buckingham had played his part well in all this. The Lord Protector, King Edward's younger brother, had been acclaimed king with great enthusiasm. The next stage in the plot had been to dispose of Lord Hastings, Captain of Calais, because he had failed to free the Earl of Oxford from Hammes Castle.

"The Bishop of Ely would not have needed me to forge documents to show Hastings was a traitor," explained Barvaux, "if Hastings had only bribed the Captain of Hammes."

"Who is the Bishop of Ely?" snapped Rocca.

"Bishop Morton of course," replied Barvaux, "but if all goes well he will become the Archbishop of Canterbury and then Cardinal."

"And the present Archbishop of Canterbury?" asked Rocca.

"He is very old. He can't last much longer," Barvaux replied. "The Bishop of Ely will not have to wait many years."

Belina wondered what the word Ely meant. Was it *illi*? Maybe it was an *Evêque Eli*, named after Saint Eli? She tried to concentrate on Rocca's swift Parisian speech and Barvaux's Flemish-accented French. It was tiring work and she missed some of the conversation.

She heard Barvaux say that the sailors would not be able to leave the Isle of Sheppey which meant that he, Barvaux, was in no danger from his action.

"Are you sure?" asked Rocca in a tremulous voice.

"Positive. Or nearly positive, at any rate."

"Go on with your story," said Rocca. "What will happennext?"

Barvaux explained that Lady Margaret Beaufort would circulate rumours that there had been an attempt to rescue the princes, but that the attempt had failed and that their whereabouts had become a mystery. At the appropriate time, King Richard would be accused of having had them murdered.

Rocca drew in his breath. So did Belina, but not so noisily.

"But the plan has been compromised," Barvaux continued. "I have this very morning received a letter from Christopher Urswick in Paris telling me that Lady Margaret has discovered that the princes who I removed from the Lanthern Tower were impostors and that the real princes were already living in Luxembourg."

"I am glad to hear it," said Rocca.

"Why?" asked Barvaux in astonishment.

"Because I disapprove of murder. The Fifth Commandment says 'thou shalt not kill'."

"So what?" hissed Barvaux. "The peace of England is worth the death of two boys."

"If I understand things rightly," said Rocca, "England is at peace now under King Richard."

"That won't last long," said Barvaux excitedly. "As I told you yesterday, in seven weeks' time the south of England will rise up against the king. He will crush the rebellion and make sure that the so-called leader of it, the Duke of Buckingham, is beheaded."

"I remember yesterday's conversation very well," replied Rocca. "Go on with your story about the princes in Luxembourg. Are they safe there? Safe from the Lady and the Bishop, I mean."

"No. The spies of Urswick and Bray have seen to that." Barvaux paused. "The letter I received this morning tells me that they are on their way to Portugal to live with Sir Edward and Lady Brampton in Lisbon." Rocca asked why. "Because Sir Edward is in reality a Portuguese merchant called Duarte Brandão who was knighted by King Edward. He knows the boys well and would be bound to look after them carefully."

"And keep them alive and safe, in other words," said Rocca.

"Much too alive and safe," replied Barvaux. "That's why it is vital that they never reach Lisbon. I am ordered to intercept them on their way through Condom, and to kill them."

"Drown them in the river Baïse, I suppose, instead of in the river Thames," said Rocca. "I take it that drowning children is a speciality of yours?"

"Perhaps.But not necessarily. I could throw a boulder on to them. I could stab them with a sword or a dagger." Belina shuddered. She wondered if Rocca, too, was shuddering. He asked Barvaux if Urswick approved of his methods of assassination and, especially, if Archbishop Cato approved of them.

"Maybe they do, maybe they don't. It doesn't really matter," replied Barvaux.

"I need to get some sleep," said Rocca. "Tomorrow morning I'm going to that unfinished building site near the Barlet Bridge. It's supposed to be the new storehouse area for diocesan tithes, rent and wine. After all the trouble I have taken to check what every single tenant will be providing, I need to have a suitable place to store it, safe from rats and – especially – from local thieves. Tomorrow morning I will threaten those lazy builders with fines and dismissal if they don't finish the job quickly."

"What if they just laugh at you and down tools?" said Barvaux. "You won't get it finished if they do that."

"They won't do that. They do not dare, and they cannot afford a fine as well as losing their job."

"They're probably just a bit slow," said Barvaux.

Belina thought so too. Obviously, Rocca did not understand the concept of a Gascon promise. It was useless in Condom to expect a builder, for example, to keep to the day stipulated for anything. Or even the week, or month. Gascons are like that, Belina knew. It was up to Rocca to learn to live with the system.

"Maybe they are planning to assassinate you," Barvaux suggested.

"Just because *you* assassinate boys does not mean that anyone here would try to kill me. *Bonne nuit.*"

"*Bonne nuit*, Claude. Sleep well if you can. Dream of the scene in the building site tomorrow." Barvaux's voice was smoother than ever.

Belina waited for a very long time before relighting the lantern and taking it into the shop and from there to the courtyard. She sniffed the air just in case there was a scent of the rosemary which always enveloped Barvaux. But there was only the scent of the climbing rose beside the shop door in the courtyard, and the only sound was of crickets chirping in the darkness. Nevertheless, it would be dangerous to cross the courtyard and go up the stairs and bump into Barvaux. She went back inside the shop, and using the lantern lit a precious wax candle because she judged that a tallow candle would smell too strongly. Shielding the candlelight as much as possible, she went slowly across the courtyard, up the stairs, and along the corridor to the door of Guillaume's chamber.

She put the candle down and felt for the door key on her belt. It clinked slightly as she turned the key in the lock and she heard Minet meow on the other side of the door. She extinguished the candle in the wooden bucket of water which the staff residence porter had left near the door, and bent down as she pushed the door open. Minet came hurtling out but Belina managed to catch her, bring her back inside and shut the heavy door as quietly as possible. She leant against it, shaking with relief while the cat struggled in her arms and scratched her.

Belina bolted the door in the dark. She felt for her tinder box and lit a tallow candle. Within a few minutes she had removed her head-cloth and her clothes, put on her nightcap and slipped into bed. The cat purred in her ear and then settled herself at the bottom of the bed. Belina pinched out the candle and lay still, pondering the story she had just heard. Even Rocca had sounded appalled, she realised. She sighed, thinking about the drowning of helpless, innocent children. It took her a long time to get to sleep.

CHAPTER TWENTY-ONE

Belina slept badly and awoke to see Minet twitching her tail and growling at the birds outside the window beside the sink. She leapt out of bed, rushed over to the open window and seized the cat's tail. Minet was furious and scratched Belina's bare arm before squirming free and landing heavily on the floor.

"Stupid cat." Belina put some water on her arm and stopped the bleeding with the towel above the sink. She shut the parchment-covered window even though it would block out the light. She washed and dressed herself while Minet sulked under the bed.

Belina forgot about the cat. Her mind was concentrating on what she had overheard the night before, of the two young princes – or two other boys perhaps – being drowned. Barvaux had not seemed to care who he had murdered. How could she have liked such a person? She felt very oppressed, both by the drowning and by her proximity to a murderer. She opened the window and gulped down the early morning fresh air. The morning was fine and the stuffy thundery atmosphere of the previous days had vanished. She breathed in and felt better.

Suddenly the cat jumped past her through the window and landed on a thin branch of the peach tree outside. The tree shook and began to pull away from the wall.

"Minet! Come back you stupid cat," Belina shouted at her.

The cat took no notice, and scrambled down on to a lower, thicker branch. Belina seized the milk jug and banged a metal spoon against it. That sound usually brought Minet straight to the jug. But not this time.

Belina tried again, holding jug and spoon out of the window. "Minet, come and have your breakfast." She leaned further over the window sill and almost dropped the jug. The cat moved upwards and the peach tree swayed again, pulling even further away from the wall.

Belina rushed downstairs leaving the door wide open and forgetting that she was not wearing her head-cloth. Minet was clinging on to a high branch which was swaying dangerously away from the wall.

"Alain," Belina called out, "please help me rescue Minet." But Alain was busy helping Sir John go indoors as quickly as he could limp.

Barvaux and Rocca were sitting in a corner of the courtyard, chatting over their breakfast, with Rocca showing Barvaux a pile of documents.

Belina interrupted their scrutiny of accounts. "Please help me rescue my cat. Please. Please."

They looked up. Rocca frowned, perhaps startled to see Belina without her head-cloth, her long black hair dishevelled and clinging to her cheeks. Barvaux stood up and put his arm round her. "Never mind the cat. It can look after itself. Sit down, Belina, and join us with our breakfast. It will make you feel better."

She pulled herself away. "Please help me rescue my cat from the tree." But Barvaux was not at all interested in Minet. His eyes were riveted on Belina's long unkempt hair.

In desperation, she went to the base of the tree and tried to reach up, calling out to Minet. The cat hesitated, testing a slightly lower branch with her paw but refusing to move down to it. Her meowing became ever more piteous as she tested the branch. She was too scared to scramble down to it.

Suddenly, Belina became aware of someone putting a table beside her and a stool next to it. She supposed that it was Alain coming at long last to her help. She put out her arm to help Alain on to the stool and then on to the table and it took her a little while to realise that the rescuer was wearing a clerical gown. He was reaching up into the peach tree calling out calmly, "*minou, minou*, come down this way. Don't be afraid. I won't let you fall."

The cat put her paw on to a lower branch, changed her mind and pulled her paw back. Rocca tried again to coax her down. The cat still hesitated. Rocca held on to the tree trunk with one hand and tried to touch Minet with the other. The cat looked nervously upwards and then sideways several times while Belina became even more distraught. Then Minet put her paw on to another branch and Rocca grabbed her before she could change her mind again.

"Don't worry. You are all right now."

With Belina holding Rocca's legs steady on the table, he cradled Minet in his arms, before turning and handing her to Belina, very gently.

"Thank you so much," she whispered.

"Don't mention it."

Belina placed Minet on the ground and helped Rocca off the stool and on to the table and then on to the ground.

The cat began to wash herself. Rocca smiled. "Typical of a cat to do that. Trying to pretend that it was never in any danger."

"And yet, she was in danger. She could have fallen and hurt herself badly. Or even have died."

He smiled again, picked up the table and carried it to its usual place. She followed him with the stool.

"Thank you so much," she said again. "I hope I did not put you in any danger."

"Perhaps a little, but a cat's safety is important." He gazed down at the ground for a moment, avoiding staring at her face and hair. "You must excuse me, Dame Lansac, but I am in a hurry. I have to go down to the new diocesan storage building site. The workmen have been working far too slowly and it needs to be ready for the harvest and the *vendange*. There's a tremendous amount still to be done. I'm sure they have been idle on purpose. It doesn't suit the folk here to have the cathedral's possessions stored safely, out of reach of pilferers."

"Perhaps it is just Gascon promises," said Belina, careful not to indicate that she already knew about his forthcoming visit to the building site. "Perhaps you were given completion dates which were in reality much too optimistic."

"I have already allowed for that pernicious, untruthful habit," he snapped. "No, the delay is deliberate. Moreover, my assistant is certain that several workmen have been stealing building materials and selling them off to a group of men from Moncrabeau who in turn have been boasting about it."

Belina smiled. "Probably not, whatever they say to Messire Loupmont in Moncrabeau. After all, that place is well known for telling lies. It is a kind of competition with them to see who can tell the biggest lie. But perhaps Messire Loupmont has not learnt about that?"

Rocca scowled and left the courtyard, banging the street door behind him. Belina picked up Minet and took her upstairs to Guillaume's chamber. The cat leapt from her arms and rushed through the open doorway. And then rushed back out again, hissing.

"Oh Minet, please do calm down," said Belina. "You really are a nuisance."

She picked the cat up again and walked through the doorway, concentrating on the cat's peculiar behaviour. And then she looked at the room. She knew she had left it abruptly and probably in a bit of a mess, but now it was in a terrible state. Chests and clothes baskets were open and their contents strewn on the bed and the floor. The jugs on the shelf by the sink had been tipped over. Her satchel with its wax tablets had been emptied on to the unmade bed and the mattress had been shifted to one side. She glanced at the secret place where she had hidden the two medallions which had been sewn inside the dead pilgrim's shirt. She lifted up her Sunday head-cloth, dreading to find nothing underneath it. But the pilgrim's two medallions were still there, wrapped inside their little silk cloths.

She sighed with relief and replaced the head-cloth over the medallions. She knew very well that Guillaume insisted that she must always lock the door, although she had not thought they possessed anything especially interesting for thieves. The first time that she had had anything of real value was now, in the shape of that gold medallion from Saint Mihiel, so much admired by Messire Benasse. How could a thief get into the secure and guarded cathedral staff residence? And how could a thief know that she had been down in the courtyard instead of having her breakfast? How could a thief know that her cat would leap on to the peach tree outside the window?

Belina pulled herself together with a big effort, and tried to ignore the thump of her heartbeats. What had been stolen? Indeed, what was there to steal? And where was the thief now?

She plucked up courage and flung open the door leading to Guillaume's workroom. That too was in disorder. Leather bags had been slit open and their contents thrown out of them. Papers and parchments were in untidy heaps. His work chest had been moved but its complicated locking mechanism had defeated the thief, whoever he had been. She stared in horror and walked towards the centre of the small room, concentrating on its dreadful state.

"Dame Belina, here I am to help you."

She spun round and saw Barvaux in the doorway with his arms stretched out towards her.

She stepped back and almost fell over Guillaume's lute. "How did you know that I needed any help, Messire?" she managed to say fairly steadily.

"The porter told me he saw a thief run off down towards the stables." He said very smoothly. "And obviously he would have come from your chamber because you had left it without locking the door. Even worse, you had left the door wide open."

Belina's throat went prickly and she felt like coughing. Unable to speak easily, she just stared at Barvaux.

"I trust he has not stolen anything valuable," he continued in his silky voice. In spite of herself, she still found his voice extremely attractive. "I think I had better help you check what is missing." He crossed the room and began to examine the lock on Guillaume's work chest.

She found her voice at last. "No, no, my husband can check if anything is missing."

Barvaux took no notice and began pulling things out of Guillaume's winter clothes chest where she had stowed the *chausse* full of the pilgrim's gold and silver coins.

"Messire Barvaux," she said as steadily as possible, "please leave my husband's possessions alone. He will be back in a moment and can check them himself."

"In a moment, Dame Belina? More like in a week or two. Your husband is on his way to Bordeaux." He got to his feet, staring at her.

Belina stepped back. "You are much mistaken, Messire, my husband is here in Condom," she said more firmly than she felt.

He laughed and pulled her towards him, lifted her chin and kissed her very fervently, taking no notice of her attempts to escape from his clutches. "Belina, my dear," he said a bit huskily, "we have a week or two in which to enjoy each other's company whilst your husband is away in Bordeaux. Let's start straight away in the next room."

She tried to slap his face, but he hugged her all the closer and pushed her into the other room.

At first he tried to force her on to the bed, but the displaced mattress and the pile of wax tablets prevented that, so he held her with one hand whilst he threw her precious tablets of botanical drawings on to the floor, breaking two of them, and damaging the hinges of the others. He tugged at the mattress. She tried to punch him but she could only reach his biceps and it was clear that she might as well have been hitting a very full leather bottle.

"Don't waste your energy on hitting me. Keep it for love-making, Belina." She kicked him, which hurt her toes in their thin slippers. "Kick me again when we are on the bed. It's good for your thighs. It will open them up for me." He laughed.

Still holding her with one hand he began to undo the ribbons of his codpiece with his other hand. She pulled her arm free and ran out of the door.

She heard the door close behind her and glanced over her shoulder. To her relief he had not followed her. She leant against the rail overlooking the courtyard, gasping. Her legs were wobbling and she had to grip the rail hard to stop her hands from shaking. Belatedly she began to wonder why he had not followed her and dragged her back inside the room. He had seemed so aroused. Why had he let her escape from him? Was that what he wanted? Was Barvaux himself the thief? She did not really believe his story of a thief rushing down to the stables. But what was he trying to steal? What had Guillaume got in his workroom that Barvaux needed so much? Was he looking for the dead pilgrim's coins? If so, how-ever had he known that the pilgrim possessed such a treasure?

Bewildered and still shaking she looked down at the court-yard. Alain was crossing it in deep conversation with Miqueu, the new stable lad. Which should she do? Request their assistance in removing Barvaux from her chamber and risk permanent damage to her reputation, or go downstairs herself and shelter in the shop? Neither option was easy. She stroked her hair back from her face - an action that reminded her that she was without her head-cloth and should not be seen by anybody. She would need to decide quickly as Alain and

Miqueu were approaching the outside door of the residence.

She inhaled deeply and called out to Alain, "there is a thief in my chamber and he's turned everything upside down. Please help me."

"Is he still there, Dame Belina?"

"Yes. I was so scared I ran out."

"But Messire Guillaume is there?" Alain asked. "Surely he can......"

"No, he's not, Alain," Miqueu interrupted. "He's on his way to Bordeaux. Dame Lansac is all alone. Or at least she should be," he added.

"Please help me," Belina pleaded.

They ran upstairs, told her to stand well back from the door and lifted the latch. Luckily, Barvaux had not bothered to bolt the door. Like Belina, and also Miqueu apparently, he must have known that Guillaume was indeed travelling to Bordeaux. Belina wondered how he knew this. The stable staff, men such as Miqueu, might have known, but surely a foreign visitor would be unaware of Guillaume's absence? Or maybe Rocca or the archdeacon had told him?

While she was immersed in her troubled thoughts, trying to unravel them, she had not noticed that Alain and Miqueu had gone into the inner room. She picked her way through the piles of her belongings strewn on her bedroom floor and stood in the doorway to Guillaume's work room. It was in even more disorder than before. The pilgrim's staff was lying on the floor. The gourd had been pulled off it and was swinging on Barvaux's belt while he searched in Guillaume's winter clothes chest. Triumphantly he held up the *chausse* containing the dead pilgrim's gold and silver coins.

"Put that back," she ordered Barvaux.

"Put what back, my dear Belina?" he replied in his silky, sexy voice.

"You know very well. That *chausse* belongs to my husband, as do all those clothes. Put them back in the chest at once." She sounded firmer than she felt.

He smiled and walked towards her, still holding the heavy *chausse*.

"Oh no, you don't," growled Alain. He tried to wrestle the *chausse* away from Barvaux, who turned and punched him in the stomach, winding him.

Barvaux pushed Belina out of the way and ran into the other room. But as he ran, he caught his right foot in a heap of Belina's clothes and stumbled. This gave Miqueu time to do a *soule* tackle and he crashed down on top of Barvaux.

Belina seized her iron frying pan and brought it down onto Barvaux's left hand so that he would let go of the *chausse*. She considered hitting his head with the pan too, but thought better of it. It could have killed him. Instead, she picked up the *chausse*, took it into the other room and put it back at the bottom of the clothes chest. She looked around for the key but could not see it among all the mess the thief had made. She assumed, with great reluctance, that the thief was Barvaux. But how had he known that the *chausse* contained so much treasure? Or indeed any treasure at all? The cathedral staff kept what valuable possessions they had - which was seldom very much - in a special safe in the diocesan strong room. Guillaume kept important, valuable documents there too. So how did Barvaux know that there was treasure in Guillaume's chamber? She could not work it out.

"What do we do now, Dame Belina?" asked Alain, still stroking his bruised stomach.

"I think the two of you should take him to the cathedral sergeant and tell him what you have seen and that this Fleming should be locked up." It was a bold statement, and Alain looked at her in surprise.

"If you say so, Dame Belina."

Miqueu stood up and tried to heave Barvaux to his feet, while keeping a grip on his shoulder. But Barvaux wriggled free, punched the youth and rushed out of the chamber, down the stairs, across the courtyard and out into the street.

Belina sponged Miqueu's bruised face very gently and told Alain to pour them all some *aygue ardente*. "We need it. What a terrible experience. I had no idea that Fleming was so rough."

"I had heard that he was trying to chat you up," said Miqueu, sipping his *aygue ardente*.

"He said he was trying to help me investigate the death of a pilgrim," replied Belina firmly. "He said he had been trained as an inquirer in Liege, which is why he could help."

The two servants looked at her, and said nothing. Then Alain began to tidy up the room.

"No please don't bother, Alain," Belina said. "I need to check to see what is missing. What you could do for me, please, is to tell Dame Quiteira in the shop that I will be a bit late. Don't tell her why."

"All right, Dame Belina, but are you really sure that you can manage by yourself to clear up all this untidy mess?"

Belina nodded.

"Thank you for the *aygue ardente*, Dame Lansac," said Miqueu, placing his cup in the sink.

Belina touched his arm, smiled at him and thanked him for all his help. "I greatly admired your *soule* tackle, Miqueu," she added.

He grinned and followed Alain from the chamber. Belina bolted the door behind them and put the chamber to rights, concentrating on checking if anything was missing. All her wax tablets were there, but damaged. Her jewel box had been thrown on to the bed, but the few things it had contained were still inside it. Evidently Barvaux had no interest in stealing them. Perhaps he had been looking for the two medallions? Just as well she had hidden them underneath her Sunday head-cloth.

The clothes baskets under the bed had been emptied on to the floor. An enormous lidded jar had been overturned and smashed, scattering lentils everywhere. It took her a long time to sweep them up and throw them away. She wondered if Barvaux had thought that the jar contained the gold and silver coins. It was about the right size for that. But again she wondered how had he known to look for coins in the first place? She was sure she had not mentioned them to anyone other than Messire Benasse. And the Pradau hospice porter was the only person who knew how heavy the dead pilgrim's cloak had been because he had carried it for her as far as the cathedral shop. Of course, he could have spoken about the heavy cloak. However, it was unlikely that Messire Benasse would have been anything but totally discreet. She stood still in the middle of the room, unaware that she was bouncing her knuckle against her mouth.

It was several minutes before she realised that she needed to find a different hiding place for the coins in the *chausse*, in case Barvaux returned. She looked around the bedroom, and finally decided to hide the *chausse* in the storage basket where she kept bags of dried peas. Then she tackled the disorder in Guillaume's work room, and found the key to his winter clothes chest under the clothes that Barvaux had tipped on to the floor. When she had replaced those in the chest, she locked it, and hung the key on its nail in the rafter. She leant the pilgrim's staff against the wall and thought about the pilgrim's missing gourd. Why was that so important to steal? The gold and silver coins she could understand. But what was so special about an empty gourd?

She returned to the bedroom and sat on the bed, thinking back on what had happened. Barvaux had acted very quickly to get up the stairs and search the chamber with such speed. Or had there been another thief and had he been the person who disturbed that thief? After all, that was what Barvaux had tried to make her believe. And he had tried to make her believe that he was only interested in seducing her in her husband's absence. But how and why was he so sure that Guillaume really was absent?

She poured some milk into a cup for her interrupted

breakfast and ate a pastry given to her by the Compagnons' *Mère* in the Place Lion d'Or the day before. Crumbs scattered over her dress and on to the rush matting. She drank the milk slowly, lost in thought. A thump at the door startled her. Was Barvaux back again? Her heart was beating fast. Her legs were wobbling. What was she to do? There was a second thump followed by a loud meow.

Belina almost laughed with relief. Then she thought that Barvaux was capable to imitating a meow. He knew she had a cat. She approached the door cautiously and heard Minet scratch the bottom of it and give a higher pitched meow. Belina unbolted the door very slowly whilst the cat on the other side continued to meow.

Belina pulled the door open a little and Minet slid through the narrow gap with a snarl and a grunt, while Belina closed and bolted the door behind her. They both sat on the bed looking at each other. Then Minet began to wash herself, which reminded Belina about Rocca. How strange that he should be so helpful and sympathetic about a cat stuck up a tree and yet so terrible in every other way. She could not understand it.

It was some time before she felt able to leave the chamber to go to work in the shop. She wondered if Alain had told Quiteira about the theft, or attempted theft, in Belina's chamber. That way, Quiteira would be less harsh about her late arrival. She brushed her tangled hair, fastened it up and put on her head-cloth. She went out, locking the door behind her this time. She kept thinking about the disappearance of the gourd. Had the wine in that gourd poisoned the pilgrim when he arrived in the hospice? Had the salty cakes made him thirsty? She was shaking so badly that she almost missed her footing on the bottom step of the staircase.

CHAPTER TWENTY-TWO

Belina was right about Quiteira. "Are you sure you still work here, Belina?" she demanded. "I'm fed up with your absences. What have you been doing? Praying in the cathedral for better behaviour?" She slammed a drawer shut and heaved another one open. "If this goes on much longer I am going to ask for a replacement. It's all wrong that I have to run this shop single-handed. What's more, Guillaume should do his own investigation work and leave you to do your work, here in this shop."

"I agree with you," said Belina. "It's high time that Guillaume took over the investigation, but he is still too busy on a report for the bishop."

"I don't believe it. Stop lying to me. I think Guillaume is miles away from here."

"I'm not lying," Belina retorted.

"We shall see," Quiteira persisted, "we shall see." She adjusted her head-cloth. "I bet you four *merveilles* honeycakes that I am right."

"I don't take bets," replied Belina. "Never."

"Aahh," gloated Quiteira, "that means that sometime next week Guillaume will walk in here, smelling of sweat and horses, give you an enormous kiss and tell you all about Bordeaux."

They continued to pretend to rearrange the contents of various drawers and it was sometime before either of them noticed that people outside were rushing past the shop, bumping into housewives going towards the market square with their shopping baskets and peasants tugging at mules laden with farm goods for sale in the market. There was a great deal of shoving and shouting.

"Quick," said Belina, "We must put the jewellery and *babiole* trays back inside the shop before someone steals them. Street disturbances mean thieves are around."

Quiteria stubbed her toe on the urn beside the counter. "Yet another reason why you should be here all the time instead of just a few minutes each day," she snapped, pulling in the last tray of *babioles*. "If we're not careful our stock of *aygue ardente* will get stolen too."

"Nonsense," retorted Belina, "it's safely in the cupboard in the storeroom."

"But it's not locked up," came Quiteira's sharp reply. "Anyway, we need to know why there is all this noise and bustle." She flounced out of the shop and stopped an acquaintance of hers in order to find out what was happening.

"There's been an accident in the building site for the new cathedral storehouse."

"When?" asked Quiteira.

"Don't know. This morning sometime. Don't waste my time. I need to see if my son is all right." The woman shoved Quiteira aside so roughly that she nearly slipped on the slimy mess in the central gutter. A man pushed past her and she shouted at him. Belina decided to stay inside the shop. She was annoyed that Quiteira had joined the crowds running towards rue Barlet.

A donkey put its head over the counter and nearly bit Belina's head-cloth. She stepped back and glared at its owner.

"What's all this fuss about?" she asked him.

"Don't know, don't care," he replied. "All these people are a damn nuisance. I can't think what's the matter with them. Daft, I call it."

A young barber-surgeon pushed the peasant out of the way. "There's been an accident in a building site. We need to see what's happened, and help the injured."

The peasant interrupted him. "And see what you can steal, I bet."

The barber-surgeon hit the donkey's rump hard and the animal made a dreadful noise and stamped its hooves, knocking down an old woman who was struggling to walk along the crowded street. The peasant punched the barber-surgeon and three other men joined in the fight.

Belina helped the old woman up, retrieved her shopping basket, and ushered her into the shop. The woman was shaking and it was difficult for Belina to sit her down safely on a stool. She gave her a few drops of *aygue ardente* from the sample flask.

Meanwhile, the fight continued outside the shop and people walked past it with difficulty, cursing loudly.

With an eye on the disturbance, Belina asked the woman if she knew anything about the accident.

She did, and she spent a long time telling Belina what she knew. Apparently Rocca had gone into a ruined building at the far end of the old timber-yard which he was having converted into cathedral storehouses. He had been haranguing the builders, and they had moved threateningly behind him, shouting at him in Gascon.

"Very bad words, Dame," said the woman. "But he's from Paris. He won't have understood." She shifted her basket. "Pity. It would have done him good to learn what we all think of him."

"Has anyone been hurt?" Belina asked.

"Yes, yes. Rocca himself has been hurt." The woman did not sound regretful.

"You mean," asked Belina, "that the builders have attacked him?"

"I don't think so." Belina waited for more. "When I left the area, Rocca was still on the ground."

"What happened?" Belina asked.

"Nobody knows. But no one will be sorry," she laughed, "and no one will say a word to the cathedral authorities." She got up. "I feel all right now, Dame. Thank you for your kindness. I must do my shopping before everything is sold out."

Belina took her arm and led her out of the shop. The four fighters had moved away. So had the donkey, persuaded with the aid of a goad perhaps.

Someone touched Belina's shoulder and she jumped.

"*Adischatz*, Dame Belina."

She turned round and saw with astonishment that it was Guillaume's groom, Antoni. She was speechless and breathless. She stared at Antoni, half expecting him to vanish into thin air, half dreading that he had returned so soon to Condom to announce that Guillaume had had an accident, or had been taken ill. She swallowed very nervously and kept touching her throat. She tried to croak a question about Guillaume but no words emerged. She continued to stare, unbelieving, at her husband's groom.

"Come inside the shop and sit down for a moment," said Antoni, "while I explain why we are back so soon."

With his back to the counter, taking no notice of the assorted people, poultry, pigs and pack animals the other side of it, Antoni told Belina how they had met the Seneschal and his staff returning to Condom from Bordeaux and that the Seneschal had insisted that Messire Guillaume had no need to travel to Bordeaux.

"The Archbishop of Bordeaux had already left for Tours, accompanied by his senior legal adviser," Antoni told her.

"And the Bishop of Condom too?" Belina asked him.

"Probably already in Tours, according to the Seneschal. Waiting for King Louis to die."

"Has he died?" Belina asked.

"Yes, on Saturday, God rest his soul." They both crossed themselves. "Bishop Montbrun is expected to stay in Tours for several weeks while the nobility fight for the top job," Antoni continued.

"What top job?" asked Belina.

"Ruling France, having power, seizing lands, raising taxes..."

"If they do that," Belina interrupted him, "people will rebel. There'll be fighting all over again." She sighed.

"If there's fighting the new young king will be able to use all those expensive Swiss mercenaries living off the fat of the land at Pont-de-l'Arche."

"Where's that?"

"Dunno. Up north somewhere, I suppose. Near Paris, I expect." Antoni sighed. "You need to shut the shop and come with me down to the stables," he added.

"I can't do that," Belina replied. "Quiteira is already down in the old timber yard, probably with the crowds gawping at Rocca lying on the ground."

"Very likely, with her closest gossips, all talking at each other." Antoni began to pull down all the shutters. "No one will be buying *babioles* today. And Messire Guillaume absolutely insists that I bring you to him. He is in the stables."

Antoni heaved up the lower shutters and they felt their way through the darkened shop to the door into the passage. Belina locked the shop door and they went down rue Barlet while Antoni explained to Belina that the Seneschal was on his way back to Condom to ensure that when the news of the king's death reached the town there would be no troubles.

"More like celebrations, Dame Belina," he said.

"But the king kept the country at peace," she replied.

"Maybe he did. But the taxes have become far too high for us ordinary folk."

"Perhaps the king did not know how much the bishops and abbots were extorting from people," she said. "My husband says that King Louis gave an enormous amount of money to the Church."

They reached the cathedral stables, still discussing Rocca.

"People will not be sorry he's injured, or even dead," said Belina, "but yet I saw another side of him this morning." She told Antoni about Rocca rescuing her cat. But the groom disliked cats and was unimpressed by her story.

Belina could see Guillaume listening to Miqueu, the stable lad who had helped to rescue her from Barvaux. Her heart thumped. Her pleasure at seeing her husband was being extinguished by anxiety at what Miqueu was telling him. Would Guillaume believe that Barvaux was the thief, or would he suppose that Barvaux and Belina had made the story up in order to conceal adultery? She deeply regretted that she had tidied his chamber so thoroughly after Barvaux had escaped. What story was Miqueu concocting? She gulped and coughed.

Guillaume spun round, opened his arms wide and strode towards her. They kissed, but not very affectionately.

"Surprised to see me?" was Guillaume's laconic greeting.

"Very. I thought you would have reached the Gironde by now." She squeezed his arm. "I'm so glad you're back."

"Really?"

"Of course I'm glad," she protested. "Why should I not be?" What had Miqueu been telling him? The truth about her being seen in shops and taverns with Barvaux was bad enough. But Miqueu might very well have embroidered on the truth. She turned her head to see where he was.

"Too embarrassed to look me in the face?" said Guillaume in his sternest manner.

"Not at all. I'm just looking to see where Miqueu has got to," she replied.

"Why?"

"Because he was very helpful to me this morning, and I wanted to thank him again," was her smooth answer. She was surprised at her own quick thinking. But would Guillaume see through her replies? His legendary perception would help him detect any lies, or near-lies, which she produced.

"What precisely did Miqueu do?"

Belina told Guillaume as calmly as she could what had happened, starting with Minet and Rocca, then her dismay at the state of the chamber and seeing 'the Fleming' in it so that she had rushed out 'immediately' and got help from Alain and Miqueu. "I was so lucky that they were there in the courtyard at that very moment," she added breathlessly.

"Yes."

"Miqueu did a *soule* tackle on the Fleming," Belina continued. "I expect he's told you all about that."

"Yes."

"But the Fleming punched his face and escaped."

"Yes."

"Have you seen the state of your chamber?" she ventured to ask him, her voice turning into a croak.

"Not yet. I didn't get further than the courtyard, talking to Sir John." He smiled for the first time. "And Alain too." He smiled again, much more broadly, and hugged her. "I gather you have been very busy with your investigations about that pilgrim's death, and also in listening to some story which Alain tells me is very important."

"Yes, yes, of course," she replied, managing to suppress a sigh of relief. She described as steadily and unemotionally as possible the plot to intercept the princes when they arrived in Condom. Unfortunately, before she had completely finished she was interrupted by the arrival of one of the Seneschal's men with orders for Guillaume's immediate presence in the building site "because there has been a death".

Guillaume stooped and kissed Belina very quickly and then ran towards the gate opposite the building site. Belina sat on a bench, exhausted and shaking. She crossed herself, lowered her head and closed her eyes.

CHAPTER TWENTY-THREE

In the nearby town of La Romieu a knight and his wife were waiting under the shade of a large oak tree for a blacksmith to begin shoeing one of their horses. Inside the forge their boys were watching the smith making the blade for a vine-pruning knife. At last the smith emerged from his forge, wiping the sweat from his brow and carrying his box of tools. He was followed by an apprentice carrying a portable anvil.

"Adischatz." The smith surveyed the horses rather than his customers.

"My wife's horse has cast a shoe," said the knight, indicating the bay ambler. "The road from Lectoure is very muddy."

The smith grunted, and suggested that if the horse had come from a place with a soggy, wet climate 'up north' it might have much softer hooves. He gently patted the bay on its rump before running his hand down its leg and lifting its foot. The horse shifted its weight on to its other feet.

The smith held the shoeless foot so that the sole of its hoof faced towards him. He selected a curved metal hoof pick from his tool box and cleaned the bottom of the hoof. Then he brushed it, chatting all the time to the knight about the bad weather that year. He had never had to shoe so many horses before. Moreover, he had mended an enormous number of carts and wagons, as well as making many more wheels than usual.

"Good business for you," said the lady as she watched the smith selecting his hoof knife from the tool box.

The smith grunted again. He cut off an excess flaky section from the bottom of the hoof and his dog snatched it away and began to chew it. "There's not much money to be earned in shoeing, Dame, but I like to be outside in the shade. Working all day in my forge is very hot." He picked up his hoof nippers and trimmed the wall of the hoof. "Are you on your way to Messire Saint Jacques in Galicia?"

"Yes, we are," said the knight, "but we are wondering which would be the best route because the rivers are so dangerously full. We only just managed to get across the ford this side of Lectoure."

"Condom has a solid high bridge," replied the smith, "but you might have trouble further west. Perhaps you could turn south at Condom instead of crossing the bridge." He began to flatten the sole of the hoof with a rasp, working very gently and with both hands. "And even if you decided to cross the Barlet Bridge at Condom you might find the Bouquerie area the other side is flooded."

"Does that mean that all the butchers' carcases will be floating down the road?"

"Sometimes it gets as bad as that, but only in the spring. That's when the Baïse flows really fast and bursts its banks." He pulled three iron horseshoes out of his tool box and examined them.

His customers waited in the shade, with the other horses. The boys shared a peach. The apprentice stood to attention beside the portable anvil.

"If you get through La Bouquerie you should be able to reach Mouchan without difficulty. Go across the stone bridge there and cross the ford of the river Auzoue the other side of Gondrin," said the smith, trying each of his horseshoes on to the newly prepared hoof.

"What if that's flooded?" said the knight, frowning.

"A group of tax collectors came through here yesterday and told me that the Auzoue ford was still passable." The smith chose a horseshoe slightly bigger than the hoof and took out his hammer. "And soon after that you will reach Cazeneuve." He placed the horseshoe on the anvil, scrutinised it and banged it twice. "At Cazeneuve you could turn south on the Tenafreza."

"What's that?" The knight took some documents out of the purse hanging from his belt, put on his spectacles and looked at the papers.

"The Tenafreza is a really ancient road. It was already ancient when the Romans came here. It goes due south without crossing any rivers. Follow that and you will get over the Pyrenees and into Spain." The smith placed the shoe on the hoof and banged two square nails into it, while he rested the hoof on the thick leather apron covering his knee. He rasped off the excess flare and hoof wall, and began to put in six more square nails so that they came slowly out of the hoof wall. He tapped delicately, his eyes fixed intently on the hoof. Using the claw of his hammer, he bent over the square tips of the nails. Finally he filed the end of the nail and then removed two rough spots from the hoof wall. At last he could lower the hoof and the lady's horse could stand on it again.

The smith examined the other three hooves and told the lady that she was too heavy for her horse.

"Not really, he's used to my weight, but we have been travelling a long way and these roads are very muddy."

The blacksmith nodded and examined the hooves of the palfrey and the other two amblers. "They should last another three weeks. Longer if you take the Tenafreza."

"I will certainly consider doing so," said the knight, paying the blacksmith. "A decision to be made at Cassaneuf, I think you said?"

"At Cazeneuve, Messire," said the apprentice, "not far from the tower of Lamothe." The knight gave him a coin.

The apprentice helped them remount, praising the horsemanship of the older boy.

"*Merci, mat beiden Hänn ënnerschreiwen!*"

"Where are you from?" the apprentice asked. "You have a funny way of speaking."

Before the boy could reply and say that he was a indeed good horseman, the lady smiled and told the apprentice that they were from Lyon, and that the weather had been bad there too that year.

The knight changed the subject again and asked which was the way to Condom.

"Past the church, through the square and then straight on. Just follow the cart tracks and hoofprints and you will get to the church of Sainte Germaine," said the blacksmith. "You could rest the lady's horse there for a while because of his new shoe. You could rest yourselves too there and have your dinner." He picked up his tool box, said "*adischatz*" with his back to them, and returned to the smithy, followed by the apprentice struggling with the heavy anvil.

The four riders walked their horses through the small town, admiring the enormous church with its two towers, and then crossed the little square with its arcades. The lady dismounted and bought some little mutton pies and some peaches. "Do you have any apples?" she asked the old stallholder.

"No, Dame, my husband has taken them all into Condom early this morning. It's Wednesday."

The lady asked if that meant it was market day and the old woman nodded. "Do you have any wine or is it too late in the season?"

"Yes it is, but I can sell you some cider if you like." The lady bought a gourd of cider and handed it to her husband, saying that it was the best she could obtain for their dinner in the churchyard of Sainte Germaine.

"Doesn't matter. The itinerary instructions say that the

Senclar mansion has excellent food, reputed to be the best in Condom."

"I wonder why that is," the lady murmured as a passer-by helped her remount her horse.

"Their high price perhaps, Alice. I asked Mautby when he gets there ahead of us to see if the Senclars would reduce their price since we are a family. I can pay whatever they ask, I suppose, but it is a good opportunity to make people think we are a family of four going on pilgrimage to Compostela."

They left the town and rode for a few miles to the Sainte Germaine church. Like all the other churches they had seen in Gascony, it had suffered from the fighting which had lasted for several generations. The wall round the cemetery was crumbling and paint was peeling off the inside walls. It smelt very damp, presumably because of the holes in the roof.

They sat on a stone ledge in the church porch and ate their rather meagre dinner while discussing the journey so far. It seemed a long time since they had fled Luxembourg, escaping from brigands sent by their enemies Christopher Urswick and Reynold Bray. They had crossed the river Loire at La Charité and then continued south-westwards on their way to Portugal, sometimes using the Chemin de Saint Jacques, sometimes taking a variant itinerary so that their enemies could not reach them.

"Sir George," said the younger boy, "are we nearly there? I'm tired of travelling." He sighed. "And will Mamm be there?"

"Your mother will take a different route from ours, for safety's sake, and later than us because she will still be in Westminster now."

The older boy launched into a series of questions. Would their mother bring all their sisters? Would she travel by sea or land? Would their uncles be with her? Would their half-brothers be with her? Had Sir George received any news about her plans? He went on and on, his voice becoming desperate. "Why won't you tell me, Sir George?"

"Because I do not know the answers, Edward," came the steady reply. "I cannot know them because we have been travelling without anyone knowing who we are or where we are. It's safest that way, you know that." The boy nodded, and began eating his apple disconsolately, his shoulders hunched.

"Did you notice all those cats in the last town, Richard?" said the lady, trying to lighten the atmosphere.

"I asked the apprentice. He said there have been too many cats in the town ever since a hundred and forty years ago and that it was all the fault of a little girl."

Sir George looked at his itinerary description. "It says here that the little girl saved La Romieu from a plague of rats which were eating all the grain, because she had hidden some kittens when everyone had been ordered to kill all cats. Her kittens became cats and killed all the rats." He put the itinerary back into his doublet. "So it was not the fault of the little girl, it was the fault of the leaders of the town."

"Bad leaders cause everyone to suffer," said Edward. "I am going to be a good leader." He stood up and looked around him. "I will make everyone mend their churches."

"Will you make them kill rats?" his brother asked but before he could receive any reply they were disturbed by two oxen drawing a cartload of wood followed by a peasant and his dog.

Sir George got up and helped the other three mount their horses before standing on a block of stone beside the gate and mounting his own horse. They walked past the peasant and his oxen and continued on their way to Condom.

CHAPTER TWENTY-FOUR

Antoni unlocked the little gate between the stable yard and the building site and waited for Belina to tidy her head-cloth. He locked it again behind them. They stared at the scene of confusion. The massive half-finished storehouse on the town side of the building site towered above the timber yard, casting it in shadow, making it hard to discern what was happening. Opposite was another half-finished storehouse with old planks and logs in front of it which was being used as temporary seating for a chattering mass of onlookers, including Quiteira who was sitting beside the cathedral seamstress. Belina noticed some women removing objects from behind the heap of planks and placing them in bits of tattered cloth. Then they sidled past behind the Seneschal's staff who were busy rounding up all the workmen. Masons stood around holding their hammers and chisels. Carpenters were sawing off bits of planks, occasionally upending the people sitting on them.

Belina tried to see where Guillaume was but there was too much movement. Perhaps he was in the ruined building or the disused stables at the far end of the timber-yard. She gazed at its wooden scaffolding and hoped that Guillaume was not in such a dangerous place. She comforted herself by assuming that he would be with the Seneschal and therefore not in danger. But closeness to the Seneschal brought another danger. She was well aware that her husband wanted to become a member of the Seneschal's staff and follow the same career path as his half-brother in Bordeaux. She had tried to dissuade him with various arguments against leaving their good life in Condom but he had accused her of cowardice and lack of adventure.

Belina craned her neck, looking in vain for the Seneschal. Several of his sergeants were evident, grouping workmen together for interrogation by the Lieutenant. She noticed that the Lieutenant frequently looked behind him, perhaps at the person who was kneeling in front of the stables who was unlikely to be the Seneschal. He never knelt, except inside a church.

"Look," said Antoni, pointing at the kneeling man, "there's a barber-surgeon."

Belina peered at him and watched him get up, holding a cloth dripping with blood, and call out to someone. Two soldiers appeared carrying a door, which they put on the ground next to the barber-surgeon. The three of them lifted a body on to the door and covered it entirely with a cloth. A dead body, therefore. Belina crossed herself.

The noise inside the old timber-yard stopped for a couple of minutes while everyone crossed themselves and stared at the trio making their way towards the Seneschal's fortress.

Where was Guillaume? Where was the Seneschal? Belina thought she saw a man with fair hair come out of the stables, threading his way through the scaffolding. She held her breath, and pointed him out to Antoni.

"That man is one of the king's Scots Guards who has been lent to the Seneschal," said Antoni. "He accompanied us on our journey back to Condom." He took her arm and led her through the crowded yard so that they were nearer the stables. "I think Messire Guillaume will be inside that ruined building."

"I hope not," said Belina. "It looks about to collapse."

They watched a soldier climb up the scaffolding and reach the wooden crane wheel on the roof.

"There's no one in this part of the building," he announced when at last he reached the ground again. "Too dangerous. The floor is rotten."

The Lieutenant ordered a roofer who was standing beside a heap of tiles near the base of the crane wheel mechanism to climb up the scaffolding and search the broken roof more thoroughly.

Everyone watched the man climb upwards, hoist himself on to the crumbling cornice and edge his way towards the centre of the building. "There's no sign of any change since I was here yesterday," he called out. "Anyway, only a roofer would dare to move about up here."

"Perhaps the assassin was a roofer?" someone called out.

"Of course not," the roofer retorted, "killing someone up here would be far too dangerous. Even for a roofer," he added. "Can I come down now Messire?" he asked the Lieutenant.

"Yes."

Antoni grabbed Belina's arm and pointed to the other end of the disused stables. She saw Guillaume peering out of a window space above an open doorway. Horrified, she watched him leaning right out over the window sill, feeling the stone wall beneath him. A bit broke off and dropped to the ground.

"Please, please, Virgin Mary, protect my husband. Make him go back inside at once and keep safe," Belina whispered. She said three *Salve Regina*, not daring to look.

Guillaume leant even further out of the window space. "I think I see what happened," he called out to the Seneschal. "Someone has dislodged the stone lintel above this door." He pointed below him. It was difficult for Belina to see anything because of the shadow cast by the half-finished storehouse. "It looks as if the lintel had been loosened beforehand – last night perhaps - and then the assassin would have waited for the right moment to hurl the block of stone down on to the Treasurer's head. Rocca wouldn't have stood a chance."

"Nevertheless, the assassin would have needed to be very precise," replied the Seneschal.

"Very precise, and very strong," said Guillaume. "Experienced too, no doubt."

"I do not recall a murder of that sort here before," said the Seneschal. He scratched his ear.

"Shall I come down now?" Guillaume asked.

"Certainly not. You are to search all that part of the stables. Maybe the assassin is still in there, hiding." The Seneschal ordered several of his men to go through the dangerous doorway and help the Rapporteur.

"Dame Belina, you are shaking," Antoni interrupted Belina's prayers. "I am going to take you to somewhere in the shade to sit down. It's too dangerous for you to stay here."

"Not nearly as dangerous as it is for my husband to be inside that horrible building."

"Your husband will take great care, Dame Belina. He always does," said Antoni. He led her to the other end of the timber-yard and sat her down in the shade on a heap of planks, telling other women to make room for her. Antoni unhooked a leather bottle from his belt, removed the stopper and handed it to Belina. "Drink this," he ordered.

Belina gulped down the warm wine, screwing up her face at its leathery taste, and handed the bottle back. "Thanks, Antoni." She paused. "I expect you want to get back to the stables and look after your horses."

"I've already done that, Dame Belina. Messire Guillaume and I crossed the Barlet Bridge quickly this morning because of being with the Seneschal."

"Oh." Belina shifted on the pile of planks. "I expect that you still want to get some rest. Just leave me here, Antoni. I will watch out for my husband leaving that ruin."

"Are you sure you'll be all right, Dame Belina? You looked a bit poorly earlier on."

"I'm recovered now, thank you, Antoni. I'm sure you need some rest. The Seneschal rides fast, or so I've heard."

"Yes indeed. He has fresh horses at every relay post." Antoni sighed.

"But my husband is always full of praise of your courser." She smiled.

Antoni tugged at his cap, bowed slightly and hurried off to the gate leading to the cathedral stables, locking it behind him.

Before Belina had had time to settle herself on the heap of planks, and in a good position to watch the ruined stables, she felt a hand on her arm.

"And who is looking after the shop, Belina?"

Belina turned round with difficulty, trying to keep her balance on the planks, and saw Quiteira glowering at her.

"No one. There are no customers. Everyone is either shopping in the market or they're down here," Belina replied, "like yourself." She paused. "Tell me what has been happening here."

Quiteira gave Belina a rather confused account of what she had overheard people saying. Apparently, Rocca had harangued all the workmen present about delays in repairing the ruined timber-yard, and there had been much muttering, mostly about his planned conversion of the yard into enormous storehouses for the cathedral tithes and as well as rents from tenants. Then Rocca had gone inside the end door of the stables followed by several carpenters. Everyone else had waited and discussed Rocca's angry speech and the threats he had made: no wages until the site was finished to his satisfaction.

"Everyone was swearing and growling," said Quiteira. "It's just as well you and I were not near to hear them."

"And then?" Belina prompted her.

Some while later Rocca had emerged from the stables looking very angry. His tonsured head was pink with anger and he was fiddling with the purse hanging from his belt, trying to get a paper out of it, or into it. Quiteira had heard both versions of this.

"And then?"

"He fell flat on his face," Quiteira announced with a beaming smile.

"Heart attack perhaps," said Belina.

"Remorse at his evil actions perhaps," replied Quiteira. "But I heard that Rocca fell because something had hit him from behind, or maybe from above. It was not clear what the weapon was, or where it had come from." She paused dramatically, and continued, "the master mason went towards Rocca lying on the ground and soon said he was dead."

"How could he know?" asked Belina.

"Wishful thinking perhaps," replied Quiteira. "Anyway, everyone cheered. Many threw their hats in the air, and two masons with pickaxes did a little dance round the blocks of stone they had been cutting."

"What about the carpenters inside the stables?" Belina asked.

"They rushed out because of the cheering, and saw Rocca on the ground. After that, no one did anything, no one moved, no one spoke."

"Why not?"

"Because Loupmont appeared and ran to where Rocca was lying. He ordered the master mason away and felt Rocca's chest." Quiteira paused for effect, and then crossed herself. "Loupmont howled, he positively howled like a wolf," she declared, "and accused everyone of murdering Rocca."

"If it was a ruined building," said Belina, looking at the crumbling stables covered by scaffolding, "it could have been a piece of decayed timber or masonry which fell down because it was mouldy."

"Why are you so much in favour of Rocca, all of a sudden?" demanded Quiteira.

"I'm not," said Belina, "I'm just trying to think rationally."

"It will be difficult to find out who threw the timber or boulder or whatever the weapon was. The choice of enemies is enormous. All the town I would say," declared Quiteira.

Suddenly, all the women sitting on the heap of planks stood up, pitching Belina forward into Quiteira's ample bosom.

"Dame Lansac, you can stay here, but all you gossips must leave the yard at once. Lieutenant's orders." The sergeant indicated the wide gateway at the end of the timber yard through which troops were herding all the onlookers who had been making so much noise.

"I am with Dame Lansac," Quiteira told the sergeant, "so I am staying here."

"No, you're not, you are leaving with the rest."

"Why is Dame Lansac allowed to stay here?" Quiteira put her hands on her hips and thrust out her chin.

"Because her husband has requested her presence. If you insist on remaining here in spite of the Lieutenant's orders I will suggest to him that you personally lured the Treasurer inside the stables."

Quiteira took the threat seriously and strode off towards the gateway.

"Who lured him into the stables?" Belina asked, sitting down again on the planks.

"Don't know exactly. I have questioned five likely men, but it seems that seven escorted Rocca inside. We can't find a couple of them anywhere. There must be some hidden way out."

"Or cellar," Belina suggested.

"Apparently not."

"Hayloft?"

"We are having that searched right now."

The sergeant left her and resumed herding the onlookers out of the gateway. Belina gazed at the disused stables, hoping that Guillaume was safe and not in the hayloft. Her heart pounded, her hands felt clammy as they gripped the planks beneath her. She swallowed nervously.

The cold, thin voice of Dame Senclar interrupted Belina's anxieties. "Lieutenant, take me to the Seneschal immediately.

I demand an explanation for what has happened to my friend the Treasurer."

"Dame Senclar, we are still trying to ascertain what has happened. All these workmen insist that they were here in this yard listening to the Treasurer address them concerning. . ."

"Concerning what?" Henri Senclar interrupted him.

"I understand that he was telling them that the Bishop required them to work more diligently."

"They wouldn't have liked that," sneered the Consul.

"No, Messire," replied the Lieutenant, "they did not. But as you are very well aware there is a tradition in Condom for its citizens to dislike their bishop."

"That does not apply to me," retorted Henri Senclar.

The Lieutenant stared at him. "There has been bad feeling betweens consuls and bishops for very many years," he pointed out, "and between consuls and abbots before then. It's been going on for centuries, *pour des siècles et des siècles*, likeprayers.»

Henri Senclar, his mother and Chézelle, his mother's physician, swept out of the main gate of the timber-yard, narrowly missing a collision with Jeanne Senclar entering it accompanied by Barvaux and the Catalan merchant. Barvaux had his arm round Jeanne Senclar's waist and Henri Senclar pulled it away with a furious growl. He punched Barvaux's face.

"You keep your hands off my wife, you dirty Fleming," the consul shouted, preparing to land a second punch. But Barvaux stepped aside very swiftly so that Henri Senclar almost lost his balance. Chézelle managed to save him from falling to the ground and led him, still grumbling, along the wharf towards the Senclar mansion. Edith Senclar followed.

Meanwhile, the Catalan merchant was scrutinising the busy scene around him. He tried to ask a labourer nearby for an explanation, but the workman just stared at him and moved away. So the Catalan asked Belina. His speech was a bit heavy and difficult to understand and she had to ask him to repeat his question.

Belina told him in slow French about the murder of Rocca. Jeanne Senclar overheard and smiled. For a moment Belina wondered if she was the assassin. After all, she disliked Rocca. But she was a very unlikely person to have climbed up to the first floor of the disused stable and hurled a block of stone on to Rocca's tonsured head. Of course, she could have hired a man to do it for her. There was plenty of choice in Condom for anyone looking for a man with a grudge against Rocca.

Belina overheard Barvaux mention the word *Luxembourg* and Jeanne Senclar telling him that four Luxembourgers were expected that very afternoon. They had sent a servant ahead to arrange accommodation for themselves and their horses. The Senclar steward had not properly understood if the group was a family with two sons or whether it was two boys being escorted by their tutors on a pilgrimage. He was a bit deaf and had found the Luxembourgish accent difficult to follow.

"Dame Jeanne," Barvaux murmured, "I understand the Luxembourgish language. It is a mixture of French, German and Dutch. I will gladly help you out with your guests. Indeed, I could take the Luxembourg boys down to the wharf, and then take them by boat across to La Bouquerie or even up-stream to the mill at Gauge. That would indeed be a treat for them. Luxembourg rivers run in deep ravines. Seeing the river Baïse would be a treat for them."

"How kind you are, Philippe," Jeanne Senclar purred. "I will get a message to you as soon as they arrive. But where will you be?"

"At the Pont Barlet inn," he told her, "with my Catalan colleague. We have much to discuss." He smiled at the Catalan. The merchant's face showed no reaction whatsoever. But Belina noticed that he was staring at Barvaux's hands. The palms were covered in dust. She wondered why such a fastidious person as Barvaux had not washed his hands recently.

She looked at her own hands for comparison and she wondered where Barvaux had been to get so grubby. Or perhaps his clothes had become dusty and he had smoothed away the dust with the palms of his hands? He had seemed clean enough at breakfast time.

She shook her head, dislodging her head-cloth. She was trying to straighten it when a hand clasped hers.

"Oh!" She turned her head cautiously, hoping it was not Barvaux.

It was Guillaume. She leapt up, dislodging one of the planks. They kissed so enthusiastically that Belina's head-cloth tumbled to the dusty ground.

Guillaume picked it up, flicked away some of the dust and, bending down, fastened it on to her head. Over his shoulder Belina could see the Catalan looking perplexed and Barvaux still deep in conversation with Jeanne Senclar. Perhaps Catalans were not very demonstrative in public? Or perhaps Barvaux had boasted to the Catalan merchant of his friendship with the miller's daughter? She hoped not. She wondered what Guillaume had already been told about her and Barvaux. Obviously Miqueu, the new stable lad, had said something to make Guillaume suspicious. Moreover, Guillaume was good at deciphering Sir John's miming, and he had told her that he had seen Sir John soon after his arrival back in Condom. And as soon as she found an opportunity, Quiteira would tell Guillaume everything, with no miming needed. Quiteira was loquacious even when she was feeling good-natured, and horribly garrulous when spreading scandal. Belina feared the worst.

"Well, you are certainly speechless, my dear," Guillaume drawled, hugging her again.

"Relieved that you have left that dangerous building." She kissed him.

"Messire Guillaume, welcome back to Condom."

They turned round. It was Brother Pierre smiling at him, with Brother Martin standing behind him and holding a bolt of cloth.

"What makes you think I have been away from Condom?" Guillaume asked, rather sharply.

"News gets around, Messire Guillaume. But Dame Belina has been deputizing for you very well." He paused. "She is very competent and clear-headed, and is a pleasure to work with. All the hospice staff have appreciated the thorough but kindly way in which she has carried out the investigation." He smiled. "And now, if you excuse me, Brother Martin and I have to get back to the hospice with this cloth. *Adishatz*, Dame Belina, and thank you for your hard work."

Belina curtseyed to him. She wondered how he had heard about Guillaume's absence, and what he had heard about her activities during that absence. She swallowed nervously.

Someone pushed past her, nearly knocking her over. It was Loupmont. He had spent his time rushing around the timber-yard, wailing about the death of Rocca, snarling at the Seneschal's senior sergeant and refusing to answer questions until the sergeant had threatened to take him back to the Seneschal's fortress and interrogate him 'more thoroughly'.

Guillaume grasped Loupmont's shoulder, not knowing (or caring) that it had already been bruised by the sergeant.

"Ouch," squealed Loupmont.

"You watch where you're going, you stupid accounter," said Guillaume, "or I'll push you to the ground, where you belong."

Belina smiled. It was a pity her brother Jordi was not there to hear that.

Guillaume took her arm. "Let's go to the inn for some dinner. I need to talk further to the Seneschal and his staff about this murder as well as that of the pilgrim." He paused. "But you can tell him about that." He squeezed her arm.

"I need to go to the Senclar stables," she said.

"Whatever for?"

"To find out when a group of Luxembourgers will arrive. It is vital."

"Are you talking about the two boys from England?" he whispered.

Belina nodded. She explained what Jeanne Senclar and Barvaux planned to do that afternoon. The boys were in grave danger.

"Indeed, they are," he replied. "But we will sort things out. Don't you worry."

"I do worry," she interrupted him. "It's really serious. I'm sure it is," she pleaded with him.

"They won't arrive in Condom until at least mid-afternoon. Plenty of time for us to have dinner and a discussion with the Seneschal." He steered her down to the wharf and into the Pont Barlet inn. Loupmont followed closely behind them.

CHAPTER TWENTY-FIVE

Inside the inn were two long trestle tables with fairly clean white tablecloths. The Seneschal and his staff were seated near the windows. They made room for Guillaume and Belina, grinning at Belina. Loupmont tried to sit down beside them and was hauled away by the senior sergeant.

"You keep out of here," he snapped. "You're not wanted. Piss off." He pushed Loupmont out of the door and returned to his place on the bench beside Belina. Everyone clapped.

In the middle of the table sat some soldiers talking loudly about the *Reconquista* against the Moors, how they would fight them, take their women, their weapons and their treasures. However, Belina found it difficult to understand their accents. Just as well perhaps, she supposed. She looked at her bowl of *garbure* and took her spoon out of its bag hanging from her belt.

It was some time before she noticed that the couple at the far end of the other table, beyond a noisy group of farmers, were Barvaux and the Catalan. They were talking earnestly and drawing lines on the tablecloth. A sort of sketch map perhaps. She wondered if it concerned the Luxembourg boys, or rather the English princes. However, she doubted that the Catalan merchant would want to get involved in murdering two unknown boys. It was common knowledge in Gascony that Catalans were excellent businessmen and not keen on fighting everything and everyone like Castillians were prone to do.

The Seneschal was discussing with his staff and Guillaume the circumstances of Rocca's death. Belina listened to Guillaume's report of finding a stash of roof tiles on the first floor inside the disused stables, in good condition, perhaps waiting to be placed on new roof timbers. There were two entrances to the stables on to the street behind them. Both had been used recently.

"By workmen presumably," said the Seneschal.

"Everyone my sergeants and I have questioned has insisted that he only used the gateway and never entered the stables," the Lieutenant declared.

"I bet they did," replied the Seneschal. "It will be very difficult to find the assassin. So many folk have a motive, or even several motives, to kill the Treasurer."

The Lieutenant continued, "They thought the stables were unsafe; some of them told me that they were haunted by the timber merchant who Rocca had harassed in order to get his hands on the yard for storing yet more goods stolen from farmers."

"Stolen?" the Seneschal looked especially forbidding.

"Extracted greedily from farmers even though they have had a very difficult year, or even two years," replied the Lieutenant firmly.

There were grunts of agreement.

"Yes, that at least is true," conceded the Seneschal. "The harvest has been rotten. People will starve this winter. I am going to insist that Bishop Montbrun releases as much grain as possible, as well as other commodities."

Guillaume said that Rocca was a typical big city person from Paris, with no idea of farming.

"But Guillaume," Belina interrupted, "Rocca does not, or rather did not, come from Paris originally. He came from a town in the east called Saint Michel, or something like that." She paused. "Not exactly Saint Michel."

"How do you know that Dame Belina?"asked the Seneschal.

"I overheard him telling Barvaux that in the courtyard."

"What courtyard?"

"The courtyard of the cathedral staff residence. Barvaux has been lodging with Rocca and they drank together in the evening." She tried to speak casually.

"They must shout their conversation if you can hear it from inside your chamber upstairs."

"No, I have been in the courtyard too," she said quietly, wishing other people were not listening.

"Why?"

"I play chess with Sir John."

"Indeed?" said the Seneschal, "I did not know you had that accomplishment."

"She has," said Guillaume. "I taught her and she picked it up very quickly." He put a protective arm around Belina.

"Who is this man Barvaux?" the Seneschal asked.

Belina explained as unemotionally as possible that he was a Flemish lawyer from Bruges who already knew Rocca.

"His Christian name?" snapped the Seneschal.

"Philippe, I think," Belina replied. She wondered how much longer she could survive close questioning by the Seneschal. Guillaume was scared of him and of his immense power. To her great relief they were interrupted by the waiter putting two bowls of *merveilles* on the table. Conversation flagged while everyone helped himself to the little cakes.

Still chewing, and leaving crumbs all over the table, the diners resumed their discussion about who was the most likely assassin. They agreed that it must have been a strong man – the size and weight of the stone lintel that had smashed Rocca's head showed that. Not necessarily a tall man because there was not a very big distance between the top of the lintel and the bottom of the window.

"I saw that he could have squeezed his leg firmly inside a clamp which was fixed to the wall. That would have prevented him from falling down," said Guillaume."I tried it myself. It was effective."

"How long would that clamp have taken to install?" asked the Lieutenant.

"It was already there. It holds back the inner shutters - although they had vanished."

"Stolen perhaps?"

Guillaume shrugged. "Not necessarily. Everything wooden inside the stables was rotting away and had been thrown into heaps."

"Good eyesight and a steady hand," the Lieutenant continued.

"A lot of practice," said the senior sergeant. "How would he get that?"

"From having done it before," said the Seneschal, "possibly several times."

Everyone agreed.

"Excuse me, my Lord Seneschal," said one of the soldiers in the middle of the table," but I have been listening to your conversation. I hope you don't mind."

"Not at all," replied the Seneschal. "An inn is a public place."

"When I was a boy there was a murderer who killed by throwing lintels, or boulders, or whatever he could find, on to his victims."

"How did he do that many times without being caught?" the Seneschal asked.

"By taking care never to be seen, in dusk or in bad weather, for example. Where I lived the winter weather was often foul, wet and misty."

"And where was that?"

"In the east. A town called Saint Mihiel,"

"Oh," exclaimed Belina.

The Seneschal glared at her.

"That is the name of Rocca's home town. I remember it now. Not Saint Michel, but Saint Mihiel. Barvaux and he knew each other there."

"Very interesting."

"A coincidence perhaps," the Lieutenant suggested.

"Not necessarily," replied the Seneschal. He turned to the soldier and asked him if the names Rocca and Barvaux meant anything to him.

The soldier scratched his head. "It's a long time ago. At least fifteen years. I need to think."

The Seneschal waited.

"Please could you repeat those two names, my Lord Seneschal?"

"Claude Rocca, a *clerc*, and Philippe Barvaux, a Fleming from Bruges."

Belina pointed at Barvaux, bent over the sketch map which he had drawn on the tablecloth in front of him. "That is Philippe Barvaux, from Bruges," she whispered.

Everyone stared at Barvaux, either by turning round or by peering over diners' heads. It was difficult to see him clearly in the dark part of the dining-room beyond the farmers shouting at each other and he had his back to the Seneschal's table. Belina wondered if he had washed the dust off his hands by now.

"I remember now," said the soldier. "The murderer was supposed to be a Fleming, but he didn't look at all like one. He had black curly hair, just like that chap. We thought he looked like an Italian or a Greek. There were lots of Italians in Saint Mihiel. Indeed, there was an Italian family of goldsmiths there called Rocca, if I remember rightly. A family that suddenly became very rich, profiting from crooked financial deals."

The soldier bit his lip, scratched his head, looked at his thumbs. The Seneschal waited. They could hear sounds from the kitchen of pans being banged about and a dog barking. Guillaume stroked the back of Belina's neck, slightly dislodging her head-cloth.

The soldier stroked the back of his own neck thoughtfully. Suddenly he stood up, turned round and walked towards

Barvaux, still bent over his sketch map, or whatever it was he had drawn on the tablecloth.

The soldier pulled Barvaux's hair very roughly and jerked it upwards. "Come and see for yourself, my Lord Seneschal, here is the same scar as the one which the murderer of Saint Mihiel had on the back of his neck."

The Seneschal and the Lieutenant got up, joined the soldier and stared at Barvaux's neck, while the soldier held Barvaux very still. Belina supposed that an experienced soldier would know how to overpower even a strong man like Barvaux.

The Lieutenant rubbed Barvaux's scar very gently. "How did you get this scar?"

"Three years ago in a riding accident."

"That scar is more than three years old."

"Four years perhaps. Tell your man to let go of me."

"He's not my man," said the Lieutenant, "and your scar is a lot older than four years. You are a liar."

"You cannot take the word of a soldier against the word of a lawyer," Barvaux persisted.

"I would take the word of anyone against the word of a lawyer," said the Lieutenant.

"Why?" Barvaux demanded.

"Experience has shown me that many lawyers have a tendency to be liars and crooks."

"Here in Gascony, perhaps, but not in Bruges."

"And in Saint Mihiel?" the Seneschal asked.

"I've no idea," replied Barvaux. "I've never been there. I come from Bruges, in Flanders, near the coast."

"Guillaume, he's lying," Belina whispered.

"Yes, I know, but it's not the moment to say so openly," he replied.

The soldier was still grasping Barvaux's glossy black curls, and the Seneschal was still peering at the scar.

"My Lord Seneschal," said the soldier, "this killer escaped hanging because he was known to two English lawyers living in Saint Mihiel. As the Lieutenant says, liars and crooks. They got him out of the Saint Mihiel prison by bribing the guards and then had him taken safely back to Bruges. Much later I heard that he was a notorious criminal in Bruges. In due course the English lawyers had him transferred to Calais so that he could take part in the attempt to rescue the Earl of Oxford from Hammes Castle."

"Why were there English lawyers living in Saint Mihiel?" the Lieutenant asked.

"Part of the miserable little Court of Queen Marguerite d'Anjou who had been exiled there."

"Ah," said the Seneschal, "do you remember their names perhaps? Although of course I realise that fifteen years is a long time ago. Same as the scar on his neck."

The soldier thought for quite a long while. "A little clergyman called Mauretonne, or something like that I think." He wrinkled his weather-beaten brow. "And the other one was Sir Jean something."

The Seneschal waited, still staring at Barvaux's scar.

"Fourtesqueue", said the soldier triumphantly. "I'm quite good at remembering names. And scars too," he added.

"I am most impressed," said the Seneschal. "And I am very grateful for your professionalism. I wish you well in Spain, lots of victories, lots of booty - and lots of women." He smiled.

"And now let go of my hair," Barvaux shouted.

"What do you wish, my Lord Seneschal?" the soldier asked.

"Yes, you can let go of him now. We don't want him to die on us. At least, not yet."

Barvaux snarled. "When I get back to Paris I will report you to the king."

The Seneschal was unconcerned. It was an empty threat. The new king was only thirteen years old and would be under the control of his sister, Anne de Beaujeu, for some years yet.

Belina realised that Barvaux probably did not yet know that King Louis had died. She wondered whether it would make a difference to the Morton-Beaufort plot to put Henry Tudor on the throne of England. Or maybe it would make it easier for King Richard tore-conquer Gascony, like the wine shippers of Bordeaux were hoping he would. She needed to ask Guillaume – but not here in such a public place. What would Barvaux do now? The word of an unknown soldier would not be enough to convict Barvaux of the ability to murder Rocca, especially since there were so many other people in the town who were known to want him dead. And the simple ability to murder would not count for much unless Guillaume and the Seneschal's staff found considerably more evidence. Or if the Lieutenant extracted a confession from Barvaux. That seemed more likely. She tried to look at the situation objectively, but it wasn't easy.

Suddenly the inn door opened and Jeanne Senclar's groom Arnaud hurtled inside.

"Messire Barvaux," he shouted, "Dame Jeanne needs you immediately. You must come straight away. She says to tell you that the boys have come."

Barvaux leapt off his bench and ran outside.

"I trust he has paid at least his share of his bill?" the Seneschal observed.

But the Catalan had not understood him, or pretended not to understand.

The Seneschal clapped his hands and the innkeeper appeared at once.

"My Lord Seneschal?"

"That curly-haired foreigner has run off without paying his bill."

The innkeeper gestured towards the Catalan merchant. "I will make sure that this," he paused, "gentleman does not run off before paying for both of them."

The Catalan unhooked his purse from his belt. "How much?" he asked.

The innkeeper thought of a number and trebled it.

Everyone held their breath and waited. The Catalan counted out the coins, added a few *deniers*, and stood up.

"Sit down again, *Señor*, I have some questions to ask you," said the Seneschal.

The Catalan obeyed, and waited.

The Seneschal began his interrogation, keeping it polite and casual. "Do you know that curly-haired person well?"

"No, my Lord. Only slightly."

"What is your business with him?"

The Catalan explained, but without declaring the amount inside the treasure chest.

"Where are you staying in Condom?"

The Catalan told him.

"Why did you choose the Senclar mansion?"

"It was mentioned in the instructions I had received from Messire Barvaux in Paris."

"From Barvaux himself?"

"From a Messire Urswick." He had difficulty in pronouncing the name of Lady Margaret Beaufort's Paris spymaster.

"What is all this treasure to be used for?"

"I do not know, my Lord. Most of it is not my own money. It has been collected from at least a dozen Catalan financiers, and is less than Messire Urswick had requested. But we financiers are rather stretched at the moment because of trying to fund an expensive long voyage by one of our members, Cristóbal Colom."

"I hope you have agreed on an agreeable rate of exchange."

"Of course, my Lord."

"What do you know about Barvaux?"

"Not much, only that he comes from Bruges, like he told you. More recently, he has been living in London working for a bishop. I don't believe this story of murdering people by dropping things on them."

"I remember very well that a Fleming looking very like a younger version of that bloke here was the murderer in Saint

Mihiel," interrupted the soldier. "He should not have got away with it. It caused a lot of distress in the town, especially because local jewellers and other *bourgeois* were being targeted. That helped the Rocca family because . . ."

The Catalan interrupted the soldier. "Is that all, my Lord?" he asked the Seneschal.

"Yes, for the time being. But you are not to leave Condom until I have given you permission. All the gatekeepers will have orders to turn you back should you try to disobey and to have you taken to the fortress."

The Catalan nodded, and stood up. "*Au revoir,* Messires." He walked out of the open doorway and strode up rue Barlet.

Guillaume put some coins down on the table, took Belina by the arm and walked outside very quickly. The others stared at him in astonishment.

"That's what comes of being away for a few days from a very pretty wife," said the senior sergeant.

The Seneschal made them all sit down again and resume their discussion about Rocca's murder.

CHAPTER TWENTY-SIX

Guillaume and Belina strode arm in arm down to the wharf. The river was almost overflowing and very swift. Belina could not remember ever seeing it that high before in summer. After winter snowmelt it could burst its banks, but in early September it was usually shallow and sluggish, creating problems for her brother operating the Gauge Mill's water wheel.

"I wonder how Jordi is coping with the water flowing so fast and carrying so many dead branches," she said to Guillaume.

"We could ask him." Guillaume pointed to a boat being tied up downstream of the Barlet Bridge. "There he is with your cousin Christau."

Belina looked and waved enthusiastically, but Jordi did not see her. Tying Christau's boat up in the swirling water was taking all his attention.

"Belina," Guillaume interrupted her waving, "Go back to the stables and tell Antoni to get three horses ready to take you down the towpath to the Autièges mill and meet me there."

"I would much rather ride pillion behind Antoni, and then he would only need to take one horse," she protested. "And who is the third horse for? And how will you get to the Autièges mill?" She clenched her jaw while staring at the swiftly flowing water.

"We will need three," said Guillaume. "We know from Dame Jeanne that these boys have two people escorting them.

Those two will not abandon their charges. Indeed, I hope that is the case, otherwise the lads might be ordinary Luxembourgers and not princes at all."

"How are we going to find out?" Belina asked.

"I don't think we can," he replied. "For now, we are going to assume that they are the princes. That frisky Fleming certainly seems to think so."

"And what do I do once I have persuaded Antoni to saddle three horses?" Belina asked, glad to be able to change the subject.

"You get out of the stables without anybody seeing you, and you find Jeanne Senclar and the Fleming and the Luxembourgers."

"And then?"

"You try to get the Fleming away from the boys."

"How?"

"That, my dear, is up to you." Guillaume stooped and looked deeply into her eyes. "Distract his attention, tell him lies, punch him in the balls, whatever seems the most effective way of stopping the rascal from getting those boys into a boat."

Belina wondered what Guillaume had heard about 'that frisky Fleming'. She shook.

"Don't shiver like that," Guillaume ordered. "Just do as I say. It's important. It's life and death." He paused. "Possibly."

"And what are you going to do while I am so busy obtaining three horses and distracting the Fleming?" she asked, looking at the river again and dreading the answer.

"Arranging with Jordi and Christau to take the princes and me down river to the Autièges mill."

"Guillaume," she gasped, "the river's far too dangerous for boats now. Why don't you take the horses yourself down to the Autièges mill? Surely that's much safer?"

"Nonsense, the Fleming will get the Senclars to send their guards after us at once with orders to kill us all. I have heard that he is very persuasive." Guillaume stared into Belina's eyes.

"Jordi is an excellent boatman," he said, "and Christau handles a boat even better. You know he does." Belina nodded, and looked away from her husband. "So we will all meet up safe and sound in the Autièges mill."

"Who do you mean by 'all'?" Belina asked, still looking at the ground.

"The five of us in the boat, and you and Antoni by land, with the escorts of the princes."

"Suppose the Fleming won't let go of the princes? Suppose he jumps into Jordi's boat?" Belina tried to concentrate on the safety of the princes instead of dreading Guillaume's accusation of her behaviour with 'that frisky Fleming'.

"I will heave him into the water and let him drown." Belina gasped. Guillaume hugged her tight. "Don't worry, he will not get into Jordi's boat. He wouldn't risk his life doing that. He's much more likely to chase us in another boat." Belina realised the sense in this practical reply. "And with any luck," Guillaume continued serenely, "he will drown in the Baïse."

He kissed her gently. "Don't worry, dear, the Fleming will drown and your brother and I will survive."

She was unconvinced. "What if he reaches the Autièges mill instead of drowning?"

"Then I will kill him and hurl his body into the river."

"Guillaume," she gasped, "you would murder someone in cold blood? Surely not."

"Don't forget what the Fleming is trying to do," he replied, "trying to drown two innocent boys." Belina nodded. "Moreover," Guillaume continued, gripping Belina's arm, "you told me that he had already drowned two boys in the Thames. He is an absolute scoundrel. The man deserves no pity, none at all."

"I wonder if the soldier in the Pont Barlet inn was right," said Belina, a little diffidently. "Perhaps the Fleming was the murderer all those years ago in St Mihiel."

"I am sure he was," said Guillaume, "but we'll discuss all that later." He made her repeat all his instructions twice over, kissed her very passionately and walked down the wharf to the Barlet Bridge.

Belina watched him for a few moments talking to her brother, then she walked into the cathedral stables by the riverside entrance.

She found Antoni in the tack room listening to Miqueu's chatter. "He's very interested in a pretty girl living in La Bouquerie. His head boatman has been sent over to La Bouquerie to fetch her." Miqueu scratched his *chausse*, and continued, "Apparently, the Consul had invited the strumpet for a dinner-and-siesta and she hasn't turned up." He chuckled.

Belina coughed loudly and they both turned round. There was an embarrassed silence before Miqueu hurried away. Belina explained to Antoni what Guillaume wanted him to do. "Please keep an eye out for when I come near the stables and bring the horses to the back entrance at the appropriate moment." She gave him her very best smile, touched his arm and was gone.

Once outside the stables, Belina breathed a sigh of relief. She looked around her, trying to locate Dame Jeanne and Barvaux among the groups of people on the wharf still discussing Rocca's death. It took her some time to thread her way through the crowd and find Barvaux. He was standing with his arm round Dame Jeanne's waist. Next to them were two youths with hair even fairer than Guillaume's, together with a grey-haired couple. Belina realised that they must be the escorts Guillaume had predicted would be with the boys. She wondered whether they were Luxembourgers and what language they spoke. Both were rather stout and Antoni would need two big horses to carry them.

"Jeanne, my dear," Barvaux was saying, tightening his grip on her waist, "could you please get someone to find this special head boatman of yours so that the boys and I can visit La Bouquerie on the other side of the river."

"I'm doing my best, Philippe," she snapped. "I have sent

two more people to look for him and they have returned to say that Troubat has taken the big boat across the river to fetch something for my husband, something too bulky to be taken over the bridge. The boat is being unloaded now, I understand, and then will be rowed down to here."

Belina did not consider the young head-cloth maker bulky. Even her head-cloths were rather slim. It was an unconvincing excuse. She supposed Jeanne Senclar saw through it too.

The grey-haired man asked why they needed to take a boat. His French was almost perfect, and certainly much better than Belina's.

"Sir 'Arliston, the boys will be much better in the boat. Much more enjoyable for children. My own sons always say so. My sons are ..."

"I am not interested in your sons. I presume they are too young to travel in a boat," the grey-haired lady interrupted her. "The river looks dangerous. We had better cross to the other side using that splendid bridge."

"That would take far too long," said Barvaux quickly.

"Why?" The lady's tone was definitely imperious.

"Because it's market day and the gatekeeper is making sure everyone pays the correct toll." With his free hand he pointed to the crowds of people at each end of the Barlet Bridge. "And the weights and measures people are checking all the merchandise coming in and out of town. Look at all those mules and donkeys waiting beside the gate tower."

They stared at the line of carts waiting to cross the bridge out of Condom and the even longer line of wagons on the Bouquerie side. A sumpter carrying a farmer's wife and her purchases was blocking the Condom gateway while the farmer argued about the toll. Mules and donkeys were protesting loudly, as were their owners.

"I am sure we could join in the line for paying our toll," said the lady. "Paying tolls for foot travellers does not take that long, or much money either. Don't be like a Hollander and refuse to spend your money."

"Sshhh, my dear," said her husband. "This fellow *is* a Hollander."

"I doubt it," she snapped. "He looks Greek to me. His glossy black curly hair, his cleft chin, and the way his eyebrows almost meet up, they are all signs of a Greek."

Barvaux's eyes blazed, but he said nothing.

"Messire Barvaux is Flemish," said Jeanne Senclar, putting her arm in Barvaux's and thrusting her bosom against his chest.

"Well, that accounts for his accent then."

"As I have already said," Barvaux purred in his silkiest voice, "the boys would be better crossing by boat."

"The river is much too rough," said the grey-haired man.

"Please, Sir George, we would love to go in a boat. Just like old times, when..."

"Old times are over now, Richard."

The younger boy bit his lip. "Sorry, I keep forgetting." He turned to his brother and said, "*t'as néirens wéi doheein*".

"*Et muss een d'Saachen huelen wéi se kommen,*"his brother replied.

"*Et muss ee sech der Decken no strecken,*" said Barvaux.

Everyone gazed at him in astonishment. "Philippe, how clever you are," gushed Dame Jeanne, "please tell me what you've said."

"As the wind blows you must set your sail."

"Is that in the Luxembourgish language?" He nodded. "And what did the boys say?" she persevered.

"I've forgotten. Nothing important, anyway."

"On the contrary," replied Sir George," they said 'there is no place like home' and 'take things as they come'. He stared at Barvaux. "Appropriate expressions for people who are travelling, don't you agree?"

Barvaux shook his head.

Belina stared at the wharf, straining to see Guillaume and Jordi. To her relief she saw that Christau and Jordi were in their boat, shipping the oars. The boat was swerving in the current, and Guillaume and two more men were needed on the wharf to ensure that it did not break from its moorings. The river was very high, and waves of muddy water were flowing intermittently over the wharf. People were getting very wet.

The older boy pushed Belina to one side and pointed to Jordi's boat. "We could take that boat there," he said.

"Certainly not," said Barvaux, grasping the boy's shirt.

"Let go of me at once," the boy commanded.

"No."

"Do as I say, Fleming."

Barvaux continued to grip the boy's shirt.

"Messire from Brugge," said Sir George Harliston, "take your hand off my nephew's shirt."

Barvaux refused to let go, while Sir George tried to prise his hand open.

Belina seized her opportunity. Grabbing the arm of the younger boy, she ran as fast as she could towards Christau's boat. Panting, she thrust the boy into Jordi's arms, saying "I'll go back for his older brother."

"No Belina," said Guillaume, "I'll fetch the boy while you keep close to the two escorts so that you can take them to the stables. Did you get Antoni to saddle three horses?"

"Yes."

"Well done." Guillaume strode towards Jeanne Senclar and seized her shoulders.

"Ouch!" she screamed, "Philippe, help me!"

Barvaux took no notice and kept his strong grip on the boy's shirt.

Lady Harliston put her arm round the boy's shoulders. "Don't worry, Edward, we'll get you away from this oaf as soon as we can."

With his other hand, Barvaux tugged Lady Harliston's arm away.

Now there were two women shouting, Jeanne Senclar

more shrilly. Guillaume pulled her backwards and thrust her into the arms of a fisherman. "Hold her as tightly as you can. Don't let her go," Guillaume told him in Gascon.

The man obeyed him with great enthusiasm, clutching Jeanne Senclar in his smelly hands. He took no notice of her furious objections in rapid French.

"Troubat, help me!" Jeanne Senclar shouted at a man disembarking gingerly from the largest boat left on the turbulent river.

He leered at her, but kept his distance.

"Is that the head boatman at last?" snarled Barvaux.

"Yes."

"Then get him to take this boy and this woman in the boat," Barvaux ordered Dame Jeanne.

"First, help me get free from this smelly peasant." She shouted. "Where's the other boy?"

"Don't know. It's the older boy who's more important."

"Why?"

"Because I say so. I repeat, order your boatman to take these two people into the boat."

"I can't."

"Why not?"

"Because he's not my boatman. He's my husband's boatman. I know nothing about boats and boatmen."

"Here's your chance to remedy that," said Barvaux curtly, still holding on to both the boy and Lady Harliston.

Belina presumed that Guillaume and the other man were hesitating to tackle Barvaux in case he hurt his two captives. She looked at the big Senclar boat with its crew of three and realised that even if Guillaume managed to get the older boy into Christau's boat and cast it off into the fast-flowing water the Senclar boat could catch it up. And then? She shivered, and said a quick prayer to the Virgin Mary.

As she concentrated on her prayer, Guillaume seized Barvaux's hair, jerked it upwards and peered at the scar.

"The Seneschal's men will enjoy investigating that fifteen year old scar," he told Barvaux. "The fortress is full of equipment to 'investigate' how you got that scar. And then the hangman's noose will cover it."

Barvaux let go of Lady Harliston and tried to punch Guillaume's face.

"Quick, Belina, take the lady to our boat and wait there," Guillaume said in Gascon.

Belina obeyed him, relieved to get away from a potential fight. Would Guillaume survive? But this was no time for another prayer. She ran with Lady Harliston towards Christau's boat. The younger boy was being held in it against his will and was protesting in a language she could not understand. Was it Luxembourgish? Was it English? After all, the only English she had ever heard spoken was by Guillaume, and a very occasional grunting word from Sir John. She explained in her best French to Lady Harliston about Guillaume's escape plan.

"I know it sounds dangerous," she assured the elderly lady, "but my husband insists that it is the only choice."

"We will wait and see – and put our trust in God of course," was the soothing reply.

They could still hear Jeanne Senclar shrieking in the arms of the fisherman, but it was difficult to see what was happening to the older boy. He seemed to be at the centre of a lot of pulling and pushing. Belina bit her lip, hardly daring to look. Now that Barvaux's right hand was free, he could easily land a punch and knock the elderly man out, or even kill him. Or he could knife both the man and Guillaume. Her heart was pounding. He could knife the boy. After all, he intended to kill him in the river anyway. She rubbed her hands desperately on her skirt.

"Don't look so worried, my dear," said Lady Harliston. "My husband is a very experienced fighter, and your husband looks very capable too. I think they are trying to find a way to trap the Fleming, to lower his guard. That way, it is safer for Edward."

"Yes," said Belina doubtfully, still smoothing her skirt.

"It is very important that Edward isn't hurt. More important than saving my husband, or yours." She paused and tried to smile. "But of course you don't realise that," she added.

"I do. I realise exactly what you mean. But this is not the moment to talk about that," Belina whispered. They were surrounded by boatmen clinging to Christau's mooring rope, and other mooring ropes. It was not an appropriate time to discuss wicked English plots. Or were they originally French plots made by King Louis? She must ask Guillaume. But not now.

They kept looking at the movement of Guillaume's fair hair, Sir George's grey hair, and Barvaux's black curls. Jeanne Senclar's shrieks continued and she was surrounded by other fishermen, some of them chuckling. She had lost her elegant head-cloth, and Belina saw it being carried away furtively by a fishwife.

Suddenly, Barvaux managed to break away and drag the boy towards the Senclar boat straining at its mooring rope.

"Let me go," Edward was shouting.

A man leading a donkey cart attacked Barvaux from behind, giving a competent demonstration of a *soule* tackle. The fishermen around Dame Jeanne clapped. But unfortunately Edward had been brought roughly to the ground as well as Barvaux and was calling out for help, or so Belina supposed from the sound of his voice.

She watched Guillaume stoop over Barvaux's twitching body and lift him away roughly. Sir George picked up Edward very carefully. He called out something to the *soule* player and together they transferred the boy as gently as possible into the cart, propping him against some sacks of vegetables. It would not be a comfortable journey, and it was just as well that it would only last a few minutes. Guillaume helped by steadying the cart as it jolted along the wharf, past the Barlet Bridge and level with Christau's twitching boat. Meanwhile, Sir George was pushing Barvaux against a bollard, taking advantage of his adversary's injured leg.

Belina wondered how Edward would manage to get into a boat, and she was very doubtful that he could survive the voyage downstream all the way to the Autièges mill. Guillaume scrambled into the boat, with some difficulty, and held out his arms for Edward, but he whimpered and refused. His younger brother tried to climb out of the boat and Jordi had to hold him tight.

Belina looked at Sir George who was still struggling against a fierce but limping Barvaux, helped rather ineffectively by Troubat. She presumed Sir George was trying to give Guillaume enough time to get both boys stowed safely in Christau's boat before the Senclar boat could chase it. And then she realised that Sir George would not know about Guillaume's risky plan of escape. He would not have dared tell him in English about it with the multilingual Barvaux listening.

"Lady Harliston," Guillaume said in English, "please persuade the boy to get into the boat immediately. It's his only chance of survival. The Fleming is determined to kill him. And I don't think your husband can delay him much longer. Indeed, the longer the boy hesitates, the more dangerous it is for your husband."

"You heard that, Edward," said Lady Harliston, "now get into the boat so that we can all be safe."

"I won't go without you, Lady Harliston," he whimpered.

"Yes you will. You will meet us later, downstream. You'll be all right. Don't worry. But please do as I say and at once. What would your mother think of you hesitating like this?"

"Will I see Mammagain?"

"I very much hope so. She is safe and well in Westminster, as you know."

"How can I be sure?"

"Your uncle will not harm her, you can be very sure of that. He's a very good, kind man."

"Yes." The boy sounded doubtful.

Lady Harliston pushed him into Guillaume's outstretched arms and said, "*Adi,* Edward."

"*Adi,* Lady Harliston."

Guillaume settled the boy very carefully on to the cushions. His young brother had been made to sit uncomfortably on the bottom of the boat and he was looking very anxious, clutching the side of the boat. His lips moved. Belina supposed he too was saying a prayer to the Virgin Mary. Guillaume and Jordi sat athwart with their backs to the bows. Christau faced them, his hand on the tiller.

"Cast off," Christau called to the boatmen on the wharf. They unwound the rope with much heaving and panting, and the boat shot into the fierce current of the river Baïse, with Christau steering it expertly through the narrow channel separating the wharf from the town mill. Belina looked on very anxiously, her hands still smoothing her skirts again and again. Guillaume and Jordi began to row. It looked very difficult and dangerous.

Belina managed to pull herself together and asked Lady Harliston to go further down the wharf and sit on a bollard while she fetched Sir George. She ran to where Sir George was pushing Barvaux against the fishermen surrounding Dame Jeanne.

"Philippe, Philippe, *au secours!*"

But Barvaux had seen Christau's boat launch into the river. He limped towards the Senclar boat straining at its two thick mooring ropes. The boatmen stared at him.

"Help me into the boat and cast off at once," Barvaux ordered them.

They continued staring, but did not move.

"Hurry up," Barvaux shouted.

"We don't move this boat until the head boatman gives us orders to do so."

"I have given orders. That should suffice."

They continued staring while Barvaux tried to clamber into the twisting boat, hampered by his injured leg.

"Well then, help me," he shouted. "Can't you see that I have hurt my leg?" He looked around for Troubat. The head boatman was a few yards away talking with two fishermen on the wharf.

"Hurry up, Troubat," Barvaux called out. "We need to chase that boat."

"There's no need, Messire. Dame Jeanne's message to me was that two boys wanted to take a boat to the other side." He pointed to Christau's boat whizzing downstream towards the town mill and its channel on the right bank of the river Baïse. "They're already in a boat."

"I know that," Barvaux snapped. "You have to catch it up. You are wasting precious time."

"The river is too dangerous, Messire. You can see that it is."

"That boat is travelling easily. So could you."

"Only if I have been given orders to do so."

"*I* have given you orders."

"Your orders count for nothing. We only take orders from Consul Senclar. And he can't be disturbed." Troubat sniggered. "He is very busy right now."

"Sir George," Belina whispered, "we must leave them to it and ride to a mill further downstream where my cousin's boat will be moored."

"But we have left our horses in the Senclar stables recovering from their journey."

"That doesn't matter, Sir George, there are three diocesan horses saddled ready to take us. My husband's groom is waiting for us at the back entrance of the stables, and your wife is waiting for us over there, sitting on that bollard." She pointed to Lady Harliston.

Belina guided Sir George through the crowd who were watching the fishermen holding Dame Jeanne. She heard bets being made on how long it would take for one of the Senclar domestic staff to arrive and rescue her.

CHAPTER TWENTY-SEVEN

Belina and the Harlistons walked to the riverside entrance of the cathedral stables where Antoni was waiting for them holding three large horses, tossing their heads against the flies. He helped the Harlistons onto the horses, and then mounted the third one himself. Belina wondered how to get up behind him with her heavy muddy skirt, but Miqueu appeared, seized her awkwardly and lifted her up behind Antoni. She was not very experienced with horses and she hoped that the animal would not go too fast.

"Hold me very tightly round my waist," ordered Antoni. "You are wet and muddy. Take care not to fall off." He tapped the horse's flanks and led the way downstream to the towpath. It was slippery after all the rain and in some places it was covered with river water and Antoni had to go very slowly. Flies and mosquitoes buzzed and whined, bothering both the horses and the riders. Water dripped on to them from the trees overhead. The going was far from easy. Belina wondered how the Harlistons would manage, especially since they would be tired from their day's journey. She turned round very carefully to check on them.

"Dame Belina, keep still," Antoni ordered her brusquely.

"But I was checking if the other two are still there, and managing all right."

"I can hear them," he replied, "and I have already noticed that they are both skilled riders."

"Sorry Antoni," she apologised.

"You just concentrate on staying still."

Belina noticed that Antoni was staring at the river on their left. "Can you see Christau's boat?" she asked.

"No. Perhaps they are further ahead. The river is running very fast. Too fast to be safe, in my opinion."

"I agree. I am very worried about my husband's safety."

"Your husband takes risks, but not ones which are too dangerous. In my experience, he has very good judgment."

Antoni continued glancing at the river. Suddenly he stopped behind a clump of trees which almost hid the river from sight, turned his head and put his finger to his mouth.

They waited in total silence while Antoni peered through the branches and watched the river. Belina was perplexed, but she kept very still.

Sir George moved his left arm very slightly and they gazed in the direction where he was pointing. The large Senclar boat came into sight, being rowed steadily by four boatmen whilst Barvaux held the tiller. He was steering the heavy boat carefully between branches floating swiftly downstream and a group of half-submerged trees lining the bank. Belina had had no idea that he knew how to steer a boat, but she supposed he must have learnt to do that in Bruges, or maybe on the river Thames. After all, she knew very little about Barvaux even though she had been in his company for several days.

In spite of the highly dangerous condition of the river, Barvaux showed no signs of panic. On the contrary, a normal onlooker might have supposed that he was closely acquainted with the river Baïse. It was very worrying. Would he catch Christau's boat?

Antoni moved forwards again and they reached a place where a stony track ran parallel to the muddy towpath. They made good time along this and soon reached the Cahuzac chateau fishponds. Antoni led them carefully across the ford in the stream east of the fishponds until they could regain the towpath.

To their horror, they saw that Christau's boat was not far ahead of the Senclar boat with its four oarsmen. Christau was manoeuvring his boat around the fishponds whereas Barvaux was taking a shorter route right through them. If he was successful he would reach Christau's boat.

Belina prayed very hard, more desperately than she had ever done before. She could not bear to watch what was happening. Antoni was making his horse go faster, which made her even more scared.

Suddenly, there was a loud crunching sound. Antoni stopped for a moment and Belina looked round fearing that the two boats had collided. If so, she would soon be a widow, however determinedly Guillaume fought against Barvaux.

But the two boats had not collided. Belina's fervent prayers had been answered. She saw with great relief that the Senclar boat had bumped into the submerged walls of the smallest fishpond. The heavy boat was spinning round, and two of its oars were floating away from it. Barvaux was shouting and cursing above the noise of the river. Troubat was cursing Barvaux and insisting on changing places so that he could extricate the boat from the fishponds. The three oarsmen were supporting Barvaux and trying to stop Troubat getting to the tiller. Barvaux held on to it tightly and punched the Senclar head boatman so hard in the chest that he almost fell out of the boat.

Meanwhile, dusk was falling. Belina realised that they still had to reach the Beauregard mill and after that the Autièges one. Their towpath journey was far from over. Antoni touched the flanks of his horse and set off quickly down the towpath. Belina concentrated on clinging on to Antoni's waist while she thumped up and down on the back of his horse.

Her heart thumped up and down too as she tried not

to remember her childhood games with Jordi, Geraud and Christau beside the Beauregard Mill on their way back from school. They used to watch the enormous waterwheel (even bigger than their own wheel at the Autièges Mill) churn the river water pouring on to it. Even more impressive was the noise of the river flowing fast over the high weir. She remembered an afternoon long ago when the four children had watched the body of a dead goat fall over the weir and the way in which its legs and head separated from the torso and disappeared again under the fast-flowing water.

When they reached the foot of a cliff Antoni made his horse stop so suddenly that Belina almost fell off. He pointed at the river, and she peered at it in the dusk, trying to see what was happening. Christau's boat was close to them, moving fast. Belina could hardly breathe, and yet could not look away. She tried to calm herself by repeating prayers over and over again. And then she watched horrified as Christau suddenly swerved his boat away from the cliff, getting Jordi and Guillaume to row towards the left bank, towards the weir. Belina squeezed her eyes shut, trying unsuccessfully to forget the memory of the dead goat shattering under the weir long ago.

Behind her came a shout and she opened her eyes. The Senclar boat hurtled into sight, still being steered by Barvaux. He too turned sharply towards the left bank. Belina clawed at her cheeks, gasped and nearly fell off the horse again. She pressed herself tightly against Antoni, trying unsuccessfully to hide her head against his back.

"Ah," whispered Antoni, "that's really clever." He pointed at the dramatic scene below them. Christau had suddenly steered completely to the right and whizzed down the narrow channel separating the cliff from the mill. Barvaux could not turn the heavy Senclar boat quickly enough, and it shot down the part of the river rushing towards the weir and the mill's waterwheel.

Still holding her breath, Belina watched Christau's boat

move swiftly down the channel and under the wooden bridge which led to the millhouse. Antoni turned round, grinning at Belina, and then rode along the path to just beyond the millhouse. They stopped and gazed at the spectacle of water crashing over the high weir, breaking on the remains of the Senclar boat, sending planks and oars rushing down the river, carrying with them the broken bodies of the boat's occupants.

Sir George pointed to the millwheel looming above them. Belina could just see a head hurtling downwards, stuck to a paddle, but the wheel was turning too fast for her to identify whose head she was looking at. Just as well.

But it was a sure sign that her prayers beside the fishponds at Cahuzac and just now had been answered. Belina crossed herself, said three *Salve Regina* and began the *Te Deum*.

However, Antoni cut short her jubilation and rode as swiftly as possible in the dusk to the Autièges mill, from time to time pointing to oars and bits of planks from the disintegrated Senclar boat floating down the river. By the time they had reached her old home, the Autièges mill, Belina was almost asleep. Guillaume lifted her down to the ground.

"I'm so glad to see you," she croaked, hugging him.

CHAPTER TWENTY-EIGHT

Guillaume helped her across the narrow wooden bridge and into the mill. Someone was lighting tallow candles from a lantern. At the far end of the room a fire was beginning to blaze. In front of it steaming clothes were draped over a fender.

"Stand here," said Guillaume, "while I take off your muddy tunic."

Belina protested a little, but her husband took no notice. He pulled off the heavy garment and wrapped a blanket around Belina in her thin summer shift. He made her sit down near the fire.

"Now drink this *aygue ardente*." He pushed a goblet into her hand and stood watching her gulp down the fiery contents.

Belina pulled a face. "Ugh."

"Nonsense, it's good medicine and you need it badly," said Guillaume, topping up the goblet.

"I couldn't drink any more, Guillaume," Belina protested.

"You're not going to. This is for the rest of us."

Belina looked at the other people in the room and hoped they had not seen too much of her when Guillaume had removed her tunic. Her brother was handing the goblet to the older boy who was sniffing the liquid doubtfully.

"Drink it, lad," said Jordi. "It will dry you much quicker than a rub-down." The prince took a very cautious sip, and then three more enthusiastic ones. "That's it, lad, you warm your insides up. It'll do you good."

The prince smiled and held the goblet to his brother's lips. "Sip a little bit, Richard. He's right, you know. It does warm you up." But Prince Richard shook his head and pushed the goblet away. "Careful. Don't make me spill it," said his brother, handing the goblet back to Jordi who passed it to Lady Harliston.

She sniffed it. "What's this?" she asked.

"*Aygue ardente*," said all the Gascons present.

She drank a little and made a face. "It certainly burns. One gulp is more than enough." She handed the goblet to her husband who drank several gulps without hesitation.

"Just what I needed. Thank you."

Guillaume took the goblet and set it down on the dresser, saying as he leant against the wall, "we must discuss the next stage of your journey now, before Antoni joins us after he has rubbed down his horses. We don't want him to learn where you are going."

"I don't think Antoni would tell tales, Guillaume," said Belina.

"Not willingly, but it's safer to keep him in ignorance." He frowned. "In case the head groom is difficult about Antoni taking three horses without permission and he demands an explanation."

Belina missed some of Guillaume's next remarks but gathered that he planned for the princes and the Harlistons to be taken across to the left bank of the river by the two millhands. Guillaume turned towards the older millhand and asked him if they could manage to do that. "Has your boat got room for this family of four plus your colleague?"

The reply was a long time coming. Guillaume began to repeat his question, but was interrupted by the man explaining that he had planned to row downstream tomorrow with a cargo of flour sacks to sell in Moncrabeau and Nérac while searching for the millowner who had been absent for over a week. "I think maybe he can't manage to return upriver in his boat, but perhaps he has been taken ill or has had an accident."

Guillaume asked if the millhands' boat was big enough to take five people as well as the flour sacks.

"No, it is too small for that." He poured out the last of the *aygue ardente* into his goblet, while Guillaume hid his impatience behind a fixed smile.

Belina recognised the tactic and hoped the millhand would make up his mind without any more delay. Would he resent Guillaume's orders?

"Mateu will row the lady and the boys to the opposite bank and leave them on the jetty there. And when he returns we will load the flour sacks, and Messire can climb aboard with me."

"That sounds like a good plan," said Guillaume, offering a genuine smile this time. "We shall tell Antoni," he continued, "that the whole party will travel downriver past Nérac to reach the Garonne and thence to Bordeaux, but in reality you will walk to the stables at Magentat – it's not very far – and buy three horses."

"Suppose the seller sees the two boys and talks afterwards about that?" asked Sir George. "He would remember their fair hair, and our grey hair too perhaps."

"A very good point," replied Guillaume. "Best to hide the boys behind a bush or something while you purchase the animals saying that you need to ride to Nérac because the river's too dangerous for going by boat. I am assuming that you are prepared to buy three horses, Sir George?"

"Of course. No problem there." Sir George patted the thick, heavy purse underneath his blanket.

Guillaume shifted against the wall and continued his planned itinerary. "You will need to get over the river Osse," he said, "but that will be narrower than this river here."

"But it might be flooded, Messire Lansac," said Mateu, putting more wood on the fire. "I'm not sure if I could cross it with three horses."

"Try the little wooden bridge downstream of the Capots de l'Osse"," Guillaume suggested, "or if it's flooded there too try the Caillaouse mill upstream." He paused. "I assume you know how to get there," he asked.

"Better the mill than the *leproserie*. I'd rather keep away from that. Don't want to become a leper."

Guillaume shrugged. "After you have crossed the river you should make for Heux and then the monastery at Romboeuf. From there turn south and make for Fourcès and then Montréal. Take care not to be seen there."

Guillaume continued his instructions. "Then go south-westwards to La Mothe and Pardelhan. Turn left on to the Tenafreza and after that cross the Grand Chemin between Eauze and Condom."

"Yes," said Mateu, gulping down more *aygue ardente*.

"At Pardelhan, search for someone who knows the Tenafreza really well and hand over your horse and your group to him, without saying where you have come from." Mateu looked doubtful. "Pretend you have all travelled from Mézin," said Guillaume. "And then you yourself will get back here on foot."

Mateu looked very glum. "Yes, Messire Lansac." He picked up the empty jar of *aygue ardente* and took it into the kitchen, followed by the older millhand.

Guillaume explained to the Harlistons that the Tenafreza was a very ancient highway going directly north-south towards the Pyrenees without crossing any rivers.

"In view of the state of rivers in Gascony," said Sir George, "that is certainly an advantage. Indeed, we were told about this dry route by the blacksmith in La Romieu."

"Does this blacksmith know who you are?" Guillaume asked, rather abruptly.

"We told him we were pilgrims from Lyon and on our way to Compostela."

"Good." Guillaume described the rest of their itinerary,

telling them they would end up at the head of the Aure valley. "Stay the night in the Monastery de Rioumajou and next day cross into the Kingdom of Aragon via the Plan Pass – it's lower than the others nearby – and continue south to Ainsa. You will need to change money at the frontier and obtain *maravedis*."

"Yes I know that. I understand that the frontier formalities are rather tiresome."

"They would be if you continued on the Grand Chemin and travelled through Béarn and then Navarra," replied Guillaume. He crossed his arms. "That would expose you not only to irritating, expensive delays but also the risk of another of Christopher Urswick's spies finding you." He paused, "and killing you. So that is why I have suggested…"

Lady Harliston interrupted him. She was looking at the exhausted figure of Antoni as he pushed the door open. "I am so very grateful to you, Antoni, for bringing us here. I do hope the horses are all right. The one I was riding must be really tired." She smiled at him. "He had to carry far more weight than he's used to."

"Dame ⊠Arliston, he will survive," said the groom. "Right now, he is enjoying his supper, including some extra oats I found in the mill stable."

Guillaume abandoned his itinerary instructions and added his thanks to Antoni. The millhands came in with some food and wine and they all ate and drank in silence.

When they had nearly finished their meal, Guillaume said to Antoni, "While you were in the stable I have been telling the others what we will all do as soon as it is light tomorrow, well before dawn."

"All of us?" queried Antoni. He paused and drank the rest of his wine, his hand shaking.

"Antoni," said Guillaume, "on the way back to Condom we will concoct a really believable tale of why you borrowed three spare horses without the head groom's permission. Don't you worry." He smiled at his groom.

"But I am worried, Messire Guillaume," Antoni protested.

Belina got up and clasped her blanket around her. She crossed the room to where Antoni was sitting trembling. She put her arm around his shoulders for a moment. "Antoni, my husband will make absolutely sure that you come to no harm. I know he will." She smiled at the groom, touched his shoulder and went back to her place on the settle near the fire.

"What about me tomorrow, Guillaume?" Jordi refilled his goblet with wine and shared it with Christau. "What are your plans for us two? There's no way we can get back upstream to the Gauge mill in our boat for several days. For all I know, it may have rained non-stop in the Pyrenees since last week's storms and the river will be impossible for ages." He sat down again. Christau sighed noisily and stared at Guillaume.

"You will ride back with us to Condom, Jordi," said Guillaume with no hesitation.

"And what about me, Guillaume?" Christau asked. "How and when do I get the boat back to the Gauge mill? Have you thought about that?"

"Yes indeed I have, Christau," said Guillaume. "I think that by far the best thing to do would be for you – and your boat – to rest here in this mill for a few days while you both recover. After all, the boat might need some repairs after such a dangerous journey."

"You're right, Guillaume," replied Christau, "several times I thought it would break up in the swirling current, especially when we were nearing the Beauregard mill."

"We watched your manoeuvres there, Christau," said Sir George. "Inspired, quick-witted, very professional. I cannot praise you enough. In my opinion it was your sudden right turn which resulted in the Senclar boat being forced into the mill race and breaking up beside the waterwheel. It was a magnificent and very brave action on your part. I think we should all drink a toast to you." They passed the goblets around, each toasting an embarrassed Christau.

The last person to toast him was Prince Edward. He held on to his goblet, smiled at the two millhands and declared, "and here in Autièges we received a really good welcome, even though the millowner is absent. We are so very grateful to you both." He raised his goblet and clicked it against that shared by the millhands. "With our gratitude," he continued.

"With our gratitude," said everyone.

The millhands mumbled something about it being normal Gascon hospitality. Then they cleared away the empty dishes and announced that they were very tired and ready to sleep in the kitchen.

"How many people can sleep in the kitchen?" Antoni asked.

They thought for a moment, perhaps also calculating how many people could sleep in the main room.

"Three more in the kitchen."

Antoni stood up. "Good. That means myself, plus Jordi and Christau," he said. "We are all three worn out. We'll leave the rest of you now. That is, if you don't object."

"Not at all. I am sure you all need several hours' sleep," said Lady Harliston.

The five of them left the room, closing the door behind them.

Sir George cleared his throat. "I would be interested to learn how and why you identified the Fleming as being dangerous."

Belina explained as succinctly as she could manage about her investigation into the death of a 'pilgrim' in the Pradau hospice, how she had identified the poison used, and how she had originally supposed that he had been killed by a well-known poisoner of Condom.

"What made you change your mind?" Sir George asked.

"There was this Fleming staying with Rocca, the Treasurer who lived in the cathedral staff residence which is where my husband and I live. He insisted on wasting my time checking on badly baked pies on sale in the street."

"And in about thirty shops, inns and taverns as well," said Guillaume sourly.

Belina took no notice. She hoped he would not accuse her in front of the Harlistons of her friendliness towards Barvaux. She gave a little cough and carried on with her story of checking the Senclar garden and kitchen, interviewing the hospice staff and residents, checking the Barlet Bridge gatekeeper's register...

Guillaume stood up and faced her. "And when did you change your mind about this excessively friendly Fleming?" he demanded.

"He was *not* excessively friendly," she replied, but could not help looking away from her husband. "He was a nuisance, wasting my time." It sounded lame to her and she feared Guillaume would not be convinced by her incorrect response.

"Miqueu and several other grooms saw you with him. So did Alain. I demand an explanation." Guillaume grasped her shoulder. "A true explanation this time. You were even seen twice going into the Serpent tavern. Not a suitable place for my wife."

Belina seized her opportunity to describe how Barvaux had dragged her out of the Serpent tavern, and how the second time when she had ventured inside it, without him, she had discovered that he and the 'pilgrim' had eaten and drunk in there on Saturday afternoon.

"So I put together in my mind all that I had seen and heard, and came to the conclusion that Barvaux had killed the pilgrim." She smiled at Guillaume. "Even though I didn't know why he had killed him, I was sure that he was the murderer. I think he put poisoned wine in the gourd stolen in the cathedral, and then he gave the pilgrim several heavily salted cakes to make him thirsty. I could not have discovered that Barvaux was the murderer if Sir John hadn't helped me." Belina explained about the two evenings when she overheard the conversation between Barvaux and Rocca.

Lady Harliston slumped against her husband's chest, rubbing her face against the blanket wrapped around him.

Her shoulders shook, but she managed not to sob, for fear of waking the boys. Nevertheless, the others kept looking in the boys' direction trying to see in the candlelight if they really were asleep.

Prince Edward was very still, his face set, his eyes shut, but Sir George thought he saw a frown developing. He asked who Sir John was, and Guillaume and Belina took it in turns to explain that Sir John Keyham was an English knight who had been on his way to Santiago de Compostela when his pilgrimage was curtailed at a stroke when he suffered an attack of apoplexy in Condom. He had nearly recovered the use of his right leg, but his right arm was still paralysed and, worse of all, he could no longer speak or write.

"We play chess with him," said Guillaume, "and he usually wins. There's nothing wrong with his intelligence."

"So," said Sir George, "the combination of his intelligence and your wife's swift actions has solved the mystery of the dead pilgrim."

"Did you discover who he was?" Guillaume asked Belina.

"I think he was a blackmailer called Robert Penge, but I don't know if he was French or English."

"Our servant Mautby learned that a killer on Urswick's staff was lying in wait for us," said Sir George, "prepared to murder us, or at least the two boys. And we already knew that he had managed to drown two other boys, in the Thames estuary, off Queenborough. There was a witness to that, and that witness was trailing the killer all the way through Flanders and Burgundy. After that, Mautby's informants lost track of both of them, but they told Mautby that they supposed that the killer, and presumably the blackmailer as well, had gone down theRhone in order to get to Cataluña to pick up treasure to fund Henry Tudor's invasion of England in October."

"So we ourselves kept well clear of the Rhone of course," Lady Harliston added.

"However, it turns out that you all took the same itinerary, and travelled to Condom," said Guillaume. "But please tell me why did you leave Luxembourg?"

"Bray's spies had discovered us there. The boys were in great danger. We had to escape in a hurry."

"To get back to the blackmailer, if he was a blackmailer," said Guillaume, "what was his name? Or perhaps you don't know it?"

"Oh yes, we do. His name was indeed Penge. Robert Penge. An ex-soldier who had fought for the Duke of Burgundy. One of many who were disgusted by the Treaty of Picquigny."

"I am still disgusted at the thought of that shameful treaty," said Guillaume. "No wonder King Richard wants to avenge that disgrace and re-conquer Gascony."

Sir George looked at his feet for a few moments. "This Robert Penge was aged about thirty, very determined, but also in need of money to pay gambling debts. We learnt that he had caught up with the killer in Ghent, and had trailed him to Brussels, followed him to Namur and then down south."

"I wonder why he took so long to get the money out of Barvaux?" said Guillaume.

"Barvaux would have given him some money," Belina suggested, "and perhaps some valuables." She explained about the beautiful gold medallion which a goldsmith in Condom had thought probably came from St Mihiel."

"Which goldsmith, Belina?" Guillaume interrupted her.

"Messire Benasse. He is always very discreet. You know he is."

"Just as well," replied Guillaume. "Did anyone see you going into his house?" She shook her head. "Did you show him anything else?"

"A silver token marked E L Y. Messire Benasse and I had no idea what that meant."

"Ely," said the Harlistons together. "*Very* interesting."

"Why ?" asked Belina.

"The Bishop of Ely, Dr Morton."

"You mean, the close friend of Lady Margaret Beaufort?" said Guillaume.

"Yes indeed."

"Barvaux told Rocca that he worked as a lawyer in London for Bishop Morton," said Belina. "Rocca wanted to know more about his work and Barvaux gave a long list: spy, forger, messenger, negotiator, briber, fixer, eliminator, lawyer. He had done all these tasks for Bishop Morton for the past fifteen years, sometimes in France, Flanders and England, and often in Calais, secretly seeing the Earl of Oxford." Belina sighed. "But Rocca made his disapproval of Barvaux rather obvious," she added.

"So that must have been why Barvaux murdered Rocca in the building site," said Guillaume. "He would have been scared of Rocca blurting out the story of Barvaux drowning the boys and the Lancastrian plans for the invasion of England and the overthrow of our good King Richard."

Before he could explain about the murder in the building site Lady Harliston said, "*our* good King Richard?" She paused and stared at Guillaume. "King Richard is the King of England and of the English, but you, I think, are French?"

Guillaume drew himself up very straight. "I am half-French. My mother is English and my parents live in Southampton. So King Richard is indeed *my* king."

"And King Louis of France?" Sir George asked him.

"King Louis is dead."

"I didn't know."

"He died last Saturday. His heir is his son, King Charles, but he is only thirteen."

"Oh dear." The remark was involuntary and everyone looked at the princes. Luckily, they seemed to be asleep.

Guillaume continued, "The Regent is Madame de Beaujeu, his elder sister. She will govern France very competently, just like her father did."

"Will she help Tudor invade England? Surely, as a woman, she would not want to do so?" Lady Harliston asked.

"That depends on how she calculates the advantages and disadvantages," replied Guillaume.

"She would not want King Richard's ideas of justice, fairness, democracy and low taxes to become known in France," said Sir George. "I regret that she may well opt for the elimination of our good king and his ideas. It would suit her to replace him with the power-hungry Lady Margaret Beaufort and the devious, ambitious Bishop Morton. Henry Tudor is nothing much, and certainly has no real claim to the throne. The one with the real ambition is his mother."

"Morton and Lady Margaret will be much too occupied with scooping up even more wealth for themselves and their supporters to care about either the people of England or the possibility of invading France and reversing the Treaty of Picquigny," said Lady Harliston. "I fear for our country." She sighed very loudly.

Both boys woke up and everyone looked reproachfully at Lady Harliston. She sat up quickly and tried to dry her eyes.

"Alice, you're tired," said Sir George, putting his arm round her. "What's more, we still have to work out what to do with Mautby. He's stuck in the Senclar mansion with our luggage and horses. By now, he is bound to have heard of our disappearance. He's highly resourceful and completely trustworthy, Guillaume, but nevertheless he will need some help and advice. Please can you give that?"

Guillaume bit his lip and walked twice around the room. "I think the best thing is for him to collect the essential parts of your luggage, no more than one bundle, and walk down the path with it to the Senclar stables."

"And how will he know to do that?" Sir George was practical.

"I will get a message to Mautby through Antoni," said Guillaume. "His brother Tomas works in the Senclar stables."

"I will write a message for him now," said Sir George, standing up and trying to see if there was paper, quill and ink in the room. "Ah yes, here's what I need." He sat down on a stool beside a low shelf full of accounts books and registers, lit a candle and thought for a few moments. Then he tore a page out of a register and dipped the quill in the ink. He wrote the message with some difficulty because the quill was in poor condition even after he had sharpened the point with his knife. He read through his message twice, added another phrase and then waited for the ink to dry.

"Guillaume, I have told Mautby to meet us as soon as possible in the fortress of Viana where a friend of ours lives. We can, I hope, wait there safely for Mautby to catch us up." He paused. "But I am relying on you to send him across the Pyrenees on a different route from us. I fear Urswick's spies."

"Belina, did Barvaux have a servant as well as a groom?" Guillaume asked.

"No idea."

"This is important. Do try to think – even if you are tired."

Belina shook her head. "I don't remember. And the Flemish merchants who told me about Robert Penge and Barvaux didn't mention any servant or groom."

Sir George suggested that Barvaux probably used his groom to spy on her. "Guillaume, you will need to be very careful that no one, but no one, follows Mautby."

"I will. Don't worry about that. I am thinking of sending him south to Auch and thence to the Somport Pass. I will arrange for him to join a messenger from Auch Cathedral who often travels south to Jaca and who is a good colleague of mine, completely trustworthy."

He hugged Belina. "I think Barvaux had a groom who spied on you – and Miqueu thinks that he did too." Belina stared at him. "I am impressed with how you solved the mystery of the dead pilgrim. You seem to have been thorough, imaginative, well-organized and tireless. I might not have discovered who the murderer was as quickly as you did." Guilllaume kissed Belina very passionately in front of everyone.

And Belina kissed him back even more fervently.

AUTHOR'S NOTE

The mystery of the disappearance of the Princes in the Tower has still not been solved. Historians are divided into those who are certain that Richard III murdered them, those who are certain that someone else murdered them, and those who think that neither of them was killed. Most historical novelists, on the other hand, indicate that Richard III did not murder the princes.

I think the reason for this very sharp difference of opinion is that novelists concentrate on character and have concluded that it was not in the character, nor in the interest, of Richard III to have his nephews murdered. However, it was very much in the interest of Henry VII, and later of Henry VIII, to have all Yorkist descendants murdered. Very many of them were killed by order of those two kings.

All historians have to examine archives painstakingly and analyse the relevant documents. Most of the archives relating to Richard III were destroyed, probably not accidentally. One of the few remaining documents about the way in which he became king is *The History of King Richard the Third*, a bilingual, unfinished description of the event drafted between 1515 and 1527 by the famous and highly respected Sir Thomas More and published in 1543, eight years after his death. Several historians quote extensively from this document and treat it as fact. Shakespeare used it too.

However, More's 'history' seems to be a satire. There is a statement in it that Richard III had a withered arm. But he cannot have had such a disability because he fought successfully in battles from an early age and died fighting. Moreover, examination of his skeleton in Leicester in autumn 2012 by Dr Piers Mitchell and Dr Jo Appleby showed that his arm had not been withered.

Another peculiarity mentioned by More was that Richard III said to Bishop Morton on 13 June 1483 (the day he arrested Lord Hastings) "My Lord, you have very good strawberries at your garden in Holborn, I require you to let us have a mess of them." This apparently innocuous remark is frequently quoted as an important fact. However, garden strawberries were not grown in England until the end of the eighteenth century and the wild strawberries which medieval people used as herbs and cosmetics had to be picked in woodland. In the sixteenth century, when Sir Thomas More was writing his satire, strawberries were considered symbols of hypocrisy and deceit.

The Luxembourg connection of the Princes in the Tower is as follows: their mother's mother was Jacquetta of Luxembourg, young widow of the Duke of Bedford. Soon after his death in 1435 she secretly married his squire, Richard Woodville, and had fourteen children. She would have brought servants from Luxembourg with her to England and they in turn would have worked for her eldest daughter Elizabeth Woodville, who became Queen and was the mother of the two princes. Possibly, they all used the Luxembourgish language in private.

It is not clear whether or not Perkin Warbeck was the younger prince or whether he was an impostor. However, it is known that he was looked after in Lisbon by Duarte Brandão *alias* Sir Edward Brampton. It is therefore possible that the princes could have travelled from Luxembourg to Lisbon along the route which goes through Condom. Their escape from more attempts to murder them is told in the next book about Belina and Guillaume Lansac.